PUNISHING IMOGEN

'Would you like me to help?' said the tall blonde, and Charlotte knew she was flushed, aroused. She felt curiously vulnerable in the face of what, ostensibly, was a humiliating exposure.

'I knew you were there,' said Charlotte, suddenly defensive and embarrassed – it was pointless to deny it, but she was slightly afraid of Petra, afraid of what she might do to her relationship with Seona, tense in her presence.

'It would help if you lay down,' Petra said, lifting the small tube of lubricant.

By the same author:

GROOMING LUCY
TEASING CHARLOTTE

PUNISHING IMOGEN

Yvonne Marshall

Nexus

This book is a work of fiction.
In real life, make sure you practise safe, sane and
consensual sex.

First published in 2003 by
Nexus
Thames Wharf Studios
Rainville Road
London W6 9HA

www.nexus-books.co.uk

Typeset by TW Typesetting, Plymouth, Devon

Printed and bound by
Mackays of Chatham Ltd, Chatham, Kent

ISBN 0 352 33845 8

Prologue

The face looking back at him is flushed, perspiring. They're waiting for him, no doubt about it; they're still there, voices dull but busy in the bedroom.

Cupped hands beneath the cold water, splash the face again. Deep breath. She'll never know. No one will know. And who would miss the chance? A fantasy come to life right there next door.

Such a long time since he last succumbed, after he'd promised and promised again, but when the older one gave him the sign in the bar it was as if choice left him, he could only allow it to take its course.

If her younger companion hadn't made her consent obvious it would've been tricky, perhaps too trouble-some to pursue, but when you get a sequence of green lights you take advantage of them, you go and hope to get the next. Now they're next door, waiting, all that remains is to enjoy.

He lightly strokes his cock with one hand, cups his tightening balls with the other and then squeezes hard on his shaft, trying to deflate a little – he's already tender after sporadic and ever-strengthening erections during the past hour. Don't want to appear too eager, not like some teenager. Not in bad shape for 53, the gut has not yet concealed all evidence of abdominal

1

muscle. He wraps the knee-length towel about him, another quick check in the mirror, quick flick of the hair. Show time.

The older one – what was her name again? – is lying back on the bed as the young blonde works between her legs, her head motionless as her out-stretched fingers span the brunette's upper thighs, gently palming as she licks. And the blonde is on her knees, exquisite arse raised, velvety, downy skin shimmering in the dim lamplight as she bucks almost imperceptibly, buttock muscles tensing and jerking.

Both completely naked. It would've been nice if the older one had kept her lingerie on. He glances down to the floor, and there, sure enough, are the stockings she'd been wearing – dark, not black, not seamed, no garter-belt, those hold-up stockings. Perhaps he can persuade her to put them back on later.

'Come over here,' she says, shifting further down the bed, raising her legs, gripping behind her knees to pull her sex up for easier access. The blonde whimpers a little, her sounds muffled by wet flesh as he nears the bed. The brunette, gasping lightly at the intensified attentions of her young partner start to take effect, reaches out and pulls at the towel. His cock springs forward and she opens her eyes long enough to locate it and grab it about the thick shaft. She pulls at it, teeth clenched, eyes shut, and he starts to thicken and harden immediately as she roughly exposes his full length, feeling about the solidity of his shaft, one finger briefly sliding down to follow the course of his pulsing vein.

She wanks him surely, carefully, pulling hard to enlarge him as fully as possible as her other hand winds through the straight strawberry-blonde hair of the girl.

'You first, dear,' she says, and the girl looks up, her lips reddened and swollen already, her eyes glazed with lust and her chin wet with the older woman's juice. And even as the blonde looks up the cock is already being pulled towards her face. Her nostrils flare as if savouring the newcomer, and she gapes compliantly as the brunette continues stroking more gently, teasing the cock to fullness. The younger woman encases the bulging head with her painted lips, taking a little more with each stroke.

'Remember what I told you before, dear,' says the brunette, and the blonde grunts acknowledgement, frowning slightly as she shifts nearer, her own hands now seeking a hold, palming his thigh and belly as she curls her thumb and index finger about his base to assess his thickness.

The blonde has his balls in her grip, lightly but firm enough to pull his scrotum down, lengthening his shaft fully. Another full, hard suck of his bulb, then she releases him, only a thread of saliva connecting his cock-head to her lower lip. She appears hesitant but eager, a low growl of frustration in her throat as the brunette sits herself up, swings her legs over the edge of the bed and positions herself directly in front of him.

'Watch,' she says, and she raises her face to him, staring straight at him as she engorges her throat, her gullet lowering and swelling in preparation for him. The blonde is watching keenly as the brunette carefully flicks her tongue-tip across his glans, loading further moisture to ease his entry.

And then she has him in her throat in one slow, painstaking swallow. He gasps, the constriction of her about his dick almost unbearably exciting as her lips become a stretched reddened cock-stuffed circle. The blonde still has the grip on his balls and she's pulling lightly, encouraging him to fuck her friend's face.

The brunette pulls her head away from him, and she studies the rigid cock in her hand as she instructs her friend: 'Get me ready for him. I want this in my arse.' Almost as an afterthought she looks up at him, unsmiling, her eyes rimmed with moisture after her exertions. 'That is, if you don't object.'

He tries to speak but can only shake his head as she raises her palms behind him, holding his buttocks and pulling to dictate the rhythm as she encourages him to enjoy her mouth again.

With her friend now crouched on the bed, behind raised, legs apart, the blonde sets about her task with obvious enthusiasm and he reaches over, only just able to assist by palming the brunette's buttocks open, watching transfixed as the blonde's fingers and tongue start reaming the older woman's bottom hole.

The tension about his cock recedes again, an audible pop from the brunette's throat as she disgorges his length, and again she gasps her orders.

'He's a bit thick, loosen me up. Come on, for fuck's sake, come on.'

The blonde frowns again as if annoyed with herself, and the brunette is already taking him back in again, her hands urging him to push into her. The blonde sticks two digits into her own mouth, drawing a glistening ribbon of spit which she briefly circles onto the puckered brown hole before twisting the index finger fully inside. The brunette issues a low grunt and the reverberation of it makes him want to come. He manages to get a finger down to the base of his cock, pressing against the vein to quell the ejaculation, and just in time. By the time he looks back the blonde has already worked the other digit inside the brunette's arse and has started brusquely fingerfucking her friend.

'I can't hold it much longer,' he hears himself saying, and he knows it's true, he's already aching to unload. The brunette clearly has other ideas though,

4

and she reaches behind her and works her own fingers about the blonde's, helping to enlarge her anal opening as another finger, and another, are twisting and delving.

'You're going to arse-fuck me, and you're going to do it now,' she says, her grip hard about his shaft, her thumb pressing so that his cock is being bent painfully.

She releases him, shifts across, her arms enveloping a couple of pillows which she sinks her face into. The blonde's fingers are still inside her backside, but the younger girl has stopped fucking with them, she's concentrating on lubing the hole, using her other fingers to deposit more spit about her embedded digits.

He gets on the bed, and the blonde takes him again, nibbling at his shaft, her tongue lapping at his tightened scrotum.

'Come on, fuck me,' says the brunette into the pillows, and the blonde is smiling now, panting as she gives him a final rub and directs his cock-head towards her arse-sheathed fingers. He shifts nearer, the brunette's calves brushing against his thighs as she draws him closer.

'Ready?' asks the blonde, looking up at him, her grip steadying his dick as she pushes her other fingers deeper into the brunette rapidly, eliciting pained grunts of frustration into the pillows before the word 'yeah' can be heard among the groaning. Suddenly the blonde pulls her fingers from the broadened brown hole and simultaneously brings the head of his cock to the already closing darkness. Then he's in and his dick is gliding into the tightness and the brunette is crying aloud and the blonde is slapping the arse-cheeks as he starts pounding, his hands at her hips, gripping, fingers trembling as he pulls at her broadness, hauling her buttocks towards him as his dick sinks into her again and again.

The brunette screams into the pillows as she climaxes. He looks down – the blonde's face is still there, smiling, looking at him, her lips open, teeth partly concealed by pink tongue-tip as he starts to come, and there's a finger at his arse, prodding. He's not sure what noises he makes as he ejaculates inside the brunette's backside, the blonde's fingers gently pumping his sac as he finishes. He slumps onto the bed, his cock still embedded as the last spasms of the older woman's orgasm ripple through her, her anus twitching about him as if calling his dick back for more. The intensity of his relief drains him so utterly that he slips into a semi-conscious slumber, a sort of waking dream, and the sounds, the movements about him, the smells and shifting of bedclothes seem disconnected from him. Coolness about his groin betrays the departure of the brunette, but she hasn't gone away, he can still hear her breathing and the mattress continues to shift, the sensation curiously marine as he wipes his face into the coolness of a pillow, the ticklish sensation of a sweat-drop tracing a path down his shoulder blade and across his back as he turns.

Minutes must have passed – perhaps many minutes – when the slight panic grips him, sensation of bristle against his chin; surely not a man? He wants to open his eyes but does not, realising, as the earthy scent of the woman's sex envelopes him, that the denuded pussy is being lowered over his face. He raises his hands slowly, finds the smooth curve of her back, the rise of her buttocks above him, and the slowly gyrating pussy finds contact with his lips and protruding tongue.

'It's her turn,' says the brunette, and he knows it must be the blonde's mouth about his cock, sucking

6

at the tender head as he starts to stiffen again. The blonde draws her knees further up to squat on her thighs as she curls nearer him, bringing her arse to his mouth. He laps at the peak of her slit, drawing the thick saltiness up to pool in her tightly starred anus and she whimpers in response. Something cool and slippery is at his own arse, and he twitches against the slight pressure, buttocks clenching involuntarily as fingers encourage the muscles to relax and part. Surely not, surely . . .

But as the brunette starts to push something into him he knows that he cannot and will not resist. Whatever it is, it's cool and ribbed and thin; it slides into him and the coursing of blood to his dick is startling enough to make the blonde shriek as she pulls him out of her mouth and firmly strokes him, her other hand going to her clitoris, fingers folding and kneading her lips, wiping herself on his face. He strains to keep her in place as he reams her, the slowly loosening hole taunting him, always just out of reach, impenetrable by tongue alone despite his best efforts. His jaw aches and the sweat runs into his eyes as the blonde resumes deep-throating him, his bulging cock-head running smoothly into the tightness of her as she opens more fully with each lunge.

'Get it all in, dear, another bit yet, come on, you're doing well,' the brunette intones, and she's now sliding that thing in and out, a little deeper each time, twisting it as if searching for something within him, somewhere in there behind the very base of his shaft, deep inside his body as the blonde increases her efforts, sliding his dick in and out of her opened throat.

Whatever the brunette's doing with that thing, she's hitting the mark and she knows it – his dick must be straining now and the blonde isn't taking as much any more as he's thickened fully. He hauls at the blonde's arse, darting his tongue into her softening ring as she suddenly shifts, lets his dick fall with a light slap against his belly and rises above him, moving herself to take him inside.

The brunette steadies his cock as the blonde pushes her arse against it, using her own hands to part her buttocks fully as her sphincter starts to expand about him. It seems impossible that he could come again so quickly, but the brunette is maintaining the maddening pressure inside him and he knows she will be able to provoke another ejaculation whenever she wants to. He screws his eyes shut and holds his breath as the blonde's growing whine is punctuated by encouraging exhortations from the brunette.

'Relax, dear, you're nearly there, that's the hardest part, keep it going, nearly there,' and it must be the brunette's fingers about the base of him, squeezing and pulling. His dick feels ready to explode. The pain is building as the blonde's back hole suddenly closes over him, engulfing his helmet, and she sinks down onto him almost in relief, already bucking and writhing as if perhaps it is her first time and she's shocked by the sensation, unsure how to move.

Then comes the unmistakable lashing of a tongue at his scrotum – it must be the brunette – even as her hand is working the tool within him, flicking at some point where she knows there is a trigger. The blonde's climax starts as his resistance is overcome by the insistent prodding of the brunette's tool and the ejaculation is staggered, at once powerful and painful. He feels the blonde spin onto the bed beside him, her breathing shallow and frantic.

He has slept, but it could just as easily have been temporary unconsciousness induced by the intensity of the climax. The sweat has cooled upon his body, a sheet has been flung over his legs. The women are still near – he can hear their breathing, calmer now but still audible – and yet there is a new scent in the room, he senses another presence, and even before opening his eyes he knows that the newcomer is looking at him.

The figure stands near the door. He sits up, squinting to focus. She is petite, completely dressed in black but her hair is startlingly bright in the dimness, almost white, perfectly straight but lightly curled in a curiously old-fashioned style. Her complexion is similarly pale, but the effect has been enhanced by the severe make-up – stark black eyeliner and dark eye-shadow give her eyes an unnaturally large appearance, and the dark red lipstick has been thickly applied to her rather small, slightly pursed lips.

She approaches the bed slowly, and he feels the hairs on his arms and shoulder prick into awareness. Something about the gown-type coat she is wearing disguises her movement, makes her appear to be floating rather than walking. There is something insectlike about her gait which alerts and unnerves him. He feels suddenly vulnerable, aware that the woman is not at all afraid of him and clearly knows the brunette and the blonde. He grabs the pillow beside him and covers his shrunken dick in a gesture which makes the strange woman smile ever so slightly, her eyes scanning his body before she glances at the brunette, then at the door.

The brunette moves to the door, picking up her dress and underwear as she crosses the room, and she flicks the lock-switch before dressing quickly, watched by the blonde who remains on the bed, exhausted and glistening with evidence of the brunette's oral attention.

9

'Who are you?' he asks, but the note of indignance intended is not evident in the rather high-pitched utterance. The woman appears not to have heard him in any case – she seems preoccupied, scanning the blonde's prone body as she nears the bedside. She sits gently on the bed, reaches her hand out towards the blonde, and he can only watch, at once disgusted and fascinated, as she starts to work her hand into the girl's pussy.

The blonde parts herself yet again, her head partly concealed by rumpled bed-linen as she writhes and massages her own breasts. The woman twists her wrist – her thumb is in there as well – and he can see the muscle movement in her lower arm as she exerts further pressure. The blonde responds, pushing herself onto the invading hand and reaching down to grip the woman's forearm tightly, bringing her pussy to cover the knuckles, the slender hand engulfed and used as a dildo. The woman begins to speak to him and he wonders, worries who the hell this person is, as he struggles to register what she is saying to him.

'I know you, Mr Allan, and I'm here to ask for your assistance.'

Mr Allan? How did she know his name? He was at the conference under a pseudonym, the papers had been meticulously prepared.

'I'm sorry, but I don't think I've ever had the pleasure . . .' he says, trying desperately to regain some control, but her eyes drift to where her wrist is showing moistly in between the blonde's thrusts – she clearly has no interest in listening to him at all.

'That's correct, Mr Allan, you never have had the pleasure. You would've remembered it, believe me. It doesn't matter how I know you, what you're doing here, all that matters is that you've been recommended to me by someone I trust, and matters are pressing, I need to move quickly.'

10

'Can I ask who recommended me?'

'You just did,' she replies testily.

The blonde's whimpers start to increase in volume and frequency, but the strange woman glances back over her shoulder to the brunette, who has now donned her bra, stockings and shoes and is just about to step into her dress. The brunette slings the dress over the back of the nearest chair and crosses quickly, kneels on the floor at the bedside and covers the blonde's mouth with an open palm. The blonde's cries, although muffled, seem to intensify immediately, and he watches as yet another orgasm racks her body, her legs tensing, midriff rippling and stretching as the climax grips her.

Suddenly the woman draws her hand from the blonde's pussy, reinserts her thumb and grips the girl's mound with the free fingers. The blonde bucks madly, a further orgasm seeming to grip her.

The strange woman gets up, takes her hand from the girl's pussy, grips his hair with one hand and rams her thumb deep into his mouth. He instinctively bites down, but she makes a warning sound and pushes harder, her thumb making him gag.

She traces her slippery fingers from his forehead to neck, smearing him with the scent of the blonde, and he closes his eyes as she speaks.

'You don't have to do anything you don't want to.'

'But I don't even know what it is you want,' he stammers, fearful, frozen camera-captured moments of his family life now surfacing as the panic starts to take hold.

'How much do you want? Is that it?' he says, trying to sound bold, defiant despite the embarrassingly obvious quaver in his voice.

She smiles again, and this time it's a broad, genuine grin exposing her teeth – he can see now that she is not as young as he first thought in the dim light, she might be 35 or thereabouts.

'I'm not interested in blackmail,' she says almost warmly, sympathetically, as if he's some kind of idiot.

She stands up, allowing her fingers to brush across the blonde's parted thighs as she moves away from the bed.

'You will be hearing from me again. Soon. When you return to London your employer will be in touch to confirm that I made contact. If you decide to decline my request, simply tell your employer that no contact was made and you will not be troubled further.'

He looks to the brunette as if hoping that she might be able to shed some light on what is happening, but her empty stare yields nothing as she palms the blonde's hair, soothing her. The woman has reached the door, and he draws the bedclothes over his thighs as she unclicks the lock. She has started depressing the door-handle, then he sees her pause, release it, and when she turns again she looks somehow different, more fragile than her garb and mien might suggest.

'Your employer is a very powerful man and I've known him a long time. I trust his judgement just as he does mine. If you want to help, just tell him we met and he will arrange everything.'

'Who should I say, I mean, what am I to tell him about . . .'

She turned away again and depressed the door handle.

'My name is Kayla,' she said.

One

Charlotte breathed in deeply and pulled the corset around her midriff to make unhooking simpler. It was a little tight, but he preferred them like that, always had, and his pedestrian tastes had not developed over the seven years of the marriage.

She dropped the article atop his discarded clothes and moved to turn off the hot tap. Catching a glimpse of herself in the mirror as she bent, she noticed the thinning white trail of his discharge across her upper chest. She wiped it off with her fingers and rinsed them under a thin trickle of cold water in the basin. The mirror was already steaming up, but she could make out the reflection showing the open door, the lump on the bed where he had drawn the thin quilt over him. He would enjoy a post-coital doze, as he always did, and when she emerged from her bath she would shower and head off to the club – the Friday-night routine had been established on the very first weekend following their return from the Japanese honeymoon, and it had never varied come what may. But that was fine.

Steve was nothing if not predictable, and that suited Charlotte down to the ground. He'd been briefly engaged to Imogen – it seemed like a lifetime ago now – and when she ditched him over some minor misunderstanding regarding his thoughts on feminism she'd recommended him to Charlotte as a thoroughly decent chap and a fantastic fuck, but very much the sort who expected women to know their place, produce children and keep the hearth warm for the homecoming breadwinner.

She lowered herself through the foaming surface of bubbles and allowed herself to become completely submerged in the long tub. Even remembering Imogen's name brought a dull pain to her belly, an ache borne of regret and anger. It could've – should've – been so different.

A twenty-year friendship in tatters, seemingly beyond repair – that was bad enough, but now, the thought that Imogen might be betraying her, threatening to undermine what was rightfully hers? It was beyond the pale.

And yet, there was always that possibility that the people at the estate and further beyond – those who controlled the controllers – were playing some kind of game in which Charlotte was merely a pawn. Not that she'd ever had any illusions that being Kayla was any guarantee of immunity against unwitting involvement in the designs drawn by these grey, anonymous people. By and large, in her decade fulfilling the role of Kayla, she had been required only to get on with the purely practical matters she had so excelled in at the illicit academy, and even now, smoothing the soap along her calves, her thighs, allowing her fingers to gently brush the lightly haired pubis, she felt again the nagging frustration that it had all been about this, her body, her flesh. She was more than that and had always known it, and for them to elevate her to the status of a sacred cow may have been wondrously thrilling ten years ago, but now it made her seethe with indignation and a determination to assert her

14

own control over the situation. The status of Kayla was, no doubt about it, a rare and highly prized attainment, one that no two living women could ever enjoy simultaneously, but now, this threat, this attack from outwith? It would have to be dealt with, and even her informants could not be trusted to appraise her fully of the situation if for no other reason than they would not, in all likelihood, know the full truth themselves.

The heat was suddenly oppressive, uncomfortable, and she flicked the lever with her toe to allow the water to drain away while turning the cold on full strength. The coolness surged along her back, about her shoulders as she undulated. She took another deep breath and slipped fully beneath the bubble-free surface, goose-pimples rising against the rapidly cooling water.

It was five years since she had last seen Imogen, that blazing argument which Steve had eventually walked right into the middle of. Perhaps it was just as well he had – there was no knowing what might've happened – but equally, there was always that chance that they would've kissed and made up as they had so many times before.

It should've been obvious, and with the great benefit of hindsight Charlotte could see now that it was on more than a few occasions, but she'd preferred to ignore Imogen's jealousy. It had come boiling out of her that evening in the Fulham flat: the furious denunciation of Charlotte, the Librarian, the man they both knew only as Dark Eyes; the bitter accusation of conspiracy between them all to deny Imogen her rightful role; the cryptic reference to Charlotte's mother; the threat that Kayla's true identity could always be exposed.

She sat up, eyes still closed, and savoured the light-headedness which always followed the sudden cooling of her flesh. In her final accusation Imogen had overstepped the mark, and they both knew it. Under no circumstances would Kayla's identity ever be revealed and that alone was the one truth they had all carried from their initiation so long ago. Seona too had undergone the training, subjected herself fully to that discipline and moulding and, although it was something they had never ever discussed together, Charlotte knew that the others fully realised there could be no betrayal which compromised the role of Kayla. It would not be permitted, and if it had ever been attempted then there existed no evidence of the effort.

There are forces at work which you know nothing about – my ignorance is less complete than yours, but still I know nothing of them. Dark Eyes's final words to them all on the day of their departure from the estate still stayed with Charlotte. She could recall the timbre of his voice, the note of sadness – or was it regret? – still see the crease of his frown as he pondered something whose nature she could only guess at. But it had been a warning and she had always held it as such. Now, with her position as Kayla apparently threatened, it was more than a little frightening to contemplate that she might well be close to encountering those forces first-hand.

The full-length mirror affixed to the bathroom door was still misted, drops of condensation descending to allow only a partial view of herself as she towelled herself dry. Thirty-one next month. Not bad. Belly, yes, but slight, no more than a gently curving arc of flesh slung from hip to hip, the musculature of her stomach still visible if she tensed, and no traces of the dreaded cellulite yet. Years before it should be a worry.

A dull shifting in the bedroom, enough of a movement to be heard above the dull whirr of the extractor, signalled that Steve was on his way to the lounge where he would have a drink waiting for her when she went in. Nice, in a way.

Then his voice, dull, not calling her, someone on the phone. She donned her robe, palmed away a clear patch in the mirror and noted how flushed she was. As always, she found it hard to look into her own eyes, it was a perpetual game with herself. A glance was OK, imagined as a quick look given to another. But to look, to actually look into her own eyes was upsetting, disconcerting for reasons she could never fathom. How often had she ended up with her nose almost touching that glassy surface, staring into herself, asking herself questions which she knew she had no answers to?

No time to get that personal tonight. Her eyes appeared greenish rather than their daylight aquamarine, no doubt a trick of the light. The door was rapped lightly, his voice was saying it was Seona.

Seona.

So, she must've got the message. Good. He'll be out and the night is young.

'Yeah, I'll take it in here, darling.'

'There's a drink waiting for you in the lounge, darling.'

Yeah, Steve. Of course there is.

Seona arrived less than an hour after he'd gone. She looked marvellous. It was three months since they'd last met, that evening in Cork Street, an uneventful but pleasant enough few hours viewing the sculptures and paintings of the latest wunderkind. Seona had bought one of the smaller canvases, an abstract landscape, but she'd taken a deep dislike to it when she'd viewed it in sobriety. No matter – the girl's pieces were a sound investment and it could be stored in the cupboard for a couple of years, accruing interest daily while mercifully out of view.

'What news?' Seona asked as she settled into the sofa, cupping the glass of mineral water.

'Not good, my dear, not good at all.'

Charlotte felt no qualms about unloading the full story to Seona. She was utterly trustworthy, had pledged herself to Charlotte all those years ago and made good on that promise. Despite being a constant focus of attention among the city's eligible bachelors, and many other men already betrothed, she had shunned the attentions of the other sex. Her devotion to Charlotte was complete, and even the marriage to Steve had never been seriously questioned as a threat to the bond between them.

Seona remained silent as Charlotte outlined what would have to be done. The man she had visited in Paris was in place – his employer had confirmed the contact, he had been appraised of Kayla's importance and had agreed to make himself available to her with immediate effect. He was already on his way to New York and would remain there until he received further instructions.

'So when do we leave?' Seona asked, smiling, expectant.

'Tomorrow evening. Arrange a diary with the outlets, sufficient to cover us for a week. That should be enough.'

Seona nodded, sipped at her water, licked her lips carefully, looked down at her lap.

'That's the business side of it. Plenty of time, dear,' Charlotte said quietly, savouring the gentle movement of Seona's crossed legs, the tapping of her kitten-heeled foot into the air between them. Bare-legged, deliciously tanned.

Seona needed no second invitation. She placed her glass on the low table, slipped onto the carpet and crawled slowly towards Charlotte, now reclining in the broad armchair. It had been a long time since it had happened like this, in here. The memory of the last time overlapped with the here and now as she shifted forward just a tad, heard the soft leather squeak beneath her. Head back, eyes closed, she twisted her bare toes into the warm pile of the carpet, anticipating the first touch, the overture.

And the first contact came from Seona's fingers, gently caressing her bare feet, smoothing the soft crevices between her toes, palming her soles. Then came the first kiss on her ankle, the warm breath of her long-term lover on her skin.

The longer they'd been together the more precious Seona had become to Charlotte – the luxury of yielding to the only woman who really knew what she wanted, the only woman who needed no bidding, no instruction, was a uniquely sweet indulgence. Palms gently smoothing her calves, fingers briefly tracing the sensitive flesh behind the knee joint as Seona's tongue gingerly licked across her toes, pressure increasing on her ankle as her foot was raised and the smallest toe taken between her lips, sucked so softly.

Charlotte gripped the broad soft ends of the chair's arms, fingernails digging into the leather as she fought to quell the increasing tension. Another deep breath, fast in, slow out, make it last, don't get carried away. Always that fight – only ever with Seona – to resist the urge to take control, seize command. But the sure knowledge that she would and could debase and dominate the girl whenever she felt like it only ever exacerbated the tension, the thrill of the possible.

Charlotte knew full well that Steve had always suspected the nature of her friendship with Seona, but had never been bold enough to confront her directly.

But it would surely fuel his solitary moments, those evenings when she left him and he masturbated. She knew where his videos were kept, his little stash of magazines. How sad it was that he had never chosen to share that part of his life with her, but it all helped to maintain the facade of their marriage, their *normal* relationship. But how he would love to see this now – Charlotte opened her eyes and took only a glimpse of her raven-haired friend's hands shifting her skirt above the knees, lips now kissing her knees, fingers caressing her inner thighs, urging her to part just a little more.

And even that shifting, that parting of her thighs was an effort, an exercise in restraint, so difficult not to entwine her fingers in Seona's hair and pull her clean fresh face into her sex.

'I've been waiting so long for this,' said Seona, and Charlotte could only moan by way of reply.

The smooth mound of her sex was sheathed in the thin cotton, but the coolness of Seona's breath on her indicated that the material was already moist, and the first hard kiss, unexpected, made her gasp aloud. Fingers digging deeper into the leather, as if resisting some G-force, a magnetic impulse to buck into Seona's face. The girl's fingers were at the panties, rimming the edges, teasing along the swelling lips but avoiding contact with her clitoris as she started to lick at the material, lapping and forcing the white cotton into the widening channel.

Charlotte raised her legs to encompass Seona's back, her calves and heels, the soles of her feet tracing the shape of the taut body beneath the thin dress, the gentle gyrations of her lover's torso indicating that she was using her hips to contain her own growing excitement.

The first flick of her thumb across Charlotte's clitoris was too much, one hand, then the other, was placed on Seona's crown and the texture of her hair was as familiar as a welcome friend, lustrous, freshly washed and wafting a fruity scent as she started to work her face deeper.

Nothing was comparable. Despite the variations she had experienced over the years, the extremes of fetish to which she had been exposed, Charlotte had never found anything so satisfying as the tongue of another woman upon her sex. There had been so many, and all so good: the Librarian had been fantastically strong; Seona was tender and had a wonderful instinct for timing and rhythm. But the best – she hesitated to follow the thought further, but knew it was there, hovering always like some unpleasant truth she would rather now deny – the best had been Imogen. She'd been the first, and remained unsurpassed.

Charlotte opened her eyes again to see Seona pulling her dress up above her waist, her fingers already soothing herself as she pushed Charlotte's legs further back and stared down at the object of her attention. Charlotte cupped Seona's face in her hands, caressed her beautiful cheeks, traced the fullness of her moistened lips before kissing her deeply.

They would make love for hours, perhaps go out for a drink later. But at some point, although it might never be spoken aloud, they would wonder, as they always did, what Imogen was up to now – where she was, how she was looking, whether or not they would ever be reunited.

Imogen's chest was heaving. The outfit was becoming uncomfortable, the rubber nipping into her skin. The others would be expecting her back soon, but were occupied for the meantime. She pulled the door open a little; the mirror in the hallway allowed a partial view of what was happening now, and although the dim light made positive identification difficult she could tell from the arrangement of limbs and hair colour of those visible that the Chinese girl was still sucking on the black man, his cock-shaft gleaming as he worked it into the girl's face, and a frantic bucking further up, behind them, revealed that the other girl had the older man on the sofa, bouncing on his lap. Yeah, they were busy enough for now.

Her scalp felt hot, and was starting to itch just a little. Well, being Kayla was bound to have some drawbacks. She palmed the hairpiece tighter against her scalp, shifted it to ease the annoyance. The boots were also starting to strain her calves – it was a long time since she'd worn heels so high, but she needed them to lift her buttocks just that little bit, accentuate their fullness. The corset straps had come away from the rubber stockings when the black man had been fucking her over the end of the sofa, but a few clips and they were once again secure. Not that the stockings needed support anyway – the thin blue rubber felt almost magnetically attached to her skin, indeed, it was difficult, thanks to the matching elbow-high gloves, to tell where the rubber stopped and her own skin started, so few were those junctures where bare flesh was visible.

But the more covering the better. That had been agreed, understood right from the beginning. The wig, she had been assured, was identical in every respect to those favoured by Kayla for so many years and had come from the same supplier, but passing off Imogen's body as Charlotte's was a different matter altogether.

Charlotte's physique had not, it seemed, changed significantly over the years. She'd always been so petite that it was difficult to imagine that any weight could be carried on her small frame which would not radically alter her appearance. But time had altered Imogen's shape. Her breasts had swollen, the small belly she bore was Monroe-esque, and her hips had certainly taken their fair share of the extra weight she had accumulated over the past five years or so, but she was happy with her shape, her carriage and posture. The only clear danger was that she would, somewhere, sometime, encounter someone who had met the 'real' Kayla within the past decade; it would be pointless even to attempt to convince such a person that Imogen's body could have been morphed from that of Charlotte. No, the physical differences were too stark to disguise, but what one lacked in terms of physical attributes and characteristics could always be made up for by strength of attitude, clarity of purpose, unshakeable confidence. Well, that's what they'd said.

So, covering up was the best option, presented the best opportunity for prolonging the great deception. Not that she objected to donning unusual wear. That period of training at the estate had confirmed her love of leather, rubber and lace and outfits of any kind. Dressing up had become a prerequisite for any meaningful sexual encounter. Of course, there was always a place for romance and the slow passionate making of love. But that was a different ball-game altogether. Real sex was different, had its own rules, its own etiquette. And Rule One was that it had to be physically demanding, tough; you had to work for the satisfaction and make sure the others did too.

Hence the sweat glistening on her breasts, working its way through the oil the girls had smeared onto her as the men watched. Her nipples pulsed, throbbed a little where the girls had nibbled and tweaked at her, and her pussy was reddened where they'd been fingering her. The Oriental beauty had been particularly rough, almost deranged at times – with any luck the equally keen black man would've taken the edge off her passion by the time she went back in.

And they would be expecting a real show, something to finish them all off for the evening. Imogen had briefed the men well, and they knew that anything might happen, but the object of the exercise was the forty-something blonde, and they were well aware that she would have to be utterly sated by the end of the evening, would have to return to her social circle carrying details of a secret tryst so utterly debauched that others would surely follow the path she had taken, would begin their own search for Kayla.

The strap-on was in the case she'd concealed below the chest of drawers in the double bedroom. It was an old favourite, a short narrow-headed black rubber gel-filled dildo with a superbly comfortable leather harness which she'd oiled the previous evening. It hadn't been used in a while and the leather was still a little rigid, but she knew from experience that after five minutes or so her body heat would render it pliable, adaptable to her shape.

Memories always resurfaced when she donned one of the toys and, curiously, even after all this time, the clearest recollection was of that very first time, that bright English summer afternoon in Charlotte's bedroom, when they'd suppressed nervous giggles as they tried to re-enact a famous blow job with a crude dildo and an instamatic camera. Ten years ago, but it could've been yesterday. She could still recall the smell of the lipstick they'd both used, the squeak of the bed as they'd ended up using the toy on one another, the sunlight slanting through the slight gap between the drawn curtains. It had been a joke, a prank, and an enjoyable one at that, but neither could've known where it would lead, how it would change their lives so completely, wreck their friendship so finally.

Well, she thought as she carefully stepped into the harness and carefully drew it up over her rubber-sheathed thighs, Charlotte had ended up enjoying the status of Kayla, and had had her time at the top. Only fair that she should move aside gracefully, show some measure of decency about it all. Of course, she'd insisted that it wasn't her say-so, that Kayla could not simply be passed from one friend to another as she'd passed on Steve. Fiancés, husbands, were ultimately exchangable, could be returned or disposed of if found faulty. But not the role of Kayla. She'd even claimed that the title was a burden she could do well without, that it was irksome at times. Irksome! To be the object of lust of so many powerful men and women, a semi-mythical character – she made it sound like nothing more than a troublesome chore.

Well, if she didn't appreciate it, she would lose it. And Imogen knew she'd already made huge headway in her efforts to unseat Charlotte – only three months in the States, and she'd already made an impact. It amused her to hear outraged mutterings about the English debutante called Kayla, the very same one who'd caused such a rumpus decades ago. How could it be? And yet there was a friend of a friend whose cousin had confided that yes, he'd seen her, he'd been there as she lashed an ex-senator to the point of tears before forcing him to suck his friend off, and yes, it was true that she was young and beautiful even now. It couldn't be true, but it was, it was. And as each story gained currency in the exclusive clubs and salons, so the power of Kayla was bolstered by recollections of the elderly, the once-powerful, and the more they wondered, the more they chatted and sought a contact, a number, a place to start their search.

A pained cry from the room brought her back to the business in hand. Sounded like one of the men had just come, and he wasn't at all shy about it, grunting loudly as his orgasm waned. Once again to the door, just a peek at that mirror in the hallway, and yes, it was the fifty-something white man, kneeling on the sofa, his hand pumping furiously at his groin as the Oriental girl knelt in front of him, her palms on his thick thighs, her mouth gaping theatrically, red lips stretched as he directed his remaining drops of liquid onto her already coated chin. The blonde was on all fours and the black man was trying to enter her anally, but his girth was obviously distressing her, her red-painted fingernails appearing between her arse cheeks, protectively sealing her backside as he ran his cock-head up and down the valley of her cheeks, obviously keen to enter but aware that she could not take it. Nice timing. The blonde would not forget Imogen – damm, she chided herself, she'd done it again, she really would have to get used to this – the blonde would not forget *Kayla*.

Indeed, the blonde looked around as Imogen entered the room, almost as if she instinctively knew that she was about to become the centre of all attention, and the look of surprise on her face was matched by the excitement registering on those of the others. The strap-on swayed lightly as Imogen slowly moved towards the group. The black man backed away, still stroking his dick as if reassuring it that it would get another chance, and the older white man on the couch, now recumbent, simply closed his eyes, smiled and shook his head as the Chinese girl continued to clean him with her tongue and lips.

The blonde was still on her knees, but she raised herself, staring all the while at the obscenely thick root springing from Imogen's groin.

'Back on your knees,' ordered Imogen, and defiance flashed in the woman's eyes.

She was considerably older than Seona, perhaps in her late forties, but like so many of her type she was extremely well manicured, the nips and tucks had been expertly done, the maintenance of her breasts and fat-management was not obvious, overstated. Her hair was the most artificial feature about her – platinum blonde streaked with white, stark, almost garish even in the dim, blueish light – and her make-up was tartish, way too much eye-shadow, the lipstick already messily smeared. But perhaps she was just one of those who favoured that particular look, who leapt at the chance to discard any trace of demure sophistication when faced with the chance of a truly bestial fucking.

Imogen steadied herself, parted her legs another few inches, purposefully ground her heels into the carpet and placed her gloved hands on her hips. The dildo was now virtually motionless, thrusting from her body at ninety degrees to her abdomen.

'I'm not going to repeat anything, so listen,' she said, staring hard at the older woman, daring her to defy her again. The woman's eyes widened, resistance was possible, but then Imogen saw the telltale wilting of resolve and knew the judge's wife was hers for the taking.

'Hands on the sofa edge, please,' Imogen heard herself saying, and the woman obeyed, her movements sluggish, vaguely drunken, as if her previous exertions were already taking their toll.

Now, with her backside raised, legs apart, Imogen could survey her in detail, see how splayed her pussy lips were, how engorged the labia were beneath the neatly close-clipped black hair. The black man had obviously tired of that orifice, tried to broaden other horizons for her, but her anus was a tight dark ring clamped against all invaders. The white man, seemingly delirious with spent lust, his heavily haired chest heaving, sweat matting the darkness about his nipples, swung a leg over the blonde's arms, the Oriental girl helping him get comfy as she arranged his wilted reddened cock and scrotum in front of the older woman.

'I can't,' the man whispered, still smiling, the weariness obvious in his voice.

Imogen advanced a couple of steps, the blonde was now directly below, the smell of her widened sex reaching Imogen, sweet and tinged with the scent of the black man. He was still absently stroking his long member, staring down at the woman as if ruing the size of his manhood.

'Yes, you can,' Imogen said quietly, 'You'd be amazed what you're capable of when you're in the right company. And you, dear –' she nodded at the Chinese girl '– keep your friend there occupied for now while we sort out Little Miss Tight-ass.'

The long-haired girl was already licking her lips as she crawled over the white man towards the sofa end, the black man content to stand as she reached out for his dick, firmly squeezing it as she brought the head to its fullness, lapping at the underside, briefly introducing it to her mouth to assess its size, the possibility of repeating the deep-throat action she had used to such effect on the older man.

Imogen knelt behind the woman, rubbing her gloved hands over the broad full buttocks. The

28

woman raised her arse higher in response as she started to suck on the white man. His groans were pained, almost sobs. Imogen raised a hand to shoulder-height, fingers relaxed but closed together, thumb protruding slightly, and brought it down on the blonde's right buttock with a loud clap which seemed to reverberate around the room. The woman jerked in surprise, but the angry growl from Imogen made her resume her position, her buttocks twitching protectively as Imogen, right hand now smoothing the slapped cheek, raised her left and repeated the action. The slender outline of her hand was already appearing on the woman's flesh as the action was repeated again, and again, and each time the woman jerked a little less, raised her backside towards the punishment just that tad more willingly, and so Imogen increased the frequency of the spanking until she had steadied into an unbroken sequence of ever-louder slaps. The blonde now bucked into the expected blows, her cock-stuffed mouth emitting squeals of pained delight.

When Imogen started to feed the dildo into her pussy the woman jerked back dramatically, almost toppling Imogen with the sudden force, and so she gripped the woman's hips, digging her gloved fingers into the flesh, locating the hip bones which would be her handles as the blonde took the slender head of the dildo easily, sliding onto it until the thickness had all but vanished.

Imogen raised herself from her knees, the strap-on still embedded fully in the woman, and she shifted forward, stepping beyond the woman's thighs to stabilise her position before gripping her shoulders. Having mounted her so completely, she could more effectively dictate the rhythm, and the blonde could do little but raise her backside ever higher to ease the strain on her pussy lips as the broad leather base of the toy covered her anus, pulling her sex up with the tension of the position.

Just as Imogen predicted, the man had found energy reserves of which he was probably unaware, and his cock, although positively glowing crimson, was once again fully erect as the blonde enthusiastically fellated him, one hand straightening and massaging his shaft as her other encompassed his testes.

Imogen started to fuck the blonde. It was not a gradual build-up, a steady increase of pace, nothing so predictable. It was a brutal shagging which neither slowed nor quickened from beginning to end. The blonde whimpered in protest as the first half a dozen thrusts brought the full girth of the toy slamming into her, the dull smack of the leather groin-pad against the woman's arse the only sound as Imogen pounded into her. And Imogen knew from experience that by being fucked in this position, with the dildo straining against her back passage, the blonde would soon have no objections to something entering her arse whether she realised it or not.

When Imogen dismounted, drawing the thick black stick from the blonde with an audible plopping sound, the woman had already lost her concentration and had effectively ceased sucking the man, the cock still stuck in her mouth but her lips slack, tired as she groaned and bucked, her gaping pussy tracing a figure of eight in the air. Imogen surveyed her handiwork – the anus was slightly distended, smeared with the woman's juices and her own sweat.

The man seemed energised as he followed Imogen's directions.

'Finger that,' she said, poking the blonde's arse with her sheathed forefinger, and he did so eagerly, straining to reach forward as the woman continued stroking him. His digit poked at her, but the ring tightened.

Imogen sucked her cheeks in, bared her teeth, then she allowed a thick steady column of spittle to snake from her bottom lip directly into the channel of the blonde's arse. The man smoothed the liquid down towards the hole and tried again, but still there was that resistance. Imogen silently directed him to move his hand away, placed an open palm on each of the heavy buttocks, then lowered her face and stuck her tongue straight into the centre of the convergent ridges of dark brown flesh. The blonde gasped with shock and Imogen steadied her, fingers digging into the soft skin, smoothing about her thigh-tops to secure her as the man helped, his broad palms parting the cheeks. Imogen stabbed her strong tongue at the hole again and again, with only a brief respite for breath and a gentle probe with forefinger at the loosening orifice. Then with another gob of spittle, another brief ream, she had her finger inside, twisting and a probing, then withdrawing to be replaced by his thicker finger.

Imogen briefly scanned the other couple: the black man was now perched on the sofa-arm and the petite Chinese girl appeared to have him close to orgasm, his face contorted, stomach muscles straining in evidence of the building tension as she worked her head up and down his length. She really was very good at that. It took a couple of seconds for the girl to realise that Imogen was motioning to her not to let him come, and she brought her mouth away from him with obvious reluctance.

The black man coming would not necessarily have ruined the plan, but better that he didn't. Otherwise, it went perfectly. Imogen re-entered the blonde's pussy with the strap-on as the man helped her to finger the backside, and within a few minutes the blonde was keen and slack enough to take the white man, his dick sliding into her easily. Then the Chinese girl donned the strap-on, helping the blonde to settle onto it as the white man brought himself over her arse. Not long after that the dildo was in the blonde's behind and she was actively encouraging the black man to fill her pussy.

Inevitably, as Imogen stood surveying the scene, the blonde demanded the black man enter her backside, rabidly sliding up and down on his cock as the Chinese girl stuffed her face with the dildo.

The blonde would return home with every orifice aching, and her esteemed husband might have a question or two about her whereabouts. But not likely. She would carry the memory of the evening for a few days, perhaps weeks, replaying the events during masturbation, her own personal set of high-lights forever imprinted on her memory. But she would crack eventually. They always did. There would be someone, somewhere whom she could not resist impressing, perhaps a best friend with whom she would like to share the experience. And so the name of Kayla would reach out again, tempting the vulnerable, the seekers of the darkest pleasures. They would seek, and if they sought long enough they would surely find, because somewhere in this city of power and passion, Kayla would be waiting.

Two

'Stay still, I'll fix it,' Charlotte said, and Seona stilled instantly.

Charlotte slipped her fingers beneath the elasticated hem of the stocking and gently teased it away from her friend's skin – just a matter of millimetres, but the line had to be corrected. In all likelihood it would've shifted before they got there, and Seona would also have to check her, but no matter – it was as well to be careful, constantly mindful that the return to the House was unsolicited, possibly punishable. Best that they should present themselves in the manner to which they had been accustomed by those who held sway at the time of their last visit.

The outfits were new, freshly despatched from the only outlet authorised to supply Kayla. Even Charlotte had never been allowed to know the address, or any details whatsoever – fittings were biannual, carried out at a dusty subsidiary in the suburbs, and she'd got the distinct impression, during her decade of frequenting the place, that they had no idea who she was, who the customer really was, and cared even less. For this latest order she had intended to pay for the outfits herself, but then thought better of it: they had always paid for everything in the past, and any deviation would seem suspicious, would alert them unnecessarily.

So they'd not queried the double order, the variation in sizes. Seona was slightly larger about the bust and hips, a couple of inches taller than Charlotte, and although it would've been distinctly dangerous for both of them to present themselves for fittings simultaneously, the apparent disparity regarding size-choice could always be explained away by necessity of occasional disguise. By the time the request had filtered through to whoever it was that scrutinised such material they would already be overseas anyway. No danger.

Charlotte knew full well that poor Seona didn't like underwear, never mind intricate, occasionally uncomfortable underwear, and never had. In that respect alone she had always been different from Charlotte and Imogen: Seona loved her flesh to be free – never wore pantyhose, stockings, panties or any other underwear and was always barefoot whenever circumstances allowed. Trying on the costumes had been an ordeal for her, and Charlotte had had to help her get re-accustomed to the sensations of mild bondage: corsets, stockings, garter belts, straps, very high heels, choker-style necklaces, bracelets and hairpieces – she hated all of it, but acquiesced to her mistress perfectly, never voicing her upset, although Charlotte knew full well the depth of her disdain for such accoutrements.

It was simply part and parcel of the task in hand, and Charlotte knew that her beloved Seona would never ever question it, would succumb completely to whatever she asked, both of them knowing full well that to resist in any way would simply require reaffirmation of their status, in which event Seona would always always be subservient, had no option but to yield. That was not a concern. The outfits of rubber, silk and leather were packed and already on their way along with the tried and trusted tools Charlotte's alter-ego had accrued over the years. But for now, the outfits would have to be rather more staid, slightly less interesting. No need to overdress for the visit ahead, but as well to present a united front, a nod towards a modicum of formality.

And so the light grey stockings were Italian, tailored seamed silk with broad lace elasticated bands – Charlotte had always favoured them; the matching panties were rather old-fashioned in appearance, finely worked lace fringing the buttock-covering material, and the brassiere was similarly conservative with just a suggestion of lift to enhance the breasts; the blouse, of course, was purest Shanghai silk, gleaming mother-of-pearl when in shadow, luxuriant material expertly designed to appear loose and casual but the perfect foil to even the sternest of suits; the shoes were moderately heeled handmade black leather lace-ups, and although they were more than six years old the design was classic, immune to the vagaries of fashion. The suits were, however, split-new, had been fitted the previous lunchtime – the dark neatly fitting woollen mix two-piece was beautifully cut, simplicity itself, but wonderfully comfortable despite the snugness about the waist.

They had done one another's hair, and the simple velvet clasps were perfect – no need for any wigs today, so they groomed one another at leisure, one hundred brush strokes each, and gathered their shoulder-length locks into simple ponytails. Seona shunned make-up completely apart from a modest smear of crimson to her lips, and this she rubbed well in so that at first glance one might surmise the colour was natural. Charlotte preferred a little more, and the foundation powder, although barely distinguishable from her predominantly sallow hue, did lend her face an air of almost surreal perfection – the delicately beige eye-shadow and subtle touch of burnt sienna to her lashes highlighted the sparkling blue-green of her eyes.

'Right, dear, that's you,' Charlotte said as Seona surveyed herself in the mirror.

'Who's driving?' Seona asked as she bent to smooth the stocking about her ankle.

'We can take turns. You first,' Charlotte replied, and within minutes they were on the road east, the soft top down, their ponytails fluttering, sunglasses on as they headed off to confront those whom Charlotte suspected were perhaps conspiring to unseat Kayla. They had given her the title – it was perhaps reasonable to expect that they could also take it away, but at the very least she reckoned she was due an explanation, and now, with dear Seona's help, she fully intended to get one.

'They are on their way,' he said, and the Librarian put her pen down.

'It seems they will be leaving tomorrow,' she said as he settled himself into the armchair by the bay window, overlooking the formal gardens that fringed the southern expanse of the estate.

'It needn't have come to this,' he said quietly, toying with his cigarette.

The Librarian pushed her chair back and rose – the sound of her heels on the floorboards was slow, solid and appeared to make him frown, so she stopped, arms folded, across from him.

'You're worried,' she said, but he did not reply or acknowledge her statement. He stared down at the cigarette, his fingers gently rolling it, smoothing along the paper tube; the sound of the tobacco crumpling seemed magnified, incredibly sharp, louder even than the shrill cries of the crows fending off an intruding magpie in the ancient trees beyond the lawn.

'Why worry?' she continued, 'we have both seen this process, it has its own shape, happens when it must. There is nothing unusual about it.'

He brought the cigarette to his lips and inserted it slowly, breathing in deeply as the sudden close passage of the harassed magpie by the window distracted him, brought his frowning glance up towards her.

'*Au contraire*, the business is inherently unusual.'

It was her turn to frown as he lit the cigarette and inhaled deeply, exhaling the steely-blue plume into the sunlit gap as she stepped back to her desk to fetch him an ashtray. As she returned, reaching out to place the flat glass bowl on the broad leather arm of the chair, his hand was suddenly tight on her wrist. She waited as he drew again on the cigarette, once again puffing out a long billowing column of smoke which drifted towards the ceiling-high drapes. He looked up, and she was relieved to see that he was smiling.

'Nonchalance is not your forte,' he said.

She tried to summon a smile by way of response but he had lost interest, his fingers slack now. She slowly drew her arm away from him and resumed her previous position at a safe distance.

He sat forward in the armchair, the cigarette cupped in his joined hands as he mumbled to himself, words forming in his throat but not emerging as words. He really was worried, but now there was a life in his eyes; whether it indicated fear or excitement she could not tell, but he was certainly steeling himself, preparing in some way for the arrival of Kayla.

'There was never one like her,' he said, and she found herself looking down at the floor, fleeting

37

images of Charlotte's face and body surfacing as she waited, wondering what his pitch would be.

'The clowns over there have no appreciation of who Kayla is. Such matters are alien to them, a different language. Perhaps, yes, perhaps there can be a surrogate, that is not beyond reason, but, what is that word, the clumsiness of it all, the childishness of it? That could present us with a serious problem.'

He proffered the cigarette, looking suddenly weary as she took it from him. He smoothed his creased brow as she drew on the pungent French tobacco.

'It will take them another two hours or so. We should prepare,' he said, rubbing his palms together with an air of resignation.

'I was hoping you might advise me as to any decision,' she said quietly, wary of him when he appeared so troubled.

He looked up at her. They had known one another for a quarter of a century, but still she could not look into his eyes or know anything certain about him.

'There has been no decision,' he said, shaking his head, 'or if there has, it may well be that we will not be informed.'

The Librarian's stomach flittered with fear – we will not be informed?

'Still,' he said as he rose from the armchair, 'we should enjoy what is here and now, and very soon we will have Kayla in this place. Let's make the most of it.'

He took the cigarette back from her and surveyed her lipstick about its end, then folded it into the ashtray.

'Today is special,' he said, and there was that warning note in his tone, the one which always alerted her, but he said no more, and with arms still folded she followed him from the office.

* * *

Light rain had started to fall as Charlotte and Seona entered the grounds of the House. A bank of heavy grey cloud had appeared from the west and seemed to be static above them, like some curtain drawn across the secret place.

Charlotte was aware of Seona's uneasiness as they walked briskly towards the main entrance, the rain hurrying them. Charlotte had returned perhaps half a dozen times in the past decade, but Seona had never been back since the day Dark Eyes sent them away with his ominous warning about unknown forces and the dangers of the world awaiting them. She was staying close, so close that her shoulder was brushing Charlotte's as they mounted the broad sandstone staircase leading to the reception hallway.

As usual, there was no one about. There was security, of that she had no doubt, but the guards were seldom seen, keeping themselves concealed at all times. The fact that the estate had no formal gateway, no barriers or fences of any kind, was a curious but clever deception designed to convey the impression that the old house contained nothing worth the attention of burglars, and that impression was surely bolstered by the dilapidated appearance of the building's facade, now moss-coated and strung with heavy clumps of ivy which completely concealed many of the windows.

But someone would be watching, no doubt about it – their entrance to the estate would have been monitored and even now they would be subject to scrutiny. Dark Eyes had not responded to Charlotte's letter – he had never been contactable any other way – and the Librarian's languid automatic request to leave a message had also drawn no reply by way of follow-up to Charlotte's query. But she had informed both – they could not have misinterpreted the nature of her contact – that she had urgent concerns and had to see them, she was coming to the House, and the date and time had been clearly stated. So, Charlotte reasoned, they would be here somewhere.

Charlotte led the way to the office upstairs, all senses at a peak. She had informed no one else of their trip, had told Steve she was shopping in the city. If anything happened to them – and the thought had occurred more than once – there would be no trail, no evidence of their journey.

The triple knock on the door of the office was strong, but elicited no response. Charlotte tried the handle. The door swung open, revealing no one inside, but there was the heavy scent of French cigarettes recently smoked. She was about to step inside when Seona's hand on her forearm alerted her. Seona had turned, was looking down the long corridor.

Charlotte had heard nothing, but she closed the office door and started off down the corridor, Seona close behind. They moved quickly; there was no need for stealth – whoever was watching them knew exactly where they were, so hiding, trying to be silent, was pointless.

Charlotte paused at the top of the staircase. She was breathing heavily, as was Seona, but she knew the cause was due more to adrenalin than exertion. They were near. Very near.

The corridor suddenly seemed familiar. Although she'd only ever approached it from the central stairwell, and had usually been led while wearing a blindfold, this was definitely it. It smelled exactly the same as it had all those years ago – somewhere in the faintly fusty odour was the trace of them both, of Charlotte and Seona. And then, of course, there was Imogen. They had all spent many hours in these room, kept apart for the days and nights of their voluntary captivity, guarded by the girls Dark Eyes had assigned to them. They had all left their mark on the place, just as it had permanently affected each one of them. The sensation was not unpleasant, but for the first time she wondered if the visit was wise.

A muffled gasp, distant but distinct, stopped the reminiscence, dispelled the mushrooming doubt – the weak bar of light across the deeply purple carpet halfway down the corridor indicated the only open door, and it was from that room that the sound had come.

Charlotte moved quickly, the fear overcome, but Seona's breathing was audible, it was getting to her too. Just a moment of hesitation before entering the room, and the heavy drapes had been almost fully drawn, the weak light fighting through a small gap. But light enough to discern the shape of the figure tethered to the simple wooden frame. It was the Librarian, standing gagged, blindfolded with her hands behind her back, her legs tight together, ankles and knees secured with thick leather straps. The simple act of staying upright in the heels must have been torture.

It was more than three years since Charlotte had last since seen the woman, and in this dull light there was little obvious sign of time having taken a serious toll on the woman's body – still the impressive, almost statuesque demeanour. Her once blonde hair appeared lighter now, perhaps white, but it had been carefully piled into a neat bun atop her crown. The blue blouse had been unbuttoned, although not fully, and her black pleated skirt had been folded and left on the chair. She had not done this alone. He must be nearby, it had to have been him ascending the stairs, leading them to her. Perhaps he was in the

41

huge mahogany wardrobe which occupied the wall facing the tethered woman. No matter – he would make himself seen in his own time.

Seona had unbuttoned her jacket and was scanning the older woman as Charlotte slowly closed the door, forcing it shut with a heavy thud which made the Librarian jerk, her face raised as she strained her neck as if using her nose to identify the scent of the newcomers. She muttered beneath the thickness of the cloth which her opened mouth had been forced to accept, and the tone of the noise suggested a question, a plea for identification. Charlotte stepped closer.

'You know who it is,' she said, and the Librarian's head shifted, lowered, as though she could somehow see through the eye-covering and was staring at Charlotte directly.

'It would've been nice if you'd returned my call,' Charlotte said, and the woman inhaled deeply, noisily, restricted to breathing nasally. The opened blouse only partly revealed her breasts, always full, pronounced, but more pendulous without the bra, tanned and tempting, the silky bumps on the blouse showing where her nipples were hardening. Surprisingly, she wore no underwear apart from the skintight G-string, also silky material, but black and shimmering. The heels were her usual court-style, black and high. Charlotte reached out and touched the woman's neck. She winced slightly, then raised her face again, turning her head as if welcoming further contact. Her flesh was not cold, but the room was very warm. Perhaps she'd been here for a while, and her almost inaudible whimper suggested that she would very much like to be free. Charlotte moved a little closer, moved her hand behind the Librarian's head and released the fastening which secured the gag. It positively sprang from the woman's mouth and she released a gasp of relief as the saliva-coated wad of material dropped away from her face. Charlotte toed it away from the woman's feet.

'Kayla,' the woman whispered, and Charlotte could not decide if the tone was adoring or mocking.

'I'm not here as Kayla,' Charlotte replied, 'and I think you know why.'

The woman smiled, her tongue wetting her stretched, tender-looking lower lip as Seona approached, looking to Charlotte for instructions. Charlotte parted the Librarian's blouse to reveal the large, low-slung breasts, and the woman inhaled ever deeper, raising her chest, her nipples now pronounced fully.

'I really don't want you to waste our time,' Charlotte said quietly, but the tone of menace had been perfected over the years and the Librarian, of all people, knew that Charlotte did not make empty threats.

Charlotte raised her open hands and cupped the heavy tits as if weighing them. She turned to Seona and showed her the tip of her tongue. Seona positioned herself closer, lowered her face and started licking at the Librarian's right breast, long rough strokes as if cleaning the woman. Charlotte's fingers located the woman's left nipple, and the gentle pressure as she twisted was sporadically increased to elicit high gasps from the woman as the interrogation proper began.

'Someone in the States is passing herself off as Kayla,' Charlotte stated flatly. The woman appeared completely oblivious to whatever was being said, her hips now shifting as she tottered on her heels, swaying as Seona's hard-working mouth found her nipple, started to nibble, teeth pulling, tongue pushing, prodding into her lightly goose-pimpled flesh.

'The point of taking that gag off was that you would talk, dear,' Charlotte said, her jaw now clenching, teeth together as her temper started to rise, the familiar tingle at her crotch as the thrill of administering punishment began to affect her.

'Yes, there is someone,' the Librarian said hoarsely, 'I don't know who she is.'

'That's not at all helpful,' Charlotte said, a note of mock pity in her voice as she gave the woman's nipple a particularly strong nip, one which made her cry aloud. Charlotte used both hands to roughly massage the left breast, Seona already using her hands to hold the other up higher, moulding it to enhance the bloated nipple which she had tongued into crimson prominence.

'Oh dear, that must've hurt,' Charlotte continued before bringing her mouth down to encompass the aureole, sucking at the engorged mound so hard that the woman started to pant furiously, panic perhaps gripping her.

'And you know I'm ever so sorry, but it'll get worse, it'll get so much worse you won't believe it unless you start talking.'

Charlotte released the tender breast, dropped her hands to the slender silky strap of the flimsy G-string where it bound the fullness of the woman's hips, slipped her fingers beneath the material and pulled at it, slowly stretching it upwards before gripping it tightly and wrenching it apart. The woman thrust her hips forward, the material trapped, still covering her pubis although it had partly slipped now to reveal her completely denuded flesh. Seona was down quickly, her arms wrapped about the broadness of the hips, hands gripping the buttocks, holding the woman steady as she started kissing at the juncture of her thighs, tongue smoothing and moistening the gentle valley which housed her compressed sex.

'Please undo them,' the Librarian begged, her voice stronger now, but Charlotte retreated, licking her lips, the subtle saltiness of the woman's flesh sparking another mild attack of déjà vu. It could've been yesterday, so fresh was the memory of those previous encounters.

'We'll undo them,' Charlotte said reassuringly, 'eventually. Give me some more, dear, I need more. This isn't a game.'

Seona continued pressing her face into the woman's crotch and belly, one hand reaching up to flick at the bulging nipples while the other hand did something behind her, probably just caressing her arse cheeks for now, softening her up.

'We can't know, we don't . . .' She stopped again, torso weakening and tensing alternately as Seona's hands and tongue bolstered the frustration.

'Enough,' said Charlotte, and Seona stood up, backed away, wiping her lips, straightening the arms of her jacket.

Charlotte stepped forward again, unclipping the blindfold and removing it. The woman's light green eyes blinked rapidly, even this dim light overwhelming her momentarily as she strained to focus on the not-unwelcome guests, and Charlotte retreated again, hands clasped in front of her, the blindfold gently swinging in front of her as she adopted her sternest expression.

'Is it Imogen?' Charlotte demanded. There was that flicker of defiance in the Librarian's expression, tempered with amusement, as if she knew, and she knew the price of her knowledge would be the fulfilment she so obviously craved.

'We don't know for sure. Even if we did, you know I can't tell you.'

Charlotte nodded gently, pursing her lips, holding the woman's stare. She knew, and she knew that Charlotte knew she knew. The usual. The game they had taught her so well, the same old charade, the blurring of fantasy and reality. It was time to persuade her that this was all too real.

Seona was unbuttoning her jacket as Charlotte moved across to the enormous double wardrobe directly opposite the bound woman, and the creak of the door as it opened was ominous, recalling some old horror-movie soundtrack. But there was no Dark Eyes in there – the cavernous recess contained plastic-sheathed dinner suits, lace dresses and a stack of old hatboxes, and although there was little evidence of dust there was the aroma of stale mothballs long-since removed. Three broad drawers revealed what she was looking for – among a jumble of braces, gaiters and spats she found a broad belt, roughened leather, perhaps once part of a uniform. It would do. She took the item from the drawer, smoothed it between her fingers, assessed the length, the thickness of it. It was hard, barely pliable, and had been lying in that position long enough that the C-shape had become rigid. It would need warming, but was suitable.

The woman smiled when Charlotte turned, as if she had seen the belt before, had no objection to its presence.

'I need to know two things,' Charlotte said as she crossed to the dresser where Seona was already hitching up the skirt, wiggling her behind rapidly as she brought the material up over her thighs, careful not to disturb the stockings too much.

Seona placed both hands on the edge of the dresser, carefully positioned her feet together some eighteen inches from the unit, straightened her arms and raised her backside. Charlotte continued to issue the carefully worded questions as she palmed the smoothness of her friend's buttocks, the peachiness of the pale skin beneath the rucked silkiness of the panties.

'I need to know if the impostor is Imogen. I also need to know the whereabouts of this person.'

She bent the belt, brought it as close to a straight length as the stiffness would allow, then allowed it slowly to recoil into the curve it originally formed. Returning towards the Librarian, she repeated the action, drawing the belt slowly through her cupped palm as she worked the leather, urging it to yield to her warmth.

'You know I can only tell you what I am permitted to tell you, and I'm permitted to tell you nothing.'

'What you are permitted to do is of no interest to me. I am interested in what you know, and you will tell me before I leave this room.'

Charlotte flexed the broad band, running the length through her palm again. It was starting to soften, succumb to flesh-heat, and the Librarian's jaw was set, her expression determined. She wanted it, nothing surer, she wanted to be punished, thrashed. Giving her what she wanted would only prolong the ordeal for all of them.

'I came here as a girl,' Charlotte said quietly, as if merely thinking aloud, 'and when I left it was with a responsibility. I take my responsibilities very seriously. I would never have been given the task unless that was proven beyond dispute.'

Seona glanced over her shoulder to see Charlotte approach, and the belt was now flexible, appeared to have been imbued with some form of life as it undulated between Charlotte's hands.

Charlotte paused, bringing her fingers to smooth over the juncture of Seona's thighs where the delicate lace-work of the stocking-bands conjoined, perfectly framing her tight smooth cheeks, the delicate crease of leg and buttock.

'Watch what I am capable of doing to my dearest friend, and know that it will never ever happen to you.'

Charlotte steadied herself as Seona lowered her head onto folded arms, her legs still tight together, her buttocks twitching ever so slightly as she anticipated the first blow.

The trajectory of the descending strap created a high hollow whistle before the crack of leather on flesh resounded about the room, and Seona's muffled cry was joined by a lustful gasp from the Librarian. Charlotte stepped forward, used her left hand to gather the pantie material together. She gently tugged at the thicker column of material, drawing it up between Seona's buttocks, her hand palming up to force the pantie-elastic further up the small of her back, the marvellous full pertness of her buttocks now revealed.

The second stroke was louder now that more flesh was available, and the white band left by the blow was already pulsing red by the time the third had landed. Seona's shoulders trembled, her face working into her arms as she successfully quelled the urge to cry aloud, but the Librarian was losing control, openly panting and groaning as she witnessed Seona receiving the treatment she yearned.

'Please, please get these things off me,' she begged, but Charlotte ignored her, concentrating on placing the lashes as precisely as she could over those already delivered, Seona now jerking against the anticipated strikes in the spilt-second before they landed.

'I want to,' cried the Librarian, 'I want to tell you, I want . . .'

Charlotte dropped the strap on the floor and moved behind Seona, pulling her raised backside towards her, allowing the relatively cool fabric of her skirt to brush across her friend's reddened backside.

'Is it Imogen?' asked Charlotte, her back to the Librarian.

'Is it?' she repeated, and the groan was a muffled yes, barely audible, but there. An affirmation of sorts.

Charlotte turned to face the older woman, her arm gently supporting Seona as she massaged her assaulted cheeks, smoothing the pain away as her friend maintained the strict posture, legs still tight together, feet exactly where they had been so precisely placed in advance of the punishment.

'OK, my dear,' Charlotte said, gently patting Seona's behind, 'that's a start, I suppose. It wasn't that difficult, was it? I sense you feel deserving of some reward. I think I may be able to satisfy you on that score, but be well warned. You haven't seen us for a very long time, and are unlikely to encounter us again. If you want there to be any chance of our friendship continuing in the future, you have to give us accurate information, and as much of it as possible. We don't have much time, so I'd advise you to get it over with.'

Seona rose from her uncomfortable position, stretching her arms behind her, allowing her fingers gingerly to assess the effects of Charlotte's attention. She carefully drew the panties down over her stockings, letting them glide down her legs before stepping away from them.

Charlotte moved quickly, unbuckling the thick belts at the Librarian's ankles and thighs, the scent of the warmed leather mixed with the older woman's

49

perspiration, the heady combination hinting at her building excitement as she groaned with relief.

Seona dragged the rug from behind the door – the thick two-metre square covering was a fur of some kind, possibly imitation but a very good one – and positioned it in front of the Librarian.

Charlotte took her jacket off, unbuttoned her blouse cuffs and carefully rolled up the sleeves to just below the elbow. The thick bands confining the Librarian's wrists were affixed to the central beam of the wooden frame with a short length of small-link chain, the securing steel padlock, small and steel and shiny-new, glinting in the dimness.

'Where is the key?' asked Charlotte, and the older woman's expression was suddenly sad, almost mournful as she glanced towards the door.

'He's got it?' Charlotte asked, and the Librarian's eyes told her, yes.

Charlotte didn't have to ask the obvious question, the Librarian now keen to assist in any way which might please, help her achieve satisfaction at the hands of the two smartly dressed women.

'You'll find him in the library,' said the woman, and Charlotte needed no further details. Pausing at the door to bend down and lift up the strap, she handed it to Seona, now divested of her skirt and blouse.

'Don't use this on her yet, but keep it warm. Lick her out, get her ready, but don't let her come until I'm back.'

The Librarian closed her eyes as Seona neared, and she eagerly parted her legs, crouching ever so slightly as Seona started to handle her bare sex, fingers roughly working against her swollen labia.

'I'll be back soon,' said Charlotte as she closed the door behind her.

* * *

He stroked the key between thumb and forefinger, rose from the armchair and crossed to the desk. She was coming now. He could hear her heels on the floor in the corridor above. He closed his eyes and remembered her legs, her hair, her scent. Of all the women he had ever known, ever been assigned, Charlotte remained the best, the very best.

Not that she was, at first sight, classically beautiful – there was that slight imbalance to her features, the way her lips creased when she smiled, the habit she had of frowning slightly when listening to someone speak as if deeply analysing every word. But there was something magnetic about her, and he knew that the Librarian for one had never quite fallen out of love with her.

But had he? The prospect of her leaving, relinquishing the role of Kayla, was unreasonably upsetting, and he was determined – more determined than, strictly speaking, he should be – that she would not be dethroned without a fight. But the preliminary reports back from his people had already indicated that the challenge, although unsolicited, was certainly being taken seriously by some very important people.

The sound of her heels on the old wood neared, slowed as she approached, and he could see her in his mind's eye, petite and smart as he'd watched her cross from the car park, the lovely loyal Seona close behind.

'Come in,' he said. The handle depressed, the door creaked slightly and there she was, silhouetted against the corridor's central window. The diffuse light captured the stray hairs about her ponytail, sheened on her dark, tightly drawn locks as she paced forward, the door swinging shut behind her as she made her cautious entrance. He lifted his hand, peered at the tiny key pinched between his fingers.

'It's been a long time,' she said and he nodded.

'Come over here,' he said and she did so, standing defiantly before him, unsmiling, and there it was, that frown. But she had improved with age, the vestiges of puppy fat had vanished from her cheeks, her exquisitely sculpted cheekbones seemed to frame her large eyes, and the make-up was perfect, complemented her naturally dark complexion beautifully.

'You know why I'm here,' she said, and he nodded again, smiling.

'Yes, yes I do. I can only apologise that you had to go to the trouble of coming here, but there are good reasons for that.'

'Really? And they wouldn't happen to include the simple fact that you and your secretary fancied a free fuck?'

He groaned theatrically. 'Vulgarity does not become you, Charlotte.'

It was her turn to smile, and he savoured the movement of her painted lips, the sparkle which brightened her eyes as she stepped forward, her open palm resting against his groin, fingertips gently contouring his semi-erect prick.

'Vulgarity? What would I know about that?' she teased, and he leaned against the desk, raising his face, shaking his head lightly as he chuckled.

Her hand was locating the zipper as he stroked her hair softly, breathing in deep to capture the scent of her.

'Seona is waiting for us, and I've a feeling that she won't wait too much longer. But I need that key. Would you like to join us?'

He stayed still as her fingers wound inside the opening, gripping his stiffening shaft and slowly wanking him. Eyes still shut as he revelled in her touch, he brought his hand away from her hair, drew it down the side of her face, the delicious warmth of her smooth cheek. He was nearing a full erection as she took the key from between his fingers with her teeth, deftly withdrew her hand from his trousers and turned away, pausing in the open doorway as she examined the tiny key, her back to him.

'We'll need something with which to finish her off.'

'I'm sure I can rustle up something. I will join you soon enough,' he said, but she did not turn around again, leaving the door ajar as he listened to her head back upstairs. His cock throbbed painfully, the coolness of exposure seeming to smart against his flesh.

Yes, he would have to join them.

The Librarian had been crying, and was still sobbing miserably when Charlotte finally clicked the cuffs off and allowed her to slump forward, her hands gripping Seona's head as she pulled her closer, bucking her sex against the younger woman's face.

'Get her on her knees,' Charlotte ordered, and Seona backed away, her face coated, shimmering with the Librarian's moisture. Charlotte could clearly see the parted labia even as the woman dropped to the rug, her fingers gripping the long thick hair, her knees drawn up and widely parted, her arse raised, smeared with evidence of Seona's intense attention.

Charlotte swiftly removed her blouse and skirt, no sign now of the slight trembling which had affected her earlier. The wig was on its way to the States, but she no longer needed it to don the persona of Kayla, it was as much a part of her as any of Charlotte's own predilections.

She picked up the strap and advanced, crouched in front of the Librarian and presented the belt to her.

'Lick this,' she said, and the woman eagerly brought her tongue against the rim of leather, sucking it.

'I said lick,' admonished Charlotte, and so the Librarian lapped at the broad length, coating it, spreading her saliva as Charlotte placed it on the rug.

'He'll be here with something suitable,' said Charlotte, and Seona followed the mimed directions to squat afront the Librarian, lowering herself on all fours before backing up, bringing her behind to the woman's face.

'In the meantime, perhaps you can make yourself useful, my dear,' Charlotte said, placing her right foot gently on the Librarian's buttock, pressing lightly, using her heel to part the buttocks and view the shaven cleft which Seona had lubed so thoroughly.

'Thank my friend,' commanded Charlotte, and the Librarian glanced up, tongue still protruding, the strap now wettened.

The older woman turned to face the proffered posterior, and emitted another groan as Seona backed up further, parting her legs to reveal the extent of her arousal. The Librarian buried her face in Seona's sex, pushing into the flesh, her shaking hands rising to grasp the cheeks, parting them as her tongue lashed at the younger woman's anus. Charlotte retrieved the strap, assumed a comfortable position, then started lashing the Librarian's backside with a fury she had not even hinted at with Seona. The woman cried aloud as the strokes increased in pressure and frequency, Seona bucking and pushing against the Librarian's face as Charlotte's fierce punishment reached a tempo which seemed unsustainable.

Seona now started to make noises, a sure sign she was nearing climax, and she had brought one of her hands to her behind, index finger gently poking at her bottom hole as the Librarian strained to lap at her pussy, both of them now groaning in unison as

Charlotte kept up the furious thrashing, the belt cracking smartly against the woman's upper thighs and arse as she fucked the air while allowing Seona to ride her face.

He came in just as Charlotte stopped the punishment, and he had donned the robe, that same black robe she'd first seen him wear all those years ago. He hadn't changed, not really – still the same military bearing, the impassive expression, the almost detached scrutiny he brought to bear on the most shocking of scenarios, and he handed Charlotte the dildo as if it was nothing more important or shocking than a cigarette. Charlotte held the thing up, scanned it carefully – yes, it too was familiar, one of the tools with which they had been trained. She'd forgotten how heavy they were, was no wiser as to the nature of the material than she had been back then, but there was no time to ponder it.

She maintained eye contact with Dark Eyes as she lifted the tool before him. He smiled and covered the smoothly crafted bulb of the black toy with his mouth, rolling his tongue around it, and then, as the saliva started to drip, she lowered it and inserted it into the Librarian's pussy. The older woman gasped with relief, her head dropping to the rug, but Seona's hands were at her hair immediately, demanding she maintain the licking, and the older woman did so as Charlotte, bending from the hip, fucked her with the tool.

He pulled at the gown-belt and the robe swung apart. Charlotte used her other hand to maintain a grip on the heavy dildo as she reached out for his cock. He was already full, getting hard, and she wasted no time on preliminaries, taking him in and sucking hard, noisily, the pre-come already welling in him as he cupped his balls and placed a hand on her head.

She knew he was close, could erupt at any time, so she pulled him away from her, hand firm against his belly to keep him back from her as she crouched and drew the thick tool from the Librarian's pussy, working it immediately against the woman's anus. She pulled on his cock, urging him to his knees as she yanked him nearer the woman's behind. He resisted, wanted more of Charlotte's mouth, so she bent forward, taking him deep into her as a final treat before wiping the end of his cock on the elasticated lacy hem of her stocking to make him a bit drier. He moaned, eyes shut, clearly getting close, so she pinched the base of him hard, compressing his vein to quell the ejaculation as she simultaneously thumbed the Librarian's pussy, widening her entrance for him.

He yielded, shifting forward to bring his cock within fucking distance of the older woman as Charlotte held him still, gently stroking him to maintain his hardness. She gave a final twist of the dildo against the woman's arse then traced it up her back, along her spine before lowering it into the gap between the woman's face and Seona's behind.

'Hold it for her,' said Charlotte, and the woman did as she was told, firmly gripping the tool as Seona disengaged herself from the Librarian's face, looked down to see the waiting dildo, then squatted and carefully positioned her pussy over its wet end.

Charlotte released him, allowed him to enter the Librarian in a full long stroke which distended her beleaguered lips to form a tight red circle as he sank completely into her, Charlotte's hand gripping his balls as he started to stroke in and out.

Seona took her time getting onto the dildo, looking down, parting her lips as she eased it in, wiggling to accommodate the thick base of it as the Librarian held firm, watching. Charlotte sat back on her calves and surveyed the scene – it would do for starters, anyway, would serve as a satisfying opening course.

'You may come on my legs,' she said to Dark Eyes, and he continued fucking at the Librarian, his cock sliding in and out of her ever faster as Charlotte thumbed the woman's bottom.

And it was the Librarian who came first, her own orgasm probably sparked by the sight of Seona fucking up and down on the artificial cock, and the building groans of the Librarian could well have proved too much for him. He pulled away from the older woman, almost toppling onto his back as Charlotte gripped his dick, roughly wanking his shaft as he started to spurt over her. She forced his cock down, covered it with her palm and milked him, the spunk splashing onto her joined thighs and stocking-tops as he released a long pained grunt.

'Right then,' Charlotte said as she pulled the final drops from him, the silver semen-thread swinging from his still stiff dick, 'before we move on to a main course perhaps you two are ready to do some serious talking. I certainly hope so.'

Three

Imogen checked her watch – almost half-nine. He'd promised to be prompt, but was already fifteen minutes late. She would have to get back to them again, persuade them that she needed a more reliable contact, but for the meantime she had little option.

She pointed to her glass and the bartender responded instantly – she'd been aware of his interest since she'd entered the hotel lounge; if business had not been so completely preoccupying her she might well have been tempted to reciprocate, but she was also aware of the attention of the senior concierge who periodically passed the entrance to the Lounge, discreetly checking if she was still there. Just as in all superior hotels, call-girls were tolerated so long as they were not openly touting for business, and it was plain he had her down as a potential cause for concern. If that clown didn't turn up soon she might well have to get back to the apartment and rearrange the meeting.

She toyed with the cocktail stick, stirring the drink, an alcohol-free concoction. The lurid green colouring was strangely repulsive, and she was swithering whether or not to order something completely different when Hans entered, grim faced and flushed. He'd obviously made at least some effort to get there on time and raised his palms defensively as he neared her. Right on cue, the concierge made another pass of the entrance, and this time he sallied casually to the reception desk, perhaps content that the potential trouble had passed.

'Did you get it?' she asked, ignoring his profuse apologies. His English was good, but he had a typically German fastidiousness when it came to language, seeming to take an age to formulate answers before allowing his mouth to release them.

'Yes. I got it,' he said, rummaging in the spacious pocket of his overcoat. Flakes of snow were fading and dying into the fabric as he finally produced the slimline wallet, placed it on the bar, then removed his coat to reveal a fashionably crumpled grey suit.

'I see you dressed for the party then,' she said, but the sarcasm was lost on him and he frowned as he mounted the high stool, flipping open the electronic diary.

'Miss Langley, I have not yet been home, this, all of this, this business is too complicated. I'm running here, running there all day, these people are calling, but they never say anything, they just give another number, and then it's the same every time. I don't know how many calls I have made today.'

He was clearly annoyed, but she was paying him well enough that he had no right to display it quite so brazenly.

'But you got the one I need?' she asked testily.

He tapped furiously at the tiny keypad, frowning as the faint blue light illuminated his features. He turned the pad towards her as the bartender approached.

'A large scotch and soda, no ice,' he said as she committed the number to memory.

'You're sure that's him?' she asked as she turned the annoying little screen away to face him again. He

60

nodded several times, peering anxiously about the spacious lounge as if looking for any familiar faces who might find his appearance noteworthy. As a private investigator he was accustomed to using the city's larger hotels for rendezvous with clients, particularly in cases of marital infidelity, but Imogen was paying him to ask questions about some seriously important people, and he'd made no secret of his building worry – colleagues, peers had intimated that his current case was not as undercover as he liked to think it was, that some awkward questions were being asked about this strange English girl, this Miss Langley and the nature of her business in Washington. He'd already refused to do any more than secure that one contact number for her, and even then she'd had to persuade him that if he walked out he would be in breach of contract and she would see to it that some of England's very best legal minds would be more than happy to cross the Atlantic for the sole purpose of kicking his balls through the highest courts in the land. He'd been persuaded of her sincerity, perhaps having checked the genuine names she was happy to give him, but now, she was quite sure, he would grab the chance to break off contact with her, mission accomplished.

But was the contact for real? Only one way to find out. She withdrew the mobile from her handbag and punched in the ten-digit number. His expression, as he lifted the tumbler to his mouth, was utterly incredulous.

'You're not . . .'

'Hi there, I'm sorry to disturb you. Is this Kyle?'

She held the tiny cellphone away from her ear, then listened in again.

'Hello? Yes. Oh, I'm so sorry, yes, well, I was given your number by a good friend.' She paused, holding the receiver away again, gawping theatrically at the stream of tinny abuse issuing from it.

'Yes, OK, point taken, my friend, no need to, now just before you do, just before you do, thank you, please tell your boss that Kayla called. Yes. Kayla. Would you like me to spell that for you? Thank you so much. Goodbye.'

Hans had not moved, his mouth remained open. Imogen lifted her forefinger to the base of his glass and gently raised it to his lips, smiling as he gulped at the drink.

'So, you're happy?' he asked.

Imogen nodded.

'Yes, yes, Hans, I do believe I am. Now, I have a tremendous favour to ask you, I know you're ever so keen to get away but there's one tiny little thing I would like you to do, one last little chore.'

He put the glass down and raised his palms again, already feeling for the coat he had slung over the neighbouring chair. She extended a hand to cover his, brought her other to his knee.

'I just need to do a little shopping for some special things, you know, bits and pieces that you can't get in the nickel and dime.'

He frowned. 'Miss Langley, you are a very interesting client for me and I will remember you for a long time, but I'm afraid that your credit was used up at three o'clock yesterday afternoon, and what is it they say, ehm, yes, you can't be running on empty.'

She squeezed his knee, gave him the smile, the look, watched as his pupils dilated. So totally, utterly malleable it was quite pathetic, but it was working.

'You know this town, Hans,' she said quietly, 'and I need a man who knows his way around. I need to find someone special but I can't do it myself.'

'Who is it now?' he said, exasperation obvious.

'I don't know yet,' she replied, picking up her drink, 'I have no idea. He doesn't have to be good-looking, he doesn't have to be sophisticated or educated or interesting in any way apart from one thing.'

Hans sipped at the remnants of his whisky, eyebrows raised, waiting.

'He has to have the biggest and best cock in the whole of this state, but more importantly, he must know how to use it.'

Hans sprayed and spluttered the whisky all over his thighs as Imogen laughed and noticed the concierge, coincidentally of course, make yet another discreet pass at the Lounge entrance.

Charlotte had finally agreed that she and Seona would stay the evening, but only after guarantees had been secured that they would be on the flight they had arranged and that they had the full support of Dark Eyes in what they intended to do.

Dinner had been a simple but satisfying Thai three-courser ordered in from the nearest restaurant, some twenty miles away. The couple he'd invited were young and shy at first, seemingly suspicious of the unexpected females, but the excellent wines had helped warm the atmosphere quickly, and the after-dinner discussion had been entertaining. The couple had allowed a decent interval before excusing themselves, and it was the Librarian who satisfied Charlotte's appetite for more details.

'They will be working in Eastern Europe to begin with, we'll see how the get on there,' she said, glancing at Dark Eyes as if confirming that she was not speaking out of turn. He seemed happy for her to speak, preferring to enjoy watching the girls as they sipped at their wine, probably recalling the afternoon's events in his mind, contrasting the behaviour of those in the room upstairs with the elegance of the females now surrounding him.

And they did look elegant indeed – the Librarian had shown them to the dressing rooms, yet more places they were familiar with but had never been allowed to find for themselves, and she left them there to select the evening wear of their choice from an exceptionally fine array of pristine designer wear, a superbly equipped trio of dressing tables complete with virgin cosmetics, and an entire ante-room with shelving to the ceiling containing literally hundreds of pairs of shoes and boots.

Charlotte had selected a stunning scarlet knee-length cocktail dress, crushed velvet with a black fur trim about the neckline and hem. It might've been made specifically for her, so perfectly did it hug her waistline and enhance her bosom, and the ideally matching slingbacks were so comfortable that she made a point of asking the Librarian if she could take them with her.

Seona had, after lengthy deliberation, finally been persuaded by Charlotte that she would do no better than the simple black silk slip of a dress which could just as easily have passed for an expensive nightie, but it was so perfectly suited to her figure that she needed only compose her hair into a French bun to become a picture of sophistication. The jewellery too was discreet and deliciously valuable, the pearl earrings and necklaces simple but appropriate finishing touches.

Dark Eyes, of course, had reverted to his ordinary tweed suit and cravat, while the Librarian had transformed herself from the sex-starved harlot of a few hours ago into a demure, quietly spoken and attentive hostess, gently encouraging the conversation along when uneasiness had threatened the earlier portion of the evening following the formalities of introduction, always a difficulty when no real names could be used.

So the young couple had been presented to Charlotte and Seona as Dieter and Petra. Indeed, they did appear to be German – not that their near-flawless English had betrayed any thickness of accent – but nationality, like real names, addresses or any other form of authoritative identification was forbidden information, and so it was neither sought nor divulged. In any event, names were never used, had no purpose – they had never met, the meal had never taken place, the whole evening, like the function of the estate and its occupants, would find no place in any records apart from the memories of those present.

Dieter was in his early thirties, of medium height, light-haired, broad-built and possessor of a truly stunning smile. His partner was equally striking, also blonde-haired and with a very similar physique: broad, athletic, but with a vaguely sinister air about her, as though she was somehow minding Dieter, protecting him. They were clearly very close, but the first and hottest flush of love perhaps had passed, and the relationship appeared rather cool for a couple so young. Nevertheless, when they'd taken their leave, both visibly tiddly, the remaining diners had watched them leave hand-in-hand with little doubt that they would soon be making love.

'I should take the opportunity, now that we have a final chance to be alone as it were,' Dark Eyes said seriously, toying with his cigar, 'to tell you what we do know, what we can be sure of.'

Charlotte tapped her fingertips together as he spoke – he had never spoken so much in such a short time. Perhaps he truly felt that this was to be their final span of time together and, if so, was making a genuine effort to equip them as best as he could for what lay ahead.

'I can confirm what we suspected, what you must have considered yourself. Imogen is in Washington, and has been for some time. Ostensibly she went there to take up a research fellowship, something to do with DNA as far as I am aware. She seems to have done rather well in that field. Anyway, her presence in the city has coincided with approaches from the representatives of several important people. Very important people. They want to get in touch with Kayla.'

He paused, looked at the cigar as if wondering when might be a good time to light it, then he carefully placed it on top of his napkin, folded his fingers into a basket, looked at the Librarian and nodded.

The woman took a deep breath before continuing.

'We believe that Imogen, or someone close to her, has embarked on a project to undermine the whole operation. The presence of Imogen in Washington at this time is almost certainly more than coincidental, though we cannot confirm that. She is, of course, a very intelligent young woman, as you all are, but we have reason to believe that she is perhaps being manipulated by someone else, someone who has convinced her that the operation is being shifted over there in its entirety.'

'And is it?' Charlotte asked.

The Librarian looked down at her hands, and her expression was rock-still, not a flicker to indicate anything one way or another.

Dark Eyes stepped in again. 'We are going no-where. We have always been here, always will be. The very idea of shifting Stateside is as absurd as it is offensive. They have their ways over there, different ways. Some say *vive la différence*. Others say nothing because they know there can be no alternative, that comparisons are futile. You both know that, as do we. And so does Imogen.'

'Have you heard from her at all?' Charlotte asked, and he sat back in his chair, passing the baton once again to the Librarian.

'She did call here several weeks ago. The message was cryptic, she sounded very tired and rather stressed, almost angry. She said she was looking forward to seeing us all again sometime, and that we would be hearing from her soon. That was it.'

'She's been turned?' Charlotte wondered aloud. No one answered. A shrill giggle from the western recesses of the House drifted through to the dining room, and Dark Eyes deemed it an appropriate moment to spark the lighter beneath his cigar.

'We can only wonder, my dear,' said Dark Eyes, rolling the cigar between his fingers as the clipped end began to glow above the steady flame. 'Whatever she is up to, she is not acting alone.'

Indeed she was not. Imogen was watching, at once fascinated and repelled, as the thickest erect penis she had ever seen slid in and out of her pussy.

Her head was uncomfortably jammed at the juncture of mattress and bedstead, her legs were raised high above her, so high at times that her toes touched the wall behind her, and her pussy was so close to her face that she could hear the slithering glide of her labia about his shaft as he pumped in and out of her.

She had donned some light make-up by way of preparation, nothing too elaborate, and had restricted her costume choice to what she considered the barest of bare mimima – a pair of fine denier lace-top black stockings.

He had been told in no uncertain terms that she wanted to be fucked, and that she would be assessing his performance closely as it could lead to an important job. He had listened attentively enough, apparently keen to please.

And he'd started so well, taking her to him with what appeared to be real passion, kissing her closely, deeply as she responded, following his lead, succumbing to his much more powerful physique as he encouraged her to remove his shirt while he fiddled with her dress straps. His opening moves were good, no doubt about it, and by the time he had lifted her to carry her to the bed she was convinced she'd found the man she wanted for the job.

But from the very moment she'd removed his bulging boxers it became clear that he knew where the spotlight was expected to focus and remain – he'd watched her carefully as she softly squeezed his cock, bringing it closer to her face as he shifted up the bed, straddling her body, and he'd been ever-more engrossed as she started to suck lightly on the fat cock-head, taking him fully into her mouth but not sucking at all, opting to roll her tongue about his ridge, tease his glans as he played with his balls, pulling them away from where her mouth had trapped him, extending his length and running his free fingers along the thickness of his uppermost vein.

And when she'd asked to be fucked he'd merely smiled knowingly, as though he'd expected as much, and it was with obvious reluctance that he shifted away from her, cupped his broad hands under her calves and raised her long legs above her, his grimace impatient, aggressive as he waited for her to locate his dick and bring it to her entrance.

She had no sooner circled her clit with the smooth saliva-coated cock-head than he was pushing, insisting on entry, and she yielded, curious to know what his next move would be.

He could not have been more disappointing. The young man, barely in his mid-twenties, kept speeding up despite her constant requests not to, and eventually, tiring of his self-obsessed preening, phoney groaning and sporadic exhortations to 'take it baby', she pulled the thick flesh-stick away from her, bent forward and used both hands to expertly bring him off.

He emitted a series of bullish bellows as the condom swelled and became milky, and she left him to lie on the sofa moaning his appreciation as she donned her jacket and left.

This was getting so fucking tiresome. The first man they'd been sent to see was ever so welcoming and interested in impressing Imogen, but he simply would not stop asking questions: why this secrecy about names and numbers? Why did the meeting have to take place in the hotel? What the hell was a nice English rose like her doing hanging around with the likes of Hans? He had, as requested, showered, and allowed her to inspect his body – first class pass as far as the physical side of things was concerned; nice natural tan, well-worked but not musclebound torso, fine long legs and a well-developed, shaved and highly presentable cock. But as soon as he came into the room, the white towelling robe arranged just so, the bulb of his cock raising the fabric, she realised that he was simply too camp to be true, it would never ever work. If he wasn't gay then he'd certainly developed his look, his mannerisms and mien to appeal to homosexual aesthetes rather than practitioners, and it was not an image that most red-blooded women would entertain in their baser, grittier fantasies. He was, in short, too *good* to be suitable for the required purpose, so she gave him a business card – one of the fakes she'd made up at the airport – and said she'd be in touch as soon as possible. He'd started to ask yet more questions but Hans had accompanied him to the door and persuaded him that the interview was well and truly over.

And the second had been at the other extreme of unacceptability – yes, he had a very impressive dick: almost a foot long, poker-straight, thickened quite magnificently from the rather slender head to the fist-thick base of the shaft from which the plum-sized balls hung full and heavy. In all other physical respects he was appalling – he hadn't shaved for weeks, possibly months, and he was smelly. He was also unreasonably hirsute; uneven clumps of thick black wiry hair appeared to have been attached to him at random, the overall effect being that he was once completely hair-covered but had been attacked or otherwise traumatised and had lost much of his covering as a result. Hans knew of three separate women, all friends of colleagues, who would happily testify that this missing link was the best fuck they had ever had in their life and yes, they would entertain him again at any time. But Imogen simply could not bring herself to inflict such a beast on anyone, particularly without warning, and so he too was given a card, thanked for his time and patience and sent packing.

She angrily punched the call-button again – the hotel was starting to feel like a prison, and she still hadn't spent a full night in it since arrival.

Hans was still waiting, but had bought himself a newspaper. When he looked up at her it was plain her disgust was plumbing new depths.

'Hans,' she said quietly as he rose and followed her to the elevator, 'let me explain something. I wanted to find a man who is a good lover, has some experience. If he's got a tremendous cock, all well and good, but that side of it is more for dramatic effect than anything else. The guy has to be at least reasonably good in the sack, has to have been about a bit. Know what I mean?'

Hans held the steel doors open as she entered, her heels clicking on the polished floor. She was tired, wanted to get the ball rolling. The women were fine, no problem there, but she just needed one man, one good guy who could be relied upon.

The elevator buzzed into action as Hans brought out his little aide-memoire and punched at the buttons.

'I have one more name here. He isn't in town right now but, let's see, yeah, we've got three film titles, he features in all. One is unavailable, the other is a little hard to get, it appears it is something of a collectors' item, but I know for sure we can get the third, it is called *Up And At Them*.'

Imogen couldn't help smiling at Hans's precise enunciation of the cheesy title, the awful gravity he brought to even the simplest of statements. His frown deepened as she tried to apologise, but eventually she formed a question to preoccupy him.

'Where is it?' she asked.

'Well, as a matter of fact, I own that particular movie. It is only on the video format, you understand, but the quality is reasonable. I can have it sent to you by courier, you will have it by, let me see, you could have it by about midnight.'

'Hans, you have this movie? At your place?'

He nodded as he folded the electronic diary and snapped the case shut.

'OK,' she said as his eyes widened with horror, 'let's go then.'

Charlotte couldn't be quite sure if she had fallen asleep or not, but she certainly felt refreshed, completely sober after the rest. It had long been dark outside the House, but there was no telling exactly what time it was.

The dinner had probably finished about nine, and although the enigmatic couple had briefly returned to have a final drink and say their goodnights to Dark Eyes and the Librarian, it had been quite obvious that the evening was not going to deliver anything more interesting than a cosy fireside chat about geopolitics and suchlike.

All of which was perfectly fine; Charlotte and Seona both had reasonable points to make about any of the subjects broached, but Charlotte had quickly formed the opinion that the chatter was a device, a stalling tactic – someone in the room was being played, and if it wasn't the attractive young couple, then . . .? Something suspicious was going on, something that even Dark Eyes had been unable or unwilling to warn them of.

But why insist on their staying the evening?

Seona was asleep, her arms curved about Charlotte's body, but she awoke silently and swiftly when Charlotte whispered that she had to get up.

The House was utterly quiet. For Charlotte, as surely as for Seona, the experience of being in such isolated countryside was always overwhelmingly unusual after prolonged periods of city-living.

So Charlotte led Seona from the room, both still wearing their glamorous outfits, but with the noisy high heels slung over hooked fingers.

It took a full five minutes to tiptoe from the second-floor guest bedroom to the ground-floor corridor, assessing each step for telltale creaks and palming their way along those sections of corridor which were not served by the intermittent pulses of faint moonlight.

The mysterious young couple had been assigned a room in the east wing, somewhere fairly close to the main entrance; the brief cry they'd heard earlier had come from that direction.

Then she sensed it rather than heard it – little more than a dull shifting, a disturbance of air, and Charlotte knew they were being watched by someone near, someone moving silently in the darkness, tracking their movements.

As if responding to Charlotte's realisation, a voice, strident and sharp, resounded in a nearby room. It wasn't the Librarian, but the voice was almost certainly female. Charlotte reached out a hand behind her, Seona's fingers found hers, and they traversed the final length of pitch-black corridor which led, not to the ground-floor guest rooms, but the staircase leading to the basement.

Now, at least, there was light, the weak electric bulb illuminating the steeply descending stairwell which led to the labyrinthine complex of stores and cellars.

Another sound, louder now, and much nearer, this time a cry, though whether borne of pleasure or pain Charlotte could not guess.

The narrow subterranean passage was lined with empty wine crates, piles of dusty books and newspapers, and they made progress carefully, slowly. Then, so suddenly that Charlotte jumped with fright, the sound of old wood being dragged across stone flooring rumbled along the dank corridor, the red light filled the shaft ahead of them, and there was Petra to welcome them.

She seemed enormously tall – she was perhaps close to six feet anyway – in the boots which encased her long legs up to her thighs, and the skintight black latex appeared to have been painted on to her flesh. The outfit, while certainly no more shocking than anything Charlotte or Seona might have chosen in similar circumstances, was utterly alluring – the woman's broad hips made the flanges of the corset appear impossibly tight, the minuscule waist surely achievable only by plenty of lace-pulling and considerable discomfort, and the low-slung cups of the black support appeared specifically designed to hold her large breasts just so. It was the bareness of her bosoms and shoulders which perplexed, made the appearance unsettling, for she had indeed been painted with latex, also gleaming black, and even her erect nipples looked strangely false. Her slender arms were, of course, gloved, her head was encased in what appeared to be a rubber balaclava, only her mouth and eyes visible. Overall, the first impression Charlotte formed was that the rather quiet young woman appeared to have transformed herself into a huge and rather menacing insect.

Charlotte entered the room first, Petra welcoming them in silently, her outstretched arm indicating that they were expected and welcome.

The ceiling was low, the atmosphere dank and vaguely salty, like the bowels of a ship might be, and Charlotte had only taken half a dozen steps when she saw Dieter sitting in the broad upright chair, his hands gripping the curved ends of the wooden arms tightly as he surveyed the Librarian sucking him. She had changed yet again, had donned her preferred rubberwear, the classic neck-high knee-length pencil dress which completely encased her body and fingers and made her sex inaccessible. Again the déjà vu threatened to swamp Charlotte – she had seen that dress before, had even been persuaded to wear something very similar during one of the many educational projects she and Seona and Imogen had so stoically endured at the House.

The cold of the stone floor registered against her toes, and Seona followed suit as Charlotte slipped her shoes back on.

Dark Eyes's voice echoed low and clear, but Charlotte couldn't see where he was.

'Good girls,' he said, and she could imagine the slight smile, the sparkle in his eyes as he surveyed them from whatever vantage point he enjoyed, 'you can judge for yourself whether you want the assistance of the newcomers. The decision is yours.'

So, the game she had suspected was little more than a tentative introduction, the extension of an offer of help. It had never been necessary before – in the execution of her tasks as Kayla, Charlotte had always been permitted to work alone, and Seona had been the only companion she had ever taken with her, had always been her first and only choice. The powerful young couple could be useful, but the statuesque Petra could conceivably be a problem – even now, as Charlotte assessed the stance of the fetishised blonde, standing with arms crossed, posing beautifully in clear sight of her partner as he was intensely fellated by the Librarian, it was clear that Kayla's role as unquestioned dominatrix might be under threat. That would not do.

Seona was close behind Charlotte, her hands on her waist as she peered over her shoulder. Dieter's eyes were closed and his chest was heaving – the leather harness he wore dug into his flesh, the fine covering of blond hair curling across his perspiring chest and midriff. He placed a hand on the Librarian's head and forced her away from him, his cock emerging from her throat with a hollow slurping sound as she sat back on her calves, the rubber stretching about her full backside. She continued to stroke his alarmingly long, thin cock as he smiled up at Petra, and then beckoned Charlotte.

'You want some,' he said, and Charlotte instantly rankled, offended that he challenge her so boldly when he had to know, must surely have been told, that Kayla was in his midst.

Charlotte folded her arms, took a couple of steps forward, and stared down at his engorged dick. She placed a hand on the Librarian's shoulder, the coolness of the rubber at once thrilling and slightly repulsive, and squeezed lightly before smoothing her fingers across the older woman's thickly gelled hair.

The Librarian wiped her lips, was still staring at Dieter's cock as it waned and settled on his thigh, still wet from her attention. He shifted in the seat, his bare flesh causing the red leather to creak, and it was only then that Charlotte realised he had been cuffed to the old piece of furniture, his ankles also manacled to the front legs.

'What I want is none of your business,' she said, and she saw the spark of indignation in his expression swiftly supplanted by the first signs of fear as she sternly met his gaze with widening eyes and an appropriately severe frown.

'You must not dare assume anything about me,' she snarled as he visibly retreated within the confines of the hard-backed seat, his cock shrinking. 'If you are going to be of any use to me, to us, then you must learn obedience.'

He glanced across to where Petra was now standing with legs apart, hands on hips as if ready and more than able to challenge Charlotte. Charlotte followed his sideways glance, caught the eye of the tall woman and silently stared at her.

'You dare to stare at me?' Charlotte said slowly, deliberately, every word a gauntlet, and the broad-shouldered woman stared on from within the heavy rubber headwear, large blue eyes unblinking, steady.

Charlotte, feeling strangely vulnerable, almost bare when compared to the voluptuously costumed blonde, crossed the flagstones to take up a position immediately in front of the intimidating woman, fully a foot taller than she. She stared up at the defiant eyes, could feel her nostrils flare, eyes narrow further as she struggled to control the hyperventilation, the tingling fear which always accompanied the initial stages of domination.

'Get over there and kneel in front of him,' Charlotte said.

Petra did not budge, but her eyes were flitting now between Charlotte, Seona and her tethered companion, the uncertainty was setting in.

'I will not ask twice,' Charlotte continued, still staring hard into the face above her, daring her to utter a word.

Petra's sudden movement could have been an effort to strike out, to make her own bid for dominance at this crucial juncture, but Charlotte remained steady, did not flinch, and the taller woman passed her, perhaps deliberately brushing her latexed arm against Charlotte's shoulder as she did so.

Seona fetched one of the many paddles hanging on the line of hooks behind the door; the old faithful design, time-tested and moulded through years of stern application. Charlotte gripped the hidebound handle, tested the tension of the thing. It was perhaps slightly larger than a table-tennis bat, but the gentle curvature of the surface and rather elongated ovoid design gave it the appearance of a solid face mask, a small shield of some kind.

The Librarian was on her feet, had retreated from the base of the chair as Petra took her place, hands on Dieter's parted knees, her posterior already presented for Charlotte's attention.

'Shift further back,' commanded Charlotte, and the woman sat bolt upright, placed her hands on her own thighs as Charlotte neared, gently slapping her palm into the spoonlike recess of the paddle.

'I'm sure you'll enjoy this,' she said, and Dieter still had that slight smile, almost knowing, deeply annoying. He probably thought he'd seen it all before, and his dick was filling again, twitching and rising as he anticipated the punishment of his partner.

So when Charlotte raised the paddle, looking up at it briefly to check its likely trajectory, he couldn't have possibly imagined it was destined for his scrotum.

The paddle came cracking against the base of his swollen dick with a fleshy smack which made the Librarian and Petra gasp aloud.

Dieter screamed.

'That's just for starters, boy,' said Charlotte as she stepped back, raised the paddle again and brought it down on Petra's bare arse.

'Get to work on him, no hands,' she ordered, and Petra leaned forward, taking Dieter into her mouth as he groaned and writhed in the seat, the first waves of shock subsiding to be replaced by what Charlotte knew would be a surging, burning pain.

'Here,' Charlotte said, passing the paddle to the Librarian, and the older woman was more than eager to continue Petra's chastisement, steadily, expertly bringing the now warming leather paddle against the younger woman's buttocks with a deceptively short swing which nevertheless achieved splendidly loud results.

Charlotte moved behind the seat, allowing her hands to rest on Dieter's shoulders.

'You would like to help me?' Charlotte asked as she looked down to see Petra's face bloated with his cock, her arse rising into the paddle blows as the Librarian upped her pace.

He was muttering, but the language was not identifiable, certainly not German. Charlotte shouted the question at him as she leaned over, running her fingers through his thick chest hair, over his tensed abdomen as she located the base of his dick. Petra's face was still sliding up and down it, her lips distended, a scarlet circle about the reddened organ.

'Perhaps, perhaps we can help,' he managed to say through gritted teeth. Charlotte was aware of her own swollen nipples straining at the crushed velvet material of her dress, her own arousal now dictating her actions as she sought the commitment which would be a prerequisite for the involvement of this couple in the trip ahead.

'You can help,' Charlotte said as she pulled at his cock, drawing it out of Petra's face, gleaming, faint concentric circles of lip-gloss where she had gradually taken his length into her, and she gripped it tightly with both hands, squeezing hard, forcing his already bloated cock-head to swell painfully, becoming gnarled and pimpled with purple blood as she hauled at him, harder with every stroke as Petra's eyes, widening and fearful, witnessed the brutal wanking.

His hands were displaying panic, arms tensing as he strained against the straps, lifting his arse off the seat to ease the effect of Charlotte's pulling, but with every inch of relief he managed to achieve Charlotte simply tightened her grip and pulled harder so that his already long cock appeared to be being hauled out of his body altogether, so distended and thin had his shaft become.

When Charlotte released the pressure his cock filled swiftly, and the pain hit him. He yelled, head thrust backwards as Charlotte brought her fingers lightly, quickly gliding up and down him as he bulged and bloated and then finally erupted, the spunk jetting across Petra's face, snaking across the rubber hood, stringing across her open lips and teeth as she closed her eyes and allowed Charlotte to stuff the end of his jerking dick back into her face.

Charlotte moved around to where the Librarian was still thrashing at Petra's crimson arse cheeks, her white hair working loose from the familiar bun, the perspiration shining on her forehead as she panted heavily, eyes savouring the proffered and punished flesh below her. Charlotte raised a hand to indicate that the chastisement should cease, and the Librarian stepped back, hands clasped afront her, the paddle still firm in her grasp as Charlotte raised the back of her hand before the older woman's face. She needed no instruction to clean the ribbon of spunk from her fingers with her tongue.

'Now then,' Charlotte said as matter-of-factly as she could, turning to the groaning Dieter, 'let's try again. Do you want to help me?'

'I suppose you could say he is something of a legend,' Hans said, adjusting his spectacles as he pushed the fast-forward button and brought the next sequence into view on the large screen.

'But how old is he?' Imogen asked, her concern obvious as she tried to assess the age of the videotape being shown. The quality was not good, the footage had clearly been copied many times previously, but it was clear enough that Orlo, whoever he was, was a very capable lover and seemed as ready to tackle men as women. The grainy fuzz of the stilled image suddenly shifted, the appalling soundtrack resumed – an absurdly inappropriate salsa-type dirge – as the close-up of Orlo's cock hammering into the backside of an extremely overweight man jerked into motion.

'Now? I guess he's in his forties, perhaps early fifties. Very little is known about him. I guess he was a big name some years ago, but now? I have no idea where he is, what he is doing. What I do know is that he had some very powerful friends, he was on the guest list for the best parties in town for a long time. It's not hard to see why.'

Indeed not. If the evidence she had just witnessed was anything to go by, Orlo was nothing if not enthusiastic about his brief forays into film, and the sheer energy he obviously possessed in great measure was impressive. Perhaps most impressive of all was his apparent ability to maintain a constant erection. Unless the editing of the film had been particularly sophisticated (and judging by its overall quality that seemed unlikely) the man suffered no loss of erection, even after ejaculation. Furthermore, he possessed the rare ability to urinate even while fully erect. Entirely possible that the poor soul suffered from some form of priapism, in which case he was perhaps more to be pitied than admired, but Imogen could see the potential there, his usefulness was plain. There was also something undeniably attractive about the slender, unremarkable looking man which made her wonder how much he had changed since the film was made, whether he still possessed that rather forlorn, lost expression. It was as if he was trying to fuck everything in sight but hadn't quite found what he was looking for. If so, the impending project might be of interest to him, might just appeal to someone who had seen and done most of the things ordinary men regarded as unachievable fantasies.

She tensed her thighs, curled a little tighter into the comfortable leather armchair and watched Hans as he replenished their glasses. What a gentleman: not once in the three weeks since she'd first employed him had he so much as glanced at her the wrong way, and although she had considered the possibility that he might be gay it was clear now, as he stretched back on the recliner and passed the glass to her, that, whatever his persuasion, Orlo was a genuine favourite. But was it the sight of Orlo servicing the lesbians that aroused him? The sight of his dick being attended to by the transexual waiter? No way of telling for sure, and the tape had already displayed such a variety of situations – some deeply arousing, some farcical – that it would be beyond most folk not to respond to some of the crudely spliced clips.

'Do you have a girlfriend, Hans?' she heard herself ask, and he didn't remove his eyes from the screen.

'No, Miss Langley, I do not. I use the services of call girls. It is perhaps shameful, but that is how it is, and in this city there are many beautiful women who are happy to spend some time with people like me. I am no trouble to anyone, my tastes are simple. It is not a problem.'

She sipped at the drink. She was getting horny, also a little tipsy, and she knew it was utterly wrong to confuse business with pleasure, but it had been a long time since she'd fucked anyone for the simple reason that she wanted to, and not because there was some gain, some angle, some requirement to satisfy.

The screen flickered and shuddered and the action shifted again. This time Orlo was standing on the balcony of a hotel overlooking a bay, the landscape unmistakably Californian. The woman sitting in the chair in front of him was mature, wore only a simple white robe, and she was jerking at the protruding inches of a white vibrator as she pulled Orlo's cock into her mouth.

'Would you like me to do that to you?' Imogen asked, and he turned slowly, removing his spectacles as he did so.

'I would like nothing more,' he replied, so straight-faced, so serious that she laughed aloud.

He drained his glass as she rose, took her hand and led her to his bedroom.

Four

'No calls,' Goodstone said as his PA gathered together the sheaf of initialled papers.

The icy snow rattled against the windows behind him as he brushed his fingertips along the edge of the desk. The door was closed quietly.

He removed his glasses, placed them on top of the open diary and pinched his nose where the specs had formed permanent indentations. The exhaustion washed over him again. Another round of meetings this afternoon, dinner with that ridiculous collection of has-beens masquerading as friends at the Club, and no doubt the usual demands to appear on the late-night news-analysis programmes. They could all go to hell.

He stood up, stretched his arms behind him, clasped his hands together and tried to yank some of the tension from his shoulders. It wasn't working, hadn't been for a while. He badly needed a break, some respite, and knew exactly what he wanted, but it was becoming increasingly difficult, dangerous to get in touch with her.

Of course, there was no realistic threat that the papers would ever run the story of the affair – there wasn't one editor he didn't know personally, and he knew full well that none would dare embarrass him publicly. But his opposition to the passage of the Bill had already drawn serious criticism, and so long as he stayed out on a limb, the casting vote in his hands, there was always that chance, that slight chance, that someone, somewhere, would drop him in it.

Besides, he had grown tired of her, and she him – it had become like a second marriage, and God alone knew one tired sham was enough to be going on with. No – she wouldn't be back in touch, and he would shed no tears over her departure.

And yet. That call. That curious call taken at the beach house. He could count on two hands the number of friends who knew he used the place as a hideaway, and a smaller number again who had the direct number. But it was not the fact of the contact that perplexed him – he'd long ago learned that no one could be entirely trusted – rather, it was the nature of the message.

Kayla? It had meant nothing at first, but the name had stayed in his mind that weekend, refused to go away. Kayla.

Calling Tom had been a hunch, nothing more, and the retired judge had seemed genuinely unable to pinpoint the name let alone determine whether it belonged to any of the mutual acquaintances they had known during their long careers. But on the Monday Tom had called the office, excited and keen to meet. No, it could not possibly be discussed on the telephone.

Tom was already the worse for drink when Goodstone had arrived at their Club, and he'd had to ask him to accompany him to a quieter corner of the smaller lounge before eliciting what he knew.

No, Tom did not know Kayla, knew of no one alive who did, but he'd had a dream that night following Goodstone's call – a disturbingly detailed, full-colour dream complete with soundtrack, scents and lingering close-ups – during which he remembered where he'd heard that name, the scenarios he'd been told about in which the mysterious woman featured.

So, it had been a full forty years since the name had been whispered to him, passed to him like some secret burden, and the man who had passed it was long since dead. But if he was to be believed – and there was no means of corroborating his claims – there was a woman called Kayla, an Englishwoman who had the power to break monarchies, lay low the most powerful of men with her charms. The woman was said to be so entrancing, so sexually explosive, that all who fell under spell and experienced her touch were unable to find satisfaction with any other mortal as long as they lived. But she was no call-girl, not this beauty. She moved among the powerful according to the dictates of those whose hands were upon the tiller of Empire, the unidentifiable men and women who forged the destinies of millions of their fellow beings without ever facing the light of scrutiny, the inconvenience of accountability. Even they were not immune to Kayla's many charms, and it was said that she remained, throughout frequent changes of government, unassailable, positioned at a permanent remove from those to whom the donkeywork of plotting global developments was but a daily task.

Old Tom – Goodstone couldn't help smiling at the memory of his friend practically slavering as he recounted Kayla's legendary antics, his rabid enquiries as to the source of the name, the origin of the curious call to the beach house.

But the call-back option had been blocked by the caller and the automatic tracing software permanently attached to his telecommunications had revealed only that the call originated in New York. No further clues.

He clicked open the drinks cabinet, reached in for the decanter but then replaced it. Still way too early, and it wouldn't help in any case. A glass of soda and ice would suffice.

A full week had passed, still nothing. Tom had kept his ears open, asked around, and although he had uncovered some interesting titbits of information which could be potentially useful to both of them, the mention of Kayla's name seemed to inspire nothing more than frowns and blank stares.

But how utterly thrilling – the very idea made his dick pulse, and it took a lot to make that happen these days. A woman who was so untraceable, so discreet that her very existence was debated. It seemed the stuff of dreams. And how could she still be alive? The voice he had heard was English, certainly, but she could not have been more than, what, thirty? Difficult to say exactly, but that had been no old woman on the phone, no way. And the voice itself had suggested mischief, a self-confidence he'd rarely encountered since assuming his present position. Fear was the default expression on the faces of those who were introduced to him, and it had been a long time since he'd been able to flirt honestly, openly with any woman on equal terms, as an anonymous man. And he knew the truth was that those days were long gone, would never be back again. He rued his fidelity all those years, the exciting, exhausting years when he'd overcome one obstacle after another, faithfully keeping Mary with him every step of the way. How many chances had there been? How many women had begged him, demanded that he fuck them? And by the time Mary had lost interest in him, and he'd finally succumbed, taking Helen as his lover, it was too late: what spontaneity had there been in the whole affair, in the pathetic clandestine meetings, the elaborately organised vacations? He could now see that the excitement of it all was reducible to his own disgust at the betrayal, an affirmation of his own self-loathing.

How delightful it would be, how welcome – a chance to recapture some scintilla of the excitement he had denied himself all his life. If only he had known then . . .

He returned to the cabinet, brusquely withdrew the decanter and sloshed some Scotch over the soda. The ice was still rattling, tinkling against the glass when the phone tringed into life, and he was about to bellow at Kyle when the door opened and the PA's face appeared.

'I'm sorry, sir, but I thought perhaps you'd make an exception. It's a young woman called Kayla.'

Charlotte eventually hung up. Steve was clearly in self-righteous mode again, demanding answers: why did she have to stay so long? What was it about the launch of the new stores along the East Coast which couldn't be done by the trusted staff she had there? Why had she suddenly taken such an interest in the couture business after years of maintaining that she was not a shop-girl and would not become one no matter how illustrious the addresses of the stores?

Bottom line – he was jealous and she knew he knew it. He couldn't stand the idea that Seona was sharing her bed again, that they were enjoying one another in ways he could only wonder at.

No matter – he would reward himself with a boisterous weekend with the lads; they would prob-ably head over to Paris, ostensibly to watch the rugby international, and she knew full well that even if he was not particularly interested in keeping up with the other chaps, he would bed one of the beautiful escorts just for the hell of it, simply because he could. And good luck to him too – he deserved a little fun.

But she couldn't help worrying. Not about Steve. Sharing the penthouse suite with Dieter and Petra had been a necessity, and although the five apartments provided more than enough space to get away from one another, it hadn't quite worked out that way so far: Petra had been demonstrating a growing fondness for, and influence over, Seona in the past week, and Charlotte knew the growing friendship was potentially catastrophic insofar as it might impact upon the job in hand.

Yes, Petra and Dieter had pledged Charlotte their unquestioning support and she had no reason to doubt the completeness of their subservience to her. It had been more than amply demonstrated back in the House, that long night during which they had repeatedly subjected themselves to her, eager to experience first-hand the pleasures and pains which came of being Kayla's slaves. And, of course, there was the quid pro quo: as initiates, the opportunity to spend time with Kayla was precious enough, but to be assigned to assist her in such an important venture was an unprecedented honour, and they had been made fully aware of that.

But now, with familiarity and boredom threatening to undermine the urgency of the mission, Charlotte was keenly aware that the pressure to find Imogen was becoming unbearable for all of them.

Dieter had enjoyed limited success in his quest – yes, Dr Imogen Langley-Boyd was currently working on a paper at the Northwoods University, but no, she could not be contacted directly; the details of her contract with the university were confidential; a message could certainly be left for her, but there could be no guarantee that she would receive or acknowledge it. So he'd simply asked that she get in touch: he had followed her work in England, wanted to do a piece for· the *Science Digest* on her latest work, and if she would care to get in touch he would love to arrange an interview for which there would be a healthy fee.

That had been five days ago. Nothing. Dieter had even taken Seona with him to the university, managed to secure a one-day pass for the library, but the afternoon spent on the campus had been a waste of time. Seona had been unable to identify anyone who might perhaps even be Imogen in disguise.

Charlotte snapped out of the reverie as the shifting lights of another passenger plane ascended into the darkness beyond the city lights below. The panorama, so stunning for the first day or so, was now becoming tedious despite the picturesque quality lent by the uniform coating of frosty snow, and the short Washington days were frustrating all of them, the increasing tension manifesting itself in increasingly spontaneous and animalistic couplings.

The nature of their introduction to one another had removed the norms of etiquette – Charlotte had fucked Dieter that evening in the House, and encouraged Seona to take him anally. Petra had been more than willing to subject herself to the attentions of the dildo-wielding Librarian, and raised no objection when Charlotte donned a strap-on to take her simultaneously from behind. The permutations had continued into mid-morning, Dark Eyes appearing at a late juncture to take over from the drained Dieter. It was difficult now to recall the exact sequence of events, but it was fair enough to say that they had all become intimately acquainted with one another before sleep committed the whole experience to the realm of memory and fantasy. Snippets still resurfaced – Dark Eyes's balls slapping against Petra's chin as he forced himself into her puffed gullet while Seona reamed her in preparation for the Librarian's fingers; Dieter yelping as Petra inserted the heel of her boot into his rectum while the Librarian pulled his scrotum high and clear to allow them all a full view; Seona's beautiful behind being sandwiched as she rode on Dark Eyes's dick; the Librarian holding the thick rubber truncheon steady in her behind as Petra dribbled her spit on the shining black stick to ease its movement.

Yes, it had been an enjoyable, interesting evening, one which left them all more than a little tender the next day.

The reverie had moistened her. She put down the cup and went to the bathroom – time to change that plug, might as well do it now. It had been a long time since she'd indulged in anal intercourse and she had to be prepared, so since their first day in the apartment she had been wearing the butt-plug which had been given her all those years ago. Seona had also been wearing hers, but they had so far managed to resist the temptation to rehearse the kind of scenario which might well lie ahead – they had both long since learned that denial, the postponement of gratification was the engine of lust, that if they were to satisfactorily convey their enthusiasm for the various arts under their command, those skills were not to become pedestrian, part of the everyday. The very fact that they both knew the other was preparing in this way was itself a stimulant, one which had made the nights more interesting than they might otherwise have been, but still they had not yielded to the pleasures they had so often taken from and given to one another. The time would come, and they would both know it, would recognise it when it did.

She removed her panties and perched on the edge of the bath-tub, slowly removed the short stubby plug and rinsed it under the tap at the basin. Always that urge to close, the bitter-sweet pain of resistance, but it was becoming easier day by day. Time for the thickest plug, unused for some years now. She was smearing the water-based lubricant over the stubby smooth end when she realised the door was slightly ajar, sensed that someone was there. There was a split-second when she could have extended a foot and closed the door fully, but she feigned concentration on what she was doing, smearing the translucent gel about the two-inch diameter of the plug's base.

It couldn't be Seona at the door – she would merely have rapped lightly and entered. Dieter had left earlier to get some cigarettes but she hadn't heard him come back. It had to be Petra.

Charlotte raised her heel to the corner of the tub, steadied herself and brought the plug behind her, approaching her anus from behind. The blouse was brushing her thighs, tickling, but she closed her eyes and focused on relaxing again, keeping herself as open as possible during this final and most important insertion.

The gel was soothingly cool against her sphincter and she responded to the pleasant sensation by gently circling the air, only just bringing the hard leather into contact with her flesh as she kept her hand steady against the bath-tub's rim, a good solid base. With eyes shut she knew that whoever was watching would be less likely to turn away. The whole sensation of being watched was one thing, but the double-bluff involved in purposely allowing it without permission was a relative novelty, one which she had rarely experienced but found intensely stimulating.

It was impossible to attend to her pussy until the plug was inserted, so she made the first tentative thrusts of her hips, pushing herself down on the widening leather roundness, savouring the slight pain as she was stretched further than she had been for some years. Her arse twitched involuntarily as she redoubled the mental effort to relax, allow it to happen – as soon as that broadest point was broached she would close about the tool and it would be a matter of hours before she no longer was aware of its presence, unless she wanted to remind herself of it by tensing the relevant muscles.

She raised her face, bit her bottom lip and pushed again – nearly there. It was getting a little sore, and she was vaguely aware of moaning lightly as she pushed again, her fist closing about the plug's flange. It was no use, she needed more gel, she was too tight. She opened her eyes, taking care to make sure that she would be looking down at the floor when she did so. She gasped as she drew the plug away from her, and it was then that the door lightly and soundlessly swung open and Petra spoke.

'Would you like me to help?' said the tall blonde, and Charlotte knew she was flushed, aroused, felt curiously vulnerable in the face of what, ostensibly, was a humiliating exposure.

'I knew you were there,' said Charlotte, suddenly defensive and embarrassed. It was pointless to deny it, but she was slightly afraid of Petra, afraid of what she might do to her relationship with Seona, afraid of her physical presence.

'It would help if you lay down,' Petra said, lifting the small tube of lubricant.

Charlotte wanted to tell her to fuck off, to go back to Dark Eyes and the Librarian and tell them that things had not worked out, that Kayla was going to do what had to be done alone, as always, that she needed no help from amateurs. But something about the woman was so casual, so natural and nonplussed that Charlotte lifted a thick towel from the rack, laid it on the floor and slipped down to kneel upon it. She brought the blouse up about her waist, raised her bottom and parted her knees. She snuggled her face into the soft towelling and waited. She was sure she heard an appreciative whimper from Petra, but had no time to dwell on it.

A slender finger traced the tightness of her still-open ring, smoothing the gel directly from the tube, allowing it to well in her opening as Charlotte fought the urge to tighten.

'You don't want to lie down?' Petra asked.

'I prefer it like this,' Charlotte replied, and the blonde woman continued gently massaging the gel into her arse as she spoke.

'That's difficult; I can never take it like that, not at first anyway. I have to lie down. Dieter likes, how do you call it, he likes spoons, that's what he calls it anyway.'

Charlotte grunted acknowledgement of what was being said, but the woman was already starting to work the plug into her, twisting it clockwise, gently fucking her with it as she delved a little deeper each time. A long cool palm was pressed into the small of her back, pushing back the blouse and persuading her to buck back against the tool as Petra continued to twist it, working the gel about the expanding rim as Charlotte made little backward jerking movements.

The scent of the woman was powerful, reminiscent of something forgotten – not perfume, not make-up or anything artificial. It was the smell of lust, young and strong unmistakably female.

Suddenly, with no warning whatsoever, the plug was rammed into her and Charlotte shrieked with shock, her buttocks clenching instinctively as the heavy leather tool filled her behind, her ring protectively closing about the flange which guarded against accidental retraction of the plug.

'There, that wasn't so bad,' said Petra. Charlotte could not answer, the dull pain radiating through her as she groaned. Petra's fingers were smoothing something else onto her, up the cleft of her cheeks, about the tenderness now covered by the flange, and then other fingers were kneading at her pussy, one in particular flicking at her wetness, encouraging her lips to part.

Charlotte felt herself weaken as she moved again, parted further, bringing her own hand down to press upon Petra's fingers, grinding her pulsing clitoris against the woman's fingertips, vicariously frigging herself with the hand of another. And the blonde woman was getting closer, her body now pressing against Charlotte as she moved both hands underneath to continue the massage.

It took several seconds for Petra's intentions to become clear, but the woman's fingers were so good, so effective that there was a millisecond during which Charlotte seriously considered allowing her to continue with the seduction. It would be easy to succumb, to let her dictate what would happen next, but the realisation that this simple submission would be precisely what Petra had been working towards since they first met was too obvious to ignore and, hard as it might be to admit it, Charlotte realised she was only seconds away from effectively throwing off her role as Kayla for the sake of a quick and furtive orgasm.

As if confirming Charlotte's deepest, most paranoid worries, Petra's long thighs started to tighten about Charlotte's legs. She was going to mount

Charlotte, attempt to dominate her. No more – the fury was volcanic.

Charlotte twisted away from Petra and, in one deft movement, sprung to her knees, tearing at the much bigger woman's blouse. The tiny blue buttons spun and scattered, ricocheting off the tiled wall as Charlotte lambasted her. Petra, shocked and unprepared for the assault, lost her balance and slipped back, hands raised protectively as Charlotte railed against her.

'Bitch! You think you can just waltz into my life and take away the thing that's dearest to me?'

Charlotte could not stop the tirade. She seldom lost her temper, usually managing to channel the anger into whatever she was doing, turn it to some positive advantage. But this time she could hear herself rant as if it was all happening to someone else, and she could see the full heavy breasts being covered as Petra recoiled, see the raw fear in the woman's eyes. But as always, if you knew where to look, there was desire and challenge, a primitive signalling of availability.

'You are beautiful, yes,' shrieked Charlotte, 'but you'll never have her. Not the way I do. Never.'

Charlotte shoved the door completely shut and advanced on the prone woman, clambering over her body as if preparing to pin her down with a wrestling move, but instead she kept going, advanced further, gripped the blonde's hair in her hands and brought her pussy down on her, grinding her wetness into the protesting face.

The cries were muffled but no doubt genuine enough as Charlotte rode the woman's face, sitting fully on her, rubbing the slender nose against her stuffed anus, grinding her distended labia against the shapely chin, fingers entwined in the fine hair as she bucked and shagged her, the long-awaited come starting to build within her.

Petra had clearly decided that co-operation was the wisest option long before Charlotte reached her climax, and the blonde prodded the flange of the plug, other fingers stuffing the smaller woman's pussy, nails digging into her arse flesh as the orgasm raged through her, transmitted to the wretched Petra via a series of violent, juddering spasms.

Charlotte toppled onto the bathroom floor, spent and disgusted with herself as the blonde gently lapped at her sex, soothing the redness of her as they panted and puffed their way to recovery, unaware that, right next door, Seona was sobbing into folded arms.

Imogen straightened her skirt and gave herself a quick double-check in the reflection cast by the highly polished teak door. The suit was rather uncomfortable but suitably business like. She had no doubt that this was, potentially, the most important piece of business she had ever attempted.

Hans placed a reassuring hand on her shoulder. It had been a good night, and he was a considerate, careful lover who abandoned his fastidious persona when between the sheets. Moreover, he was big and strong and she knew he always carried a small pistol, so his presence was a very welcome support.

Orlo's voice crackled through the intercom, and it was Hans who replied. The heavy buzz and click signalled they should enter, and when they did so it was to face a steep flight of navy-blue carpeted steps.

Hans went first, and was nearing the top of the flight when Orlo appeared, hand extended in welcome, his greeting muttered and muted, although his smile seemed genuine enough.

Imogen offered her hand and he took it gently, placing a kiss on her joined fingers before standing back almost theatrically and scanning her from the toes up, eyebrows indicating his approval of what he saw.

'You are very welcome,' he said, indicating with an open palm that they should enter the enormous living room dominated by the four-seater fake leopard-skin sofa and the biggest domestic aquarium Imogen had ever seen. He noticed her interest, brought her to the long tank and introduced individual fish as though they were friends.

She declined the bourbon offered, plumping for a glass of white wine as they settled down to discuss her proposal. Hans had already aroused Orlo's interest by contacting his ex-agent, but details remained sketchy, largely because Imogen had never divulged them to anyone.

'Hans, I'm sure you wouldn't mind leaving us alone for a few minutes,' Imogen said, smiling sweetly at the big German and, although his expression betrayed mild annoyance, he did get up and leave, muttering something about getting some cigarettes, but she noted the firm way he said he wouldn't be long, and his obvious concern was warming, welcome.

Imogen waited for the sound of the heavy front door clicking shut, smoothing the pleats of her black skirt over her stockings as she prepared her opening gambit.

'I've seen some of your work,' she said, affecting a look of mild embarrassment, and the Texan merely nodded politely, expression impassive.

'It's really quite impressive,' she continued, finding his stare rather disconcerting.

'I want to cut to the chase here,' he said, fingering his moustache before taking another gulp of the straight whisky, 'I was told you might have a job for me, something unusual. Now, I don't know what you consider unusual, but I want to tell you something which, under normal circumstances, I would never dream of saying in front of a lady.'

Imogen smiled, genuinely complimented.

'Fact is, Miss Langley, I've been retired for a long time. Almost nine years now. I was only ever in the business six years, made me some money, lost me a whole lot of friends, lost me a good woman too. I ain't never going back to that. Got me a good business now, for some reason I got nostalgia value, least that's what my commercial manager says. Nostalgia value.'

He said the final two words slowly, smiling as he did so, and with another gulp the glass was drained.

'I'm rather hoping that your status, if I can say it, your cult status is what interests me. I've been looking-for a man with a particular blend of qualities, and to be honest, I think you're the closest I've seen to an ideal candidate.'

She sipped at the wine and watched as he frowned, staring into his empty glass.

'Can I ask you a personal question, Miss Langley? A real personal question?'

She nodded, and he leaned forward, perched on the edge of the enormous sofa, the empty glass cupped in his hands.

'Do you remember the first time you made love?' he said, staring straight into her eyes. She felt the blush begin, not because the question was in any way salacious, but because it was so disarmingly sincere, his voice loaded with emotion.

She looked down into her own glass, remembered. Charlotte. That afternoon. The many men she'd known didn't matter when such recollections surfaced or were otherwise summoned. It was always her, always that sunny afternoon with the drapes almost fully shut, and she knew that it would always be, for her, the first day she'd ever made love, the day Kayla's destiny had been decided.

'Yes, yes I do,' she said, and she knew her eyes were filling, her voice was breaking.

He wiped at his moustache again.

'It don't get no better. Never does. Miss Langley, I have fucked many women, and I dare say you know I even fucked some men. There was a time I was screwing to order, five, six times a day. It was a job. But I want you to know that there was only ever one woman I made love to, that was the woman I married, the woman who bore my two children, and it don't happen again. You get it once, and if you're too dumb to realise it, that's too bad. Yeah, I fucked plenty people, after a time I didn't bother counting no more, and I was good at it. But it's over now. I don't know what you got in mind that you feel might interest me. If you want to talk merchandising, franchise, that kind of thing, that's fine, we can do all of that, it's straightforward enough. I could use someone in England. But from what Hans told me, your business is a little more complicated.'

She had regained her composure, dispelled the unexpected yearning for Charlotte. He seemed a reasonable man, and she had come this far. It was worth a try.

'Mr Orlo, I'm very close to arranging, let's just say, an evening of entertainment for someone very special, someone you will certainly know of. Nothing has been finalised yet, it's likely to take another few days, but if I know you're on board then the chances of it happening are tremendously increased.'

'So you're talking a guest appearance?' he said flatly, unimpressed.

'There is no publicity attached to what I'm doing. It is highly sensitive. The subject of my attention has no idea what I'm doing, is barely aware of my existence.'

'Well, let me say right off, young lady, I need to know that what you have in mind is not illegal, and I also need to know who this person is.'

Imogen swilled the wine.

'On the first count, please don't be alarmed. There is nothing whatever illegal about what I'm planning. The morality of it, well, that's for others to decide. I'm talking about a straightforward seduction.'

'And on the second point?' he said, his mounting interest now plain.

Imogen rose from the sofa, carefully negotiated the deep-pile rug, and bent to whisper the intended subject into his ear.

Orlo settled back into his seat, released a long high whistle, and resumed stroking his moustache.

'Holy shit,' he muttered, reaching for the bourbon bottle.

Imogen carefully returned to her seat, aware that he was watching her closely. The night was young, but she was tired and had already had a long day. If he was interested in having a closer look at who he might be working with, he would have to wait.

Goodstone could barely contain himself. The call, so brief, so cryptic, had left him weak-kneed and shaking. He had never believed in karma, destiny, any of that garbage, but for her to have called just at that moment, at that very moment when he so very nearly started drinking the one which would have led to another and, inevitably, the cancellation of his appointments for the rest of the day? It was certainly curious.

He replayed the one-sided conversation over and over again in his mind, the richness of her English accent impressed indelibly. '*You're a hard man to get in touch with . . . I hope you don't mind me calling you speculatively like this . . . I really do think we ought to meet up some time . . . please consider my interest . . . I realise you have to do checks, all that troublesome security related stuff . . . I'll quite understand if you don't want to . . . I'll leave you to think about it, but I promise I'll call again . . . soon.'*

Kyle had, within minutes, confirmed that the call was made from a public call-box downtown, and although he'd alerted the boys and they'd been there within five minutes of the call, there was nothing by way of evidence. The owner of the delicatessen outside which the box was situated confirmed being pleasantly distracted by a young woman using the call-box at the time of the call, but she had been well wrapped up against the weather, wearing a furry Cossack-style hat and a muffler which concealed her face. However, he could confirm that he did see her face briefly as she spoke – she had a very pale complexion, was wearing bright red lipstick and had large dark eyes. She also had a great pair of legs shown to their best effect in a pair of high-heeled boots. Yeah, she was a bit of a stunner, but she'd disappeared quickly; perhaps she'd had a car nearby or jumped a cab, he couldn't be sure. Other locals and shopkeepers confirmed the basic description, but no one recognised her, saw what her mode of transport was, in what direction she'd headed.

Kyle buzzed through to confirm that Tom had arrived. Goodstone got up, met his old friend just as he came through the door, and he could tell immediately that his buddy was semi-drunk as well as intensely excited about something.

'I got it, I got it, wait until you see this, my God,' he said breathlessly, heading for the armchair in front of the log fire.

Goodstone picked up the poker and stabbed at the greying pieces of timber. Little fountains of bright red sparks spurted out in protest as he flung a few fresh cuts of aromatic dried pine onto the glowing embers. Tom dumped the folder on the side table as he struggled to get his snow-specked overcoat off.

'You'd better fix yourself a drink,' said Tom, 'and get me a good stiff one while you're there.'

Goodstone did as he was told while Tom rubbed his hands, standing with his backside to the rejuvenated fire. He tried to use the tongs to negotiate some ice-lumps from the bucket to Tom's glass, but his hand was trembling so badly that he couldn't get a grip of the damn things. Eventually he grasped a couple of lumps, tossed them into the glass and swamped them with Irish whiskey, splashed a similar amount into an ice-free glass for himself and approached Tom, trying to remain as calm as possible. Tom's cheeks were rosy, not due entirely to the cold, and Goodstone had no doubt that the matter had to be serious indeed to drag him from the dinner, particularly when he knew for a fact that some interesting 'entertainment' had been arranged to celebrate the impending wedding of one of the Club's younger members.

'My God, Paul, you know, when you mentioned that woman's name that day, I don't know what it was, but something clicked. My God, it must've been buried there for years.'

Tom sat down and dragged the low table across to occupy the space between himself and Goodstone.

Tom tapped on the large manila envelope as if drumming out a code of sorts.

'It's all here. OK, not all of it, but she's here. No one ever asked for this stuff before, likely because no one else ever thought to. It's been available under the

Information Freedom legislation for almost ten years, but today was the first request to see it. I got one of the interns to go down, it cost five bucks, the package came back within three hours, sealed. No one apart from me has seen it. The whole system there is, as you know, automated. This is hot stuff, Paul, maybe too hot.'

Tom slurped at the whiskey, the ice rattling against his false teeth as Goodstone carefully placed his glass on his own chair-side table and reached out for the envelope. He was about to slip it off the table when Tom's hand suddenly covered his, and Goodstone could feel now the extent of his friend's excitement, the palpable tremble in his fingers. Between them they were shredding a lot of nerves over this, and it was clear that Tom had spent some time following through the logical ramifications of what they were both doing.

'If you look at this stuff, Paul, I mean, once you've seen it, that's it. I can't deny that you've seen it. Right now? I still can. If you want to, just let's finish our drinks and go back down to the Club, the girls are due to appear about eleven or so. I'm only saying it because you're a dear friend and you know I'd never allow myself to compromise you in any way, intentionally or otherwise.'

Goodstone looked down at the inoffensive plain envelope, then back at his friend.

'Thanks, Tom, I appreciate that,' he said quietly, as if perhaps the room was bugged, 'but you know I have to see it if it concerns her, that woman.'

Tom nodded, took his hand off Goodstone's forearm, and sat back in the chair as the logs started to crackle and spit.

The pictures were old, from the thirties and forties. The only conventional portrait showed a young woman, rather chubby cheeks and a pretty Cupid's-bow smile with face angled wistfully, staring up at something beyond the camera. It was a normal studio piece, inexpensive and probably a sepia original, but the copy gave no clue as to the size or current state of the image.

It was the only 'normal' image in the package. All of the others depicted sexual acts, many involving heavily costumed participants, and in all of them appeared the same slim-waisted but broadly hipped and generously bosomed Kayla. It was perhaps coincidence, but more likely not that her face was never shown in any detail. A blurred profile was the closest available to an actual likeness, and even then the severe cut of the light-coloured wig made proper identification all but impossible. He reverted to the first portrait, the innocent-looking twenty-something, anonymous, captured at some time in the twenties at an unknown location. Who was she? And was she the same person who appeared in these other photos, here impaled on two monstrous cocks, one clearly false and worn as a toy by a laughing brunette? Or here, in profile with a limp penis strategically placed to hover above her nose as she craned up, tongue out, showing only so much profile? And another, where her blonde hair was buried deep in the complicated underclothes of a stern-looking madam?

He couldn't even begin to start reading the inane intelligence data – if there was anything of note in there Tom would already have told him. This woman, if she was still alive, would have to be more than a century old. It made no sense whatsoever, and he knew he looked as perplexed as he was frustrated.

'She's perfect,' said Tom, as if reading Goodstone's thoughts, 'absolutely perfect. The Brits devised her, we don't know exactly when. She's the bête noire they needed to keep their top dogs under some kind of control. You know how the Brits were when they had their goddam empire, running here there and everywhere organising everything. There was no law they didn't hold themselves above, and nothing, no matter how heinous, there was not a thing they couldn't do that King and Country wouldn't happily excuse on the grounds of bettering the rest of mankind. Perverse, perhaps, but that's the way it was back then. But for many of them, bear in mind this was Victorian England, Paul, some rather quaint old values in play, and a lot of those fellows took them very seriously indeed, certainly insofar as they could impact upon their suitability for high office. So, Kayla probably did not exist, probably never has, but someone invented her, had to invent her. She proved valuable, so valuable that she has never been allowed to die.'

'And we've never known of her before?'

Tom gestured to the sheaf of documents.

'Yes, we have. But why would anyone ask questions about someone they've never heard of? Why would anyone protest about the complete absence of knowledge on an unknown subject? How can a negative be described without reference to a positive, a reality? Kayla is a genuine secret, one that has evaded even the most fervent of conspiracy theorists. Ostensibly she does not exist. Certainly, for us she did not exist before you got that call, before we saw these photographs. She has been around for almost a century, maybe even more, but we never heard about her until now, we didn't realise that she exists until right now. She is real, Paul. We know that now. But *why* does she still exist? That's the more important question. Why has she revealed herself to you, and why now? There must be reasons. And Paul, for

chrissakes, be very very careful, this is deeply dangerous shit we're getting into, particularly as we can't go
to anyone about it.'

Goodstone slipped the papers back into the envelope, smoothed the envelope, then folded it and
lobbed it into the fire, and the two friends watched in
silence as the packet slowly succumbed to the flames.
He leaned forward, grabbed the heavy tongs – it was
still possible to retrieve the images. The surge of fear
which had compelled him to ditch the envelope into
the hearth was making him feel nauseous, but he
knew that merely burning the evidence Tom had
brought would not dispel the mental images he had
already created of the mysterious woman. He had to
see her, somehow. It would have to be arranged, and
only he could successfully, safely ensure that the
preparations were properly secure. Not even his
oldest and dearest friend could be allowed to harbour
any serious suspicion that he was going to attempt
contact with such a wild card, and so he replaced the
tongs as the first blue flames started to lick at the
edges of the paper, then raised his glass, drained it in
a series of small slow swallows before leaning forward
to gently pat his friend's knee.

'Come on, Tom. We're getting too old for fairy
tales. Let's get down to the club and see some real
action.'

Five

Gerry Allan checked his tie one final time. He raised his chin, angled his face slightly. As good as it was going to get.

It had felt like a lifetime since that evening in Paris, the encounter with that strange woman. But she clearly had more clout than he'd given her credit for, and the instructions from the CEO had been crystal-clear: go to New York, drop into the office every now and then but don't shift, don't leave town until her people get in touch.

And they finally had. It could have been the same woman on the phone, but impossible to say for sure as she had refused to confirm her name, insisting that he listen rather than speak. But the instructions had been clear enough – he would be provided with an escort to accompany him to the function at the Embassy. Her name was Seona. More than that he didn't need to know, but she would stay close to him all evening. His task was to socialise, nothing more, do the usual glad-handing, work the room as comprehensively as possible. He was experienced in such situations, that was why he had been chosen to help. This was it.

No explanation. Even the CEO had been evasive, almost nervous during the briefing on the morning of his departure. There was every chance that absolutely nothing would happen, that he would spend two, three weeks in the Big Apple then be recalled. But if anything did happen, if they got in touch and wanted anything, he was to comply utterly with their every request. Enquiries as to the identity of Kayla were flatly brushed off. It didn't matter who she was, what her business was – all that mattered was that Gerry be where he was supposed to be for as long as it took. If he wanted explanations then he would have to wait for the debriefing.

The phone buzzed just as he was drawing his jacket on – reception letting him know his expected guest had just arrived, was waiting for him.

Seona. He wasn't sure what face to put to the name, no idea where she came from, what her business was. Perhaps she had some connection with the Embassy, or perhaps she was involved in the development of the project whose completion was being celebrated at the dinner. And a big function too – plenty of big names sure to be there, plenty of ambassadors, foreign ministers, and no doubt a few familiar faces, those senior business-folk who seemed to spend their lives jetting from one junket to the next. Gerry had long dreamed of being one of that set, and so long as this strange game continued he was determined to make the most of it.

He slung the heavy overcoat over his arm and left. Reception was busy, but no sign of single ladies standing waiting for him. He assumed that this woman would have been given some idea who to look out for, shown a photo perhaps, but no one in the spacious circular lobby made any move towards him. He approached the desk, where he was given a profuse apology – she was waiting for him outside.

He stepped out into the cold evening air. The bright spotlights gleamed on the bodywork of the limos and Cadillacs, some bearing small flags denoting various countries and organisations. He scanned the people, looking for anyone to make eye contact, and when the door of the black limo opened he didn't take too much notice of the chauffeur until he was mounting the broad steps.

'Mr Allan?' asked the man, and Gerry nodded.

The driver gestured towards the opening door of the dark-glassed vehicle, and he was almost ready to double check that there hadn't been some mistake when he caught sight of the two women inside, both peering at him, the smaller dark-haired one smiling a warm welcome. He got in.

His senses were swimming as the car pulled away, so smoothly that he wouldn't have known it was in motion but for the shifting lights of the passing buildings.

The blonde woman offered him a glass, had already opened the champagne, and he allowed her to half-fill his glass as he felt the sweat break out on his brow.

'You must be Seona,' he said, addressing the blonde, but she shook her head. 'I'm Petra. This is Seona.'

'And you are Gerry. Gerry Allan,' said the smaller dark-haired one. He gulped, wanted to loosen his tie but it had taken ages to get right.

'I like your suit,' said Petra, and he summoned a weak smile by way of response as she extended a leg to brush against his. The dull hum behind him indicated that the smoked glass partition between them and the driver was being raised to give them some privacy, and he took a slow deep breath – it really was happening.

'I just have to check, Gerry,' said Seona, 'that you have your instructions.'

He sipped at the champagne again, declined the offer of a cigarette from Petra.

'Yes, well, I was told not to ask any questions, that you'll stay close to me, we have a good evening and socialise. That was it really, I can't . . .'

The brunette leaned forward in the spacious seat, her eyes glistening brightly, lips deliciously plump and glossed shimmering pink, eyes that practically promised the best sex you could ever imagine. Every inch of her was pampered and perfectly groomed. The fur coat was white and thick but the sparkling blue cocktail dress showed enough of her cleavage for him to forget his manners, blatantly savouring her as she spoke, the mere sight of her so engrossing that he was barely aware of the blonde tracing the heel of her shoe behind his leg.

'That's pretty much it, but I can also tell you that I'm looking for someone in particular, an old friend, and although she's unlikely to be here there's every chance that we might encounter someone who knows where she is.'

He wanted to ask the identity of the missing friend, but the instructions had been clear and he had listened well. No questions.

'I know you want to know, and it's good you're not asking. We're trying to find out about someone called Kayla.'

He frowned, looking at the blonde who merely sipped seductively at her bubbly and gave him a broad smile.

Seona's hand was then on his knee.

'Yes, I know, it is a tad confusing. We're looking for an impostor, and that impostor was once a friend.'

He sat back, nodding, trying again to smile. But the smile cracked when he realised that Seona had no intention of taking her hand off his knee, had started rubbing along his leg, sumptuously painted finger-

112

nails parting and radiating up across his lower thigh, and Petra was putting her glass down on the little table and slipping from the seat, her thumbs hooking beneath the slender silk straps as she manoeuvred her magnificently tanned torso from the sheer sparkling white material.

Seona patted his knee and sat back.

'I've a feeling you're going to enjoy this evening, Gerry,' she said, her smile revealing pearly teeth as he leaned back to allow Petra access to his belt and zipper.

Seona gingerly fingered her nails, checking them, holding them up before her, examining each in turn as Petra, emitting deep low grunts, flicked back the loose belt and hauled at his trousers. He grasped at the upholstery, sought a handle on the door as the blonde's strong hands pulled insistently, forcing him to raise his arse as she pulled the fabric clear of his thighs. His dick was not swelling at the attention, and he shut his eyes, praying that he could respond. Nothing like this had ever happened to him before. Sure, he'd fantasised about it. Who hadn't? But now that it was actually becoming reality he realised that he was terrified.

Seona crossed her legs and shifted just a little to let Petra have some more space as she pulled at his boxer shorts, again forcing him to raise himself as they joined the trousers, now crumpled below his knees.

Petra's mouth had taken in his shrivelled dick when Seona next spoke, and he found it difficult to concentrate, only briefly glimpsing her as she watched what was going on with obvious amusement.

'I'd love to help out, Gerry,' she said, 'but I don't want to get messy. Perhaps later. Who knows, we might get another opportunity, all three of us. That would be nice, wouldn't it?'

He nodded dumbly as Petra, humming and groaning dramatically, started to suck hard on him, forcing his reluctant dick to respond. He closed his eyes, breathing becoming ever more shallow as she found his balls and squeezed them. The vibration caused by her mouth, the deep noises she was making acted as an effective vibrator, and he could feel his cock-head rimming the head of her throat, the completeness of the tight fit about his helmet as she slurped, still groaning as she hardened his shaft with strong fingers.

He gawped at the sight below him, the shining blonde hair which had been sprinkled with something like glitter, the deliberate movement as she worked up and down on him, his cock now hard and forcing her to rise on her knees the better to take him as the angle became trickier for her.

Seona, still smiling but preoccupied with searching in her little clip-bag for something, drew out a small packet and passed it to him. A condom.

He tried to open the little foil packet but his fingers were trembling terribly, and it was Petra who glanced up and, realising his difficulty, moved quickly, entrapping the base of his now stiff cock with thumb and forefinger as she took the packet, tore it open with her teeth and withdrew the slippery black rubber.

She drew the tight circle of her fingers up his shaft, once, relaxing the grip, back to the base. She drew up again hard to force him fuller as she capped the end of him with the fine sheath, and then her mouth was over him again, the sensation of her strong lips forcing the rubber ring down his shaft as she continued to squeeze hard, so hard that the pain made him groan.

'She's ever so good at that,' Seona said matter-of-factly, 'and it's terribly difficult. Years of practice.'

The waft of cherry – or was it blackcurrant? – drifted up to him as Petra sat back again, lip-gloss smeared messily about her chin as she surveyed her handiwork. With a little bit of tweaking she drew the thin tight band a tad further down his shaft, making it all neat before assaulting it again with her teeth and tongue, lapping at him, running her tongue up his shaft from base to tip, watching his reaction, smiling with each long lick, flicking at his rubber-coated dick-eye, rasping the tenderest flesh against her tongue, closing about him and pulsing the vibrations of her groans through him again and again. He started to jerk, his thighs now trembling, but she sensed his peaking excitement, drew back from him and bent his cock down towards her, gently smoothing her long fingers down his broadness as she quelled his impending climax.

'Don't worry, Gerry,' said Seona, 'there's no hurry. We can take as long as you like. The whole point is to enjoy it, so why not make it last? In any case, being a gentleman you wouldn't want to leave poor Petra unsatisfied, would you?'

As if on cue, Petra turned from him, positioned her bare chest over the seat she had been occupying, reached down to the fringed hem of her dress and hauled it up over her long, strong bare thighs. He shook his head, trying to recover his breath as he took in the sight of her, the raised arse, the gorgeous peachy-textured skin, the tight brown star of her proffered anus, the already moistened crack below. And she was shaved too? It was getting too much. He knew that if he so much as touched his dick he would come there and then. But Seona was right, of course she was right, this was the chance of a lifetime and he was going to make the most of it.

He slid off the seat, pushing his trousers and boxers as far down as they would go. No time to try and get them off entirely, it would ruin the moment, so he waddled across on his knees, his stiff and rubber-blackened cock swaying in front of him. That night, the session in Paris had been fantastic, but this was something else. He was pondering, wondering how far he could or should push his luck when Petra's hand appeared at her sex, fingers smoothing over her cleft, pushing herself further open, and the other hand appeared at her arse, massaging her cheek, wet index finger pressing down against her anus.

'Come on, Gerry, she's obviously ready,' said Seona, her tone now sterner, as if she was getting impatient, perhaps annoyed. He glanced around, met her stare, and there was something about her which reminded him of that strange woman, the one who said she was Kayla. Her expression had been similar – stern, but almost sad.

Petra released a loud groan, an appreciative, smile-laden whine which regained his attention, and he covered her broad, well-muscled cheeks, savouring the sheer size of her, the sight of his engorged dick nearing her openness as her fingers reached further, her shoulder lowering as she strained to locate his balls, gripping them hard within her grasp as she pulled him, urging him to enter.

He allowed her to squeeze him several times before sinking into her pussy. The sensation of heat, of pressure and the instant working of her inner muscles was overwhelming, and he knew he would not last long. He gripped her about the waist, reaching down for her heavy breasts as she raised herself, pushing down on his cock as she brought his hands up, helping him massage her breasts, pulling at her nipples as she started to buck madly against him. She slumped forward again as he responded to the rhythm she had established, the impending orgasm somehow suspended, time itself warped and meaning-less as he gave up any thought of controlling the scenario. But her cries were impossible to ignore, the passion undoubtedly real as she started to come, the sudden splash of warm liquid on his balls as she spurted. It was then he gripped her hips, held her as close as he could and fucked into her so hard that he felt his heart would burst. His breathing was sus-pended, vision misting and blurring as the climax started from his fingers and toes, surging across every inch of his body, concentrating and peaking with the first vein-filling discharge as she tightened about him, pussy clamping, milking him.

He slumped over her, her body still moving, the rhythm slowing.

'Well done, Gerry,' he heard Seona say, 'now, best get yourself tidied up. We've got a long evening ahead.'

Goodstone leaned forward in the seat and cupped his hands behind his head. Another wave of nausea washed over him, his stomach fluttering with a nervous tension he hadn't experienced for years. There was still time to leave. And the option would always be there throughout. That had been made clear.

The bodyguards remained at the gatehouse where he had ordered them, as required, more than an hour before. The closest panic button was concealed in the ornate woodwork forming the centrepiece of the fire-surround. So long as he stayed exactly where he was the alarm would always be within reach and the boys would be with him in less than fifteen seconds.

The light cast by the dwindling fire created vast shadows against the walls of the study, the dull orange flickers dimly highlighting the contours of the furniture like some slowed and weakened strobe.

He sipped at the whiskey, wondered whether it was all perhaps some fantastic hoax. If so, he had fallen for it completely. Security had certainly been compromised. If questions were asked, if she did attempt blackmail? Too late now. The contact had been made, the arrangement had been his suggestion. Too late to back out now.

And yet, nothing had happened. Nothing untoward. Nothing to explain or conceal. Not yet.

He got up and crossed to the patio doors. The long, tree-framed lawn was dark, the slender denuded trunks waving their sturdy branches in the stiffening wind. More snow had been forecast to add to the six or more inches carpeting the grass and flower beds. So picturesque, so alluring, and so horribly soulless when there was no one to share it with. But even that could change. He saw that now. Everything could always be changed.

The steady, cautious click of heels in the corridor alerted him, and he quickly returned to his chair, settled into the seat as the footsteps stopped outside the door. There could be no doubting the correct portal to use – his instructions had been specific. She would perhaps be checking that her colleagues were ready.

The loud crack of burning timber was shocking, the spurt of sparks into the hearth seemed almost to be a final warning, notice of a last chance to hit that button, have this strange woman and her companions arrested for trespass. Questioning by the authorities would at least clear up the matter of her true identity. But plenty of time for that.

The door opened slowly, and she came in followed by three other figures, all entering in silence, their thick dark clothing muffling the movement of their feet. With the door closed again, the fiery splutter of the glowing logs was the only sound. He surveyed them standing in the darkness, no doubting now that she was indeed the woman portrayed in the file Tom had passed to him, the file which now formed part of the ash beneath the flames. It was her – the same hair, the cherubic face, pale and painted and large-eyed and unquestionably in charge.

She moved towards him, fingers working together as she removed the gloves to reveal not flesh but a layer of black shininess in the dimness, latex of some kind. Her gown was clasped at the neck with a gleaming brooch, and she unhooked it as another, taller, female figure approached behind her, similarly clad, to take the garment from her shoulders.

He felt suddenly vulnerable, small in the chair and dreaded what she might say. But she said nothing, merely looking down at him with an expression he could not fathom – was it disdain, perhaps, or pity? Whatever she thought of him, her expression gave no clue. The eye contact appeared to be little more than a visual confirmation that he was there and that he was awake. She turned from him, her figure now easier to appreciate as the flamelight gleamed reflectively on the skin tight latex dress, the sharp stiletto-heels.

He was not to be touched. That had been her suggestion, one he didn't think to question. It had sounded like a reassurance at the time, but now he could see that it was, potentially, a threat. He would take no part in what was about to happen, he was merely a spectator.

The others had removed their cloaks, and he could see now that they were more conventionally dressed. The man, perhaps in his early forties and less than average height, wore his long hair in a neat ponytail, his dark moustache neatly clipped, and the dinner suit was of a cut which suggested it was bespoke, neatly fitting his slim torso and broad shoulders. The smaller of the other women was Oriental, perhaps in her mid-twenties – so difficult to say in this light – although it seemed that her taller brunette companion, a strong-limbed woman with voluminous dark hair, was older, perhaps late thirties.

The man gathered the outer garments and placed them on a chair by the door as the women stood across from Goodstone, eyes cast down to their feet, hands clasped in front of them, waiting for Kayla to make her directives known.

Whatever system they used to communicate, Goodstone could only guess. They did not speak. If the whole procedure had been rehearsed then they had managed to do so without access to the geography of the room. It was as though some fundamental form of telepathy was at work, compounding the surreal nature of the performance.

Kayla had the man manoeuvre the armchair which Tom had occupied just the other evening, turning it fully around so that the broadly curving expanse of studded crimson leather was facing Goodstone, slightly angled towards the fireplace. The Oriental woman took up her position, hands gently resting on the waist-high back of the chair as her brunette friend knelt on the chair. The two women faced each other, staring into one another's eyes as they entwined their fingers and gently kissed, noiselessly, lips working softly as the man stood watching, hands behind his back as if awaiting some form of quasi-military inspection.

Kayla returned, occupied the space between Goodstone and the Eastern woman. Her shiny black dress was close enough that he could touch her tight firm behind if he extended a hand, but he knew he wouldn't dare, not yet anyway. Then she crouched, her calves touching as she lowered herself, and when she stood up he realised that she was working the girl's dress up her legs, exposing her as she continued kissing the dark-haired beauty on the seat, and the man stayed stock-still, eyes shut as if composing himself.

Kayla stepped back nearer the fire, and Goodstone was aware of his own breathing becoming heavier, more rapid as he took in the sight of the smaller woman's bared sex, her legs slightly apart, arse raised as Kayla looked down, inspecting it. The flesh was so smooth in the firelight, so perfect that Goodstone wanted to moan aloud at the perfection of it. Her buttock muscles were clearly visible, well-developed, hinted at the power in her stocky but pleasantly defined thighs and calves. No great surprise that she wore no underwear, but always that special thrill for him, the lack of any hair. He'd bedded a Japanese girl once, while stationed abroad – forty years ago now? – and still the memory of touching her down there, the strange thickness of hair, at once fascinating and mildly repellent, a texture he had never ever forgotten.

The brunette's hands were smoothing across the girl's behind, not grasping or probing, merely scanning the peachy flesh, the dark fingernails tracing intricate patterns on the firelit surface as Kayla beckoned the man to approach.

Goodstone wanted to get up, to witness the scene from further back, take it in in its entirety, but he was rooted to the spot, afraid that even the merest movement of a finger or limb might shatter the spectacle unfolding before him.

He heard the man's zipper slowly descending, but the man's hands were still clasped behind his back. It was impossible to see if Kayla had drawn his cock from his trousers or was working him within the cloth, but the slight tugging of the material at the crotch suggested he was being manipulated in some way. Goodstone looked up, and was shocked to find Kayla staring directly down at him, and now, with her so much closer, he could detect the smile, so slight it might possibly be a trick of the dancing light, perhaps painted on, just a flick of a brush, but he fancied it was a smile and it was for him as she pulled at the man's cock, readied him.

And perhaps she was purposely shielding him from an explicit view, wanted to tease him further, for she stepped back, an arm extended but the hand out of view, pulling the man towards the woman's exposed sex, and still she maintained the eye contact with Goodstone as if assessing his every blink, only occasionally taking a languid glance at what she was doing as the Oriental girl's faint whimper indicated that contact had been made.

And still the man did not react, remained utterly impassive, his head raised as if perhaps staring at the shifting shadows on the ceiling as the girl started to work herself against him, her leg muscles twitching and straining as she raised her left leg to make the task easier, while Kayla's hidden hand continued to do heaven only knew what at the juncture of the bodies, the rustle of the man's clothes being pushed against by the woman's backside the only sound to rise above the dull crackle of the fire.

Then the first spank, loud and sharp and clear, Kayla's latexed hand rising into view; then another stinging report as the woman raised herself further, tiptoeing within the shoes, the heels coming away from the ground as she bucked, bringing her sex higher.

Sudden sharp pain made Goodstone shift – his swelling cock was pulling trapped pubes, but even the slight movement required to ease the discomfort seemed liable to disrupt proceedings, and the surge of fear at the very notion he might incur Kayla's wrath was an ancient terror resurfacing. He knew he wanted Kayla, wanted her to punish him, but she would not: somehow she knew him, had access to his deepest, most forgotten yearnings, and so she would know that he dared not upset her in any way.

The man stepped back at Kayla's bidding, turned towards Goodstone, and now he could see the long thickness of the man, the wetness on the topmost third of his shaft where he'd entered the girl, the bulbous knot of his helmet gleaming with her moisture, and about the centre of the thick shaft, Kayla's slender pale fingers, tightly gripping him, slowly moving his circumcised skin up and down. The girl's pussy was already closing, her distended lips relaxing about the air which had been occupied by hard cock, and Goodstone wanted so badly to slip his hand into his own trousers, to ease the building itch to touch, to be touched. How long had it been? The thought had no time to form fully, the memories of the last unsatisfactory fuck were dusty, unworthy of recollection in the face of this unfolding scenario.

The brunette's hands were still in place, massaging the raised cheeks of the girl as Kayla continued stroking the man's cock lightly as if teasing him to further fullness, and as the man moved aside his dick was released by Kayla to gently sway afront him. He remained with hands still knotted behind his back, side-on to Goodstone as Kayla lowered her hand to the girl's cleft and slowly worked her fingers into the bared, shaven lips, and whatever signal she gave then was acted upon

123

immediately, the brunette disengaging herself from the Oriental's face, her lips reddened and opened and only briefly licked before covering the man's cock-end, not sucking or nibbling but simply taking him into her throat in a single long concentrated swallow which made her throat bulge, her eyebrows furrow with effort as she gaped to accommodate him.

Goodstone wanted to take his cock out, but knew it would not be permitted. Such rules had not been discussed, but he knew it would appear unseemly, desperate. This was all just the foreplay, it was what she had implicitly promised and now she was delivering. To respond so crudely would be to show disrespect for her, and he knew that would mean a premature ending to what he wanted and needed, the completeness of debasement that she must surely already know he was praying for.

The Oriental started fucking the air as Kayla's hand smoothed the crevice above her arse, but her task now was to hold the brunette's head still, grip it tightly as the man started to fuck her face. With his hands still tightly clasped he appeared to be in stern control of himself, but even in the dim light Goodstone could discern the man's shoulders tensing and flexing as he strove to control his gentle rocking, the gradual building of thrusts into the brunette's face, her darkly glossed lips forming a now-widening, now-contracting painted flesh circle about his shaft as he worked his tool in and out of her.

Kayla stood still, hands on hips, still staring at Goodstone as if waiting for some reaction. He was aware that his mouth was open, that his chest was heaving, but action was out of the question, his body rigid with trepidation. He would do whatever she told him to do, and the calm boldness of her look left him in no doubt that she knew it as well as he did.

A loud groan from the brunette attracted Kayla's attention, and Goodstone also caught the sudden withdrawal of the man's dick from her mouth as she pulled her face back and gripped him tightly, not moving her fingers but squeezing hard about the base of his shaft, perhaps quelling orgasm, and the man's pained expression, eyes screwed shut, confirmed that he was struggling to contain himself.

Kayla moved again, and the bodies started to shift, rearrange themselves on cue. Goodstone caught a waft of the brunette's perfume as she neared him, her long strong legs only feet from him, her broad, beautifully shaped behind still contoured within the slinky velvet cocktail dress as she positioned herself. Again, Goodstone's view was blocked, but he could hear Kayla and the others moving. The urge to raise his hands, to savour the texture of the brunette's backside was growing, his fingers shaking as he resisted, and in his mind's eye he saw the dress slip away, the magnificent roundness of her buttocks bared for him.

He closed his eyes, took a deep breath and tried to calm himself. The tightness in his chest was not yet serious enough to make him consider calling a halt to the display, but he would have to be careful. The brunette stepped to the side, her hands behind her back at the short zipper holding the material together about her body, and she was peeling it off, helping it over her hips as Kayla's new arrangement of the bodies under her command came into view for him. The Oriental girl was crouched over the prone man, his clothing still intact, his thick hard cock protruding obscenely from the tangle of shirt and trouser material, his hand maintaining the erection full and perpendicular as the girl looked down, assessing his position as she lowered herself nearer, one hand

125

easing her lips apart, the other gathering the material of her dress clear, Kayla's hand on her shoulder, helping to steady her.

The brunette dropped to her knees, and she enveloped the cock in her mouth again, briefly lapping at it, further lubricating it as she smoothed her saliva over the broad stump of the dick-end, her hand replacing his to maintain the rigid position as the smaller girl slowly, gently settled onto the end of it, taking in only the first couple of inches as she closed her eyes and started to rotate her hips, moving the stiff shaft along with her. Kayla shifted again, now straddling the man's head as she placed both hands on the girl's shoulders.

Again, she was staring at Goodstone as if trying to read his thoughts, and she turned her face slightly, still eyeing him as she raised her fingers and gently tapped the girl's bare arms.

The girl sank down fully onto the man's shaft, her sharp intake of breath indicating the shock of taking him fully as the brunette's hand worked inside the material, presumably in search of the man's balls.

Kayla stepped back again, apparently bored now, looking up at the fireplace, at the framed portraits hanging either side of the antique clock. Perhaps she had given her signal that the others could do as they wished, for now the Oriental girl seemed to cut loose, eagerly riding herself on the thick cock fully stuck inside her as she leaned back, Goodstone now enjoying a fuller view of her stuffed sex as the brunette peeled back the opened trousers, her hands easing the shirt material away from the base of his dick, his balls now visible in her grasp as she pulled at him.

The Oriental's hand was at her clitoris then, frantically fingering herself as she pulled away, raising

126

herself so that the cock emerged glistening, falling with a heavy slap against the man's belly before the brunette gripped it, pointing it towards the Oriental's gaping pussy as she bucked forward again, perhaps purposely allowing the solid cock-end to bump at her entrance, not going in now but acting as a super-digit against which she could pound herself. Then she pulled at her clit as she slid onto him again, her fingers tightening the entrance to her passage as she took him fully again, the brunette's hand now squeezing rhythmically at the engorged testicles as if urging him to unload.

Kayla seemed to deign to return her attention to proceedings when the increasingly frantic panting of the Oriental signalled that she was surely about to come, and Goodstone could only watch in astonishment as Kayla raised her rubber dress hem, crouched over the man, and started to piss on him. The Oriental must have realised what was happening as she flung herself back on the man, her face straining back to enjoy the shower as Kayla's thick stream of urine gushed over the faces below her. The brunette's hand was steadily working the man's cock, keeping him inside as the Oriental went berserk, thrashing about, her hips and thighs convulsing. The thick cock started to jerk, the brunette only pulling it from the girl's sex with some difficulty as it released its first powerful stream of whiteness into the brunette's face, her mouth opening in anticipation of the second spurt as she used her hand to help the Oriental frig herself into orgasm. Kayla's piss still sprayed over the couple as they came mutually, his cock jerking under the brunette's wanking hand, her tightened fingers frustrating the smooth release of his spunk, forcing him to come in staggered, spitting bursts as she wanked him vigorously as if determined to shake every last drop from the shaft before she would start sucking it again.

As suddenly as she had started to release her fluid, Kayla was back on her feet, her dress pulled back down.

The man's cock was dwindling as the brunette stuffed him back inside his trousers. The Oriental was on her feet, still panting heavily as she drew the dress material back over her bare and glowing sex, Kayla's long fingermarks clear on her backside.

Kayla stepped nearer Goodstone. Her voice was calm, but he detected a note of anxiety, perhaps annoyance.

'I would so like you to join us,' she said, no longer looking at him but scanning the fire, the flickering flames dancing on the sections of charred log, 'but this is not the right time, and this is not the right place. Perhaps I will call you again.'

Then she raised her hands to accept the gown being draped over her shoulders by the man, and she snapped the clasp shut, raised the hood and made her exit, the others following as closely and as quietly as they had entered.

Perhaps? That's what she'd said, he thought as the door quietly closed and the shadows calmed on the walls and the ceiling and the fire spat another series of dying sparks into the hearth.

Perhaps.

Six

Charlotte hurled the full glass across the room, her raging stare fixed upon Seona as the crack and scatter of the shards upon the tiled floor echoed about the penthouse.

Dieter crossed his legs, Petra appeared to be willing the sofa to swallow her. Seona alone stood, eyes meeting Charlotte's, her defiance clear in the determined set of her jaw.

'Do I have to do everything myself?' Charlotte said, her voice deceptively low and calm.

Seona slipped the coat off and folded it over the back of the sofa next to Petra, and she was reaching down to unbuckle the strap of her shoe when Charlotte turned her gaze to Dieter, so quiet all evening, preoccupied with the little electronic chess set he seemed to carry with him wherever he went. And then Petra, now fascinated by her fingernails, eyebrows raised as if blissfully unaware of everything bar the violet sheen of the gleaming varnish.

Charlotte turned on her heel and paced across to the door. Things were falling apart, no sense denying it any longer. Seona's sortie had yielded nothing, not a sign of Imogen, and no indication from any of the many she claimed to have spoken to that Kayla's presence in the city was known, causing the sort of fuss she had been warned about.

It had always been so straightforward, so simple – life was normal, undisturbed, and the alter-ego she'd come to feel was hers had only ever emerged as and when required. But now, with the cryptic calls, the feigned ignorance all around, Petra's apparent growing influence over Seona, it was crumbling at the seams; the very foundation of Kayla's identity was being tested to destruction with no clear input from Imogen or anyone else.

She quelled the urge to grab her coat and head off into the night, get a cab to somewhere, anywhere away from this dammed hotel. But running away would solve nothing, might well encourage whatever conspiracies had already been instigated, if not in reality then certainly in her own befuddled mind.

Arms crossed, nostrils still flaring as the anger gradually subsided, she turned to scan them again. Seona had perched herself on the sofa beside Petra and was soothing her feet, rubbing hard at her ankles where the strain of high heels always affected her. Dieter's expression as he stared at Petra was almost forlorn, removed, as though he too might be wondering what to do about the blossoming relationship now becoming so obvious. It was a bloody awful shambles, and Charlotte knew she had no one to blame but herself. She should've stayed at home, ignored the unsourced warnings, refused to rise to such childish bait. But it was too late – the search for Imogen could not end now, would have to be seen through if for no other reason than to satisfy her rampant curiosity, the increasingly desperate need to know exactly what had happened, whether Imogen had indeed betrayed her so deeply by stealing the identity she had no right to own.

'Why not call back, double check?' said Dieter, still staring down at the tiny chessboard, as if the whole sorry mess was little more than a distraction.

Charlotte bit her lower lip, keeping her arms crossed as she returned to the centre of the huge open-plan suite. It was at these moments, these superficially informal moments, that she felt most vulnerable; without the benefit of the hairpiece, the costumes, the make-up, she was physically bare in a way which surely emboldened those who assumed she shed the persona of Kayla along with the protective, fetishistic accoutrements.

She could tell he wasn't really concentrating on the game in hand any more, although he continued to stare down at the little board, his fingers poised over a bishop.

'Dieter,' she said, 'if that's even your real name, perhaps you would care to tell me when this whole project became subject to committee decisions?'

He looked up, momentarily confused, but as his English was near-perfect she knew his frown indicated something more akin to insolence.

'I just think it would be –'

'You're not required to think,' Charlotte snapped, 'not unless explicitly instructed to do so. The terms of your presence here were made very clear back in England.'

He sat back in the seat, clasping his hands behind his neck, gazing up at the ceiling, his jaw twitching as if the next sentence he wanted to deliver was rattling about in his mouth as he chewed it.

'And what about you?' Charlotte said, turning to Petra, 'do you have any smart suggestions about what we should do now?'

Petra glanced at Seona, but the look was not acknowledged or returned. Charlotte nodded as she stared at her friend, her dear Seona, now so distant, becoming a stranger with every passing day.

'The call I got said that the woman we were looking for had been invited to that function tonight.

I've got no reason to doubt the source, it's always been accurate in the past. So, I'm guessing that one of two things happened. Perhaps she wasn't there, but given the guest list and the setting I can't imagine for one second that she would miss it. The alternative explanation is that she was there, but you missed her.'

Seona looked suddenly guilty, embarrassed, but Petra's reaction was more interesting: the statuesque blonde appeared to writhe, drawing her knees up to her chest, clasping her calves protectively, and Charlotte felt sure she could detect Dieter also squirming behind her. She'd touched some kind of raw nerve.

Then it registered.

If it was possible for a realisation to dawn with an audible click then it would've been loud and clear. She paced towards the patio windows as she followed the thought through, and she'd mounted the three broad steps facing the floor-to-ceiling glass doors when it all came together, made sense.

She turned and scanned them again. Seona had moved to the drinks cabinet, was idly fingering the bottles, checking labels.

'There's a third possibility,' Charlotte said, smiling, and Seona looked up. Dieter turned in his seat, pushed his spectacles further up his nose, squinting to focus on her as she descended the steps.

'Someone in here tipped her off and she decided not to show.'

Charlotte committed their instant reactions to memory, and would replay them many times before the night was over: Dieter laughed; Petra smiled weakly while shaking her head; Seona's face drained of colour, her hand tightening until the knuckles went white about the neck of the wine bottle.

* * *

Imogen wanted to skip and dance, hadn't felt so happy in years. The swift trip to Goodstone's beach house had gone exactly as planned, she had known within minutes of entering the room that he would pose no problem, that he was as acquiescent as she'd suspected from the phone calls. He would have to wait now, wait and hope that she would get back in touch. And she would. Of course she would. But in her own good time.

Hans had waited for them in the car, dropped the girls off in the city centre where they'd arranged to meet some friends. Orlo had accepted the offer to stay, seemed tired and preoccupied after the late-evening trip to the coast.

She drew the moisturised wipe down hard behind her ear, along the line of her jaw to clear away the final traces of the thick stage make-up. Her skin was glowing, cheeks rosy and grateful for fresh air, and it was great to get the clinging rubber and heels off at last. She felt energised and ready to take on Charlotte first-hand.

And dear Seona, the poor soul, going to all that effort, getting all dolled up to attend the function where she'd been told Imogen would be. The recorded message had confirmed that a young woman matching Seona's description had indeed attended the soirée, had been asking questions, and the informant had also left the name of Seona's companion. His name was not at all familiar, but they would find out in due course, they would let her know, and so the entrapment of Charlotte would continue.

She squeezed another thick pool of cleanser onto the cotton-wool pad and firmly fingered the coolness across her eyebrow, down across her closed eyelid. Charlotte would be getting increasingly frustrated, anxious to get it all over with. She would be seeking a showdown, a face-to-face clash. OK, she'd come team-handed, but that was only to be expected. What was surprising, and pleasantly so, was that Charlotte had agreed to take that young couple with her, the tall German man and his impressive girlfriend – surely her antenna had been temporarily out of order if she was prepared to keep two relative strangers so close to her on such an important trip. Perhaps she was just getting careless.

Another blob of cream, the other eye. She squinted at herself in the mirror as she carefully wiped away the dark cosmetic, and she realised that she was smiling. And why not? Why the hell not? Losing the companionship of Charlotte and Seona had been a painful, bitter episode, one which was still hurting, but more galling was the apparent ease with which the pair had continued their lives and their own intimate relationship. No effort to reconcile, apologise, although it was very clear who should be offering any olive branch. If Charlotte really believed that she could dump those who had helped her reach such dizzy heights, fair enough, but her fall would be long and hard and Imogen would make sure she witnessed it first-hand.

The wig was safely back in its box, the outfit had been wiped and carefully folded back into the case. There would be more business, much more, but for now she wanted to relax, unwind. Orlo was waiting for her, would undoubtedly be partaking of a shot or two of bourbon to calm himself after the evening's excitement. He had done well, as she had known he would, but now she wanted to enjoy him for herself. She drew on the towelling robe, raised the collar to caress her bare neck, checked the hair clip was secure, took a last look at herself in the mirror and wondered what Charlotte was doing, what she was wearing, how she looked.

One thing seemed pretty certain – she wouldn't be smiling.

Gerry Allan told the cab driver to keep the change and hurried through the windswept snow, raising his collar against the icy wind. He'd been asleep when the call came, and although he'd been told by Seona to expect another call he certainly didn't expect it so soon.

But it hadn't been Seona who'd called – it was that woman again, that strange platinum-haired beauty he'd encountered in Paris. And she sounded angry, her demand that he get himself over to their suite pronto was not one to be quibbled with despite it being almost two in the morning.

He felt entirely sober. The function had been immensely enjoyable, not least because he had the beautiful Seona on his arm, and the mesmerised stares from the distinguished men in the company had left him with a satisfied glow he hadn't experienced before. It had been an illusion, of course, and a necessarily brief one, but what a deeply enjoyable episode, to pretend that she was his, and little drink had been needed to produce a uniquely memorable intoxication.

But now, waiting for the elevator, he recalled Seona's building anxiety as the evening had progressed. He had been shown some recent snaps of Imogen, and was fully aware that she would be heavily disguised, perhaps not in the 'Kayla' wig, but she would certainly be going to some lengths to change her appearance. Nevertheless, there was no one who could possibly have been her, and those who were even vaguely similar in terms of build or colouring had all been closely checked by Seona. The search had intensified as the night wore on, and

Seona had even, at one point, contrived to get 'lost' as she checked the catering quarters and staff rest rooms. No. No doubt about it, Imogen had not been at the function, and Seona had maintained a thick, murky silence during the drive back into the city, although she'd been entirely civil, thanked him for his help and assured him that there was no more he could've done.

The hasty, terse phone call and abrupt summons suggested that Seona's mistress perhaps had other ideas, and the trepidation was only controllable because he knew he had acted strictly according to instructions and had behaved impeccably. Moreover, he was prepared to do anything he was asked or instructed to do; the CEO had not had to remind him that total compliance was expected and he would not have been chosen otherwise. And anyway, what was the worst that could happen?

Seona greeted him at the elevator as the doors slid apart, and although she made an effort to smile she looked awful: her make-up was streaked, clearly the result of crying, and her eyes were puffed and red-rimmed. The dress now looked tired and crumpled, she was in her bare feet and her hair was gradually slipping from the exquisite bun she'd clearly spent so much time preparing before their night out. He wanted to embrace her, but she turned with the air of a tourist guide, an extended hand inviting him to follow her.

As soon as he entered the dimly lit studio apartment he knew something was terribly wrong – the atmosphere was laden, heavy with rage and fear. Those years in the forces – so long ago now that he sometimes wondered if the experience had been entirely imaginary – had left him with an instinct for trouble, and he knew instantly that it was here in spades. Seona walked on towards the main living area as he followed, unbuttoning his coat, loosening his scarf.

'It shouldn't take long,' Seona said, 'she just wants to ask you some questions.'

She? It had to be her. That woman who'd so calmly entered the room in Paris, who'd disturbed the greatest sex session of his life but left him with more than a promise of yet more should he choose to commit himself to helping her. And now the moment had arrived – he had been there as required, had helped as requested. What further demands would be made of him before there was any sign of pay-back? He quelled the selfish thought – there had never been any mention of inducements beyond the obvious bonus of being given an open-ended fully paid vacation. So far, he really had little to complain about bar a nagging curiosity which he was finding increasingly difficult to assuage.

The atmosphere thickened as they neared the room, door open, and the flickering candlelight signalled the movement of air within, the movement of the bodies responsible for the raw earthy scent of exposed and perspiring flesh.

Seona stepped inside first, turning briefly with hand on the brass knob as he entered, the door swiftly closed behind him.

His eyes struggled to adjust to the dimness, struggled still further to take in what he was seeing: the blonde woman who'd given herself to him in the car only a few hours ago was on the high modern-style steel four-poster bed, her ankles and wrists tied together, mouth gagged, jaw open, her mouth obviously stuffed with something bulky. Her eyes were closed, hair matted and messed, her body entirely naked, but she had ruffled the bedcovers with her feet, perhaps attempting to draw the material over herself. She raised her head slightly, made eye contact with him, then returned her face to the crumpled pillow and turned it away from view with an air of resignation which made him want to release her immediately, although he dismissed the insane notion no sooner than it had occurred.

The woman standing in the corner would probably have something to say about it if he did. It was her. He recognised her instantly thanks to the distinctive platinum hair, so curiously old-fashioned and yet so utterly suited to her almond-shaped face, perfectly complementing her huge painted eyes. It was certainly her, but the rather passive, almost melancholy creature he had encountered in Paris had been transformed into an utterly menacing figure, bare-breasted, broad-shouldered and positively pulsing with strength. Despite her diminutive stature she was so imposing, so utterly in command of herself and the room that her eyes were, in effect, the focal point of the entire scenario, and once he had met her stare he knew he could not, dared not look away as she spoke.

'Your coming here at such short notice is appreciated. It will count in your favour. Go and shower.'

Her raised hand indicated the en suite beyond her, and he proceeded cautiously, Seona staying close behind then passing him as he neared the doorway. Kayla's stare had returned to the prone and tethered figure on the bed, and he felt a shiver as he passed her, an almost visceral sense of what the petite figure was capable of. It was not merely her austere attire: the knee-length dark cotton tunic was simple, unadorned and would have been a perfectly normal dress were it not for the fact that it had no covering for her chest and her pert breasts were completely bare, elevated by the close-fitting material where it

138

hugged her diaphragm; her shoes were rather plain, dark low-heeled lace-up brogue-style, reminiscent of some schoolmarmish ensemble; it was not even the severity of her make-up, the dramatically darkened eyes and black lipstick. No, it was something about her mien, her posture, the clarity of her eyes and purposefulness of her voice which frightened him. She was not to be messed with, and he had no intention of doing so.

Imogen held the heavy cock in her hand, idly remembering the many she had seen and tasted over the years, those she had brought into her front and back passages, those she had merely handled or witnessed in action from a distance.

Orlo was still asleep, naked beneath the covers, but the initial disappointment had receded as she cuddled into his warmth, enjoying the silence and steady rhythm of his breathing.

It felt good. To be able to smooth her cheek into a lightly haired chest, a strong arm about her back, every now and then the light brush of his fingers on her skin as he dreamt, fidgeted, perhaps the effects of the nervous energy generated during the evening finally dissipating as deep sleep enveloped him. She would wait, could always wait.

It had been close with Steve, so close he would never recognise it, but Charlotte had taken him too. Imogen had made light of it all – *you're very welcome to him* had been her actual words. But Charlotte didn't love Steve and never had. It was so obvious it was embarrassing, and if he wasn't so thick he would've recognised it years ago and moved on. But too tempting for them both – two trophy-hunters satisfied in one fell swoop? Who wouldn't have jumped at the chance? But it was yet another reason to rub her face in it: the totemic role of Kayla had become just the most grating of all their differences, the most heavily symbolic proof of unfairness and betrayal. Poor deluded Charlotte couldn't even accept that her own mother had once been Kayla. OK, there was no documentary proof of it, but Imogen had always known, Dark Eyes had, in his own way, confirmed it. Denial was simply another of Charlotte's less alluring traits to add to an embarrassingly long list.

Orlo's cock twitched, pulsed in her grip and he sniffed deeply, sighing long and hard as if in the grip of a particularly interesting dream. She wanted to tighten her grip and start rubbing him, but plenty of time yet. He would stir in his own good time, and when he did she would give him the wake-up call of his life.

Plenty of time yet? She knew there wasn't. Not really. She wanted the home and the children and the career, all of it. Normality. The career side of things was ticking along nicely, no problem there. But she knew she would not and could not accept any single man fully into her life until she had exorcised Charlotte from her life, and taking her alter-ego, making it hers was the only sure way of doing it. If Charlotte could be made to feel the rejection, the awfulness of being second best for just once, that would be enough. Who could tell? There might even be a hope that they would once again be friends.

He twitched again, his hand closing on her shoulder, gently gripping her, and his dick pulsed harder, swelling. It would be so nice, one day. This could be normality, simple and uncomplicated. She had been pretending for so long that it was easy to pretend that here was her man, this was a normal night, and she was doing a normal act with one she loved.

Loved? It didn't matter. She slipped her head from beneath his arm, shifted down the bed and lifted his cock to her face, locating the limp velvety end and gently taking it into her mouth, fingers tracing down along the thick central vein. There was the slight saltiness, that aroma she'd encountered so many times but which she'd always found exhilarating, primally arousing. Resisting the urge to start sucking, she rolled the bulbous smoothness about her tongue, careful not to graze with her teeth, using her lips to keep him clear. And he pulsed again, the surging energy transmitting itself through her fingers as she allowed him to grow at his own rate, her hand now cupping his base, his testicles rising steadily against her.

But still he slept, sporadic snores interspersed with lengthy exhalations. She would've given anything then to see his dream, to glimpse the unsullied nature of his fantasies, view them directly as they formed. He must surely have seen many things she could not even imagine, and yet she too had seen enough, perhaps more than she should've. The memories were dulling with the passage of time, but still they resurfaced – the expression on Charlotte's face when she'd taken that strap-on from the box on that sunny afternoon so long ago; the sensation of having two cocks fuck her simultaneously, both in her pussy to begin with, then the sweet unforgettable pain as the smaller one had been introduced to her tongue-slackened behind; the sight of Seona wetting the end of that ridiculously thick white rubber dildo as Imogen prepared the Librarian with her fingers; Charlotte's face, mouth agape as Dark Eyes pissed on her, soaking her hair and bare swollen tits; the peculiar noise that man had made when she wanked him into Seona's open mouth.

Orlo's cock-head had swollen enough and he was starting gently to buck. She tightened her grip about the bulging flesh and started to work on him, her fingers digging into him as he hardened and expanded.

Just normal. Not covered in oils and leather and latex and lace and rubber and god only knew what else. Just normal like this was abnormal for her. It had been turned inside out and upside down, and she knew she might never ever be able to reverse it all, set it right. But no harm trying.

He stirred, his hands moving to her head as she raised his cock using her mouth, her hands urging him to part his thighs as she massaged his base, fingers grooming the thick hairiness of him, easing down towards his arse cheeks.

His hands were on her then as he awoke, reaching for her behind, his torso bending and hands urging her to take him deeper into her mouth as he sought to bring her sex nearer to him. She shifted quickly, smoothly, keeping his cock tight and full inside her mouth as she manoeuvred herself over him, opening her legs to allow him access, and he shifted them both bodily further down, giving her the space to extend her legs in comfort as he started licking her inner thighs, his strong broad fingers already kneading her buttocks, thumbs expertly tracing the outer sensitivities of her pussy and anus.

She settled into a slow rocking rhythm, taking him into her mouth smoothly, not even sucking but gaping, enlarging her mouth so that he could feel her capacity, know that she could and would take much more of him. But no rush – soft stubble grazing her, firm tongue prodding at her clitoris, flicking at the peak of her, teasing the tiny cock-shape into fullness as she restrained herself, resisting the urge to rub against him.

His hands were cupping her buttock muscles, pressing her further down as he intensified his oral attention on her mound, tenderly sucking her bud, and the sensation spurred another rapid sequence of flashbacks: Seona favoured that method, the gradual build-up centred on the clitoris, while Charlotte had always been rougher, tended to nibble, lash rather than lick with her tongue. Orlo was good, certainly, but Seona was still the best, had always been the best.

Orlo's earlier ejaculation had been spectacular and copious, but his balls seemed heavy and full again, rising high and tight in his scrotum as she briefly buried her face in his groin, lipping his orbs with her mouth, sucking just enough to loosen the constriction, tease his testes away from the base of his cock. She didn't want him to come too soon, and from the patient nature of his tonguing it seemed he was similarly content to make the session last.

His cock-vein was cable-like, thickly sinuous down the perfectly straight shaft, the knot midway down the column a gnarled ridge of pulsing blood as she resumed taking him deep in her mouth, the thick helmet nudging at her throat-head, filling the hole completely, expanding her tissue as she relaxed further and felt the soft ridge of his glans broaching the gentle ribbing of her own throat and pulsing, hardening further, forcing her to grip him hard and raise her face to better allow the deepening entry.

His tongue had located the exquisitely fine apex of her responsiveness, and he was at once pushing with his tongue-tip while sucking at the minute and stiffening shaft of her clit. She took his entirety, her throat now fully expanded and gliding easily over his length, his gentle bucking in perfect tandem with her gaping lunges as she completely engulfed him again and again. His thumbs were pressing against her arse, not invading.

His vein jerked spasmodically, signalling his inevitable come, but she withdrew him, easing herself away from his face and tumbling over onto her back, pausing only to wipe her stretched lips as he rose to cover her, his mouth on hers, tongue transmitting her salty muskiness as he kissed her deeply. She fumbled for his cock again, her saliva already cooling on the hot flesh as she steadily worked her hand about him, pulling him towards her, and he allowed her to guide him in easily, her legs wide and raised to make accommodation as swift and full as possible.

His hand urged her thigh to lower, then the other, and he widened his own legs, maintaining the tight fit of his dick within her as he straddled her hips, her legs now tight together, her compressed pussy stuffed with him as he rose higher, bringing the broad shaft against her clitoris directly as he slid in and out, the friction maddeningly intense. The pressure seemed to be lifting her arse away from the bed, so solidly had he impaled her, and movement was difficult under his weight, his strong thighs and calves forcing her legs still tighter together as he fucked her.

Imogen closed her eyes, pulled his head against her neck and dug her fingers into his tight buttocks, urging him to shaft her fully, but he merely pushed harder, already fully in, his groin grinding hers as the come sparked in her belly, irreversible, overwhelming.

She heard her own cries as if from afar, distant and high, the staccato shrieks combining with his lower rumbling groans as he gripped her shoulders and pumped his orgasm inside her, her backside and pussy clamping, jerking in response to his final deep thrusts.

The sudden withdrawal of him seemed to spark a supplementary come as the pressure was released, her legs parted and the heavy cock was above her again, coated with his fluid, but still hard and long and ready for more attention.

She raised a hand, languidly stroked the wet cock, her fingers gathering their mixed juices as she wondered how he managed it. That was certainly a first. The come seeping from her pussy was dribbling coldly over her anus, and she placed a finger there, assessing her slackness as she smoothed the come over his sack. Yes, she wanted it in there, and he would surely be happy to oblige.

She got onto her knees in front of him, raised her arse high and, with two fingers already reaming herself, used her other hand to guide the still-solid cock-head towards her anus. He voiced no objection as she carefully pressed him home, her hole easily closing about him, and then, with eyes closed, head snuggling into the pillow, she relaxed and let it all happen.

Charlotte had become Kayla again, completely and effortlessly. The task in hand could not be left to Charlotte, naïve and generous-hearted as she surely was. Only Kayla could exert the pressure now required, and it would have to be consistently increased, relentlessly ratcheted up until one of them cracked.

There was nothing to keep any of them here. The betrayal she suspected might be nothing more than a figment of her imagination, a paranoid reaction to the frustration and boredom of being cooped in this blasted apartment for so long.

Yes, they could simply walk out of the door if they wanted to, but she suspected they had much more reason to stay. That poor man Mr Allan, so desperate to please, so utterly submissive: there was no doubt he was innocent, that he would no more jeopardise this unusual vacation than he would dare defy the explicit instructions of his boss, a formidable man she had known for some years. He sat quietly on the hard-backed chair, his eyes flicking from figure to figure as if checking that everyone was still there, that he wasn't hallucinating the whole thing. Always the chance that he had been used, that he was working for Imogen without knowing it, but she seriously doubted it.

Petra was still bound on the bed, Dieter cuddling her protectively as she sobbed into the pillow, and Charlotte couldn't help wondering if she was upset because it was not clear whose side Seona was on. Her friend stood stock-steady in the thigh-high suede boots, magnificent and calm, ready to take her orders. She'd balked at wearing the hood – she had always been mildly claustrophobic and the rubber was indeed tight, allowing little room for breathing – but hadn't had to be reminded that this was a serious test and it was crucial that they both looked the part.

'This is going to be as quick and painless as you decide to make it,' Charlotte said, and it was as if her words alone were enough to make the candlelight flicker. Kayla had arrived.

'I need to know that all of you can be trusted, and if I decide that you cannot then you will no longer be welcome.'

'It isn't your place to issue such demands,' said Dieter, his voice trembling with a mixture of fear and outrage.

The poor soul probably hadn't liked being instructed to strip, perhaps fearing that he too was to be bound as his girlfriend had been, but he had known the nature of the assignment from the beginning, there could be no excuse for his insolence.

'Oh, Dieter,' Charlotte said as she paced towards the high mattress, her low thick heels clicking ominously on the thick rubberised tiles, 'you really have trouble controlling that mouth of yours, don't you? That could well be the source of all the problems here, a loose word here, an eavesdropped conversation there. You like talking?'

He frowned, unsure how to respond. Charlotte turned to Seona, flashed an index finger across her lips, and her loyal assistant reacted immediately, fetching the gag from the sideboard where the other tools had been neatly arranged.

Seona attended to him quickly, and he offered no resistance whatsoever bar the defiant glances sporadically aimed at Charlotte. The leather ball was of a diameter which he could barely accommodate, but the strap held it firmly in place. That would keep him quiet for as long as they wanted and might encourage him to release something of value when he did next get the opportunity.

But what to do with him? How best to impress upon him the absolute necessity of total compliance to her, to the whole concept of what Kayla meant? He was an amateur, as was Petra, that much was now clear. Yes, they had been sanctioned by Dark Eyes, and they would never have set foot in the House to begin with unless those in control of Dark Eyes had deemed it desirable that their visit should coincide with Charlotte and Seona's visit.

Looking at them now, Charlotte could see the allure for the young couple: if her own experience was anything to go by then they had probably been seduced by continental affiliates, persuaded that heady career options lay ahead if they were prepared to endure some short years of inconvenience and mildly offensive situations which would require participation in some rather overt, occasionally unnatural sexual acts. It would've been presented as an almost irresistible offer, most probably in the context of already-established friendships, business relationships.

But the minutiae of their CVs was not Charlotte's concern now – she needed to know that this couple would submit entirely to her, pledge themselves to her just as she herself had pledged herself to honouring the role of Kayla. If they did, all well and good, but if they did not? The notion that there could be any further insurrection, that challenge could present itself from within the present company was almost too horrible to contemplate. Imogen was already out there causing mayhem, skilfully avoiding Charlotte's efforts to track her down. There was complicity at some level, no doubt about it, but did the conspiracy extend into the room? She simply could not tell. It would have to be a harsh and utterly unforgiving demonstration of her power, one which left them in no doubt that defection to the other camp, to Imogen, could not possibly be worth it.

The heat had built up quickly, and Charlotte was aware of the perspiration cooling on her upper chest, on her forehead. Seona would be getting increasingly uncomfortable in her tight rubberwear and keen to take out her frustration on someone.

And it really had to be Dieter. The most visible defiance had come from him, so Charlotte gave Seona the strap and set her to work. He got to his knees on the bed, curled into a ball, backside tight, muscles rigid as the strap was brought across his upper thighs. Petra appeared to wince in sympathy as her man groaned into the sheets, his shoulders and upper arms solid, flexing against each stroke in the milliseconds before the resounding impacts were made. Charlotte paced around the bed as the punishment continued, arms folded beneath her bare breasts.

'Dear Dieter,' she said as Seona continued the steady thrashing of his buttocks and thighs, 'so keen to get involved, so confident that you could take whatever might be thrown at you. Did you really think you could just come along for the ride? That there would be no pain involved?'

His grunting took on a semblance of structure, as if he was trying to say something, but it was way too soon for that. Seona was merely warming up.

Charlotte crossed to where Gerry Allan was trembling in his seat, legs tight together, his hand cupped protectively over his shrunken genitals as his widened eyes took in what was happening before him. She extended a hand and gently stroked his white-flecked hair. How many men had she seen wearing precisely that same expression, that combination of utter fascination and fear? He would never ever forget this, had probably fantasised about such a scenario for most of his adult life, but now that it was unfolding before him he was, like so many others, utterly petrified. He glanced up at her warily, his chest static, breath suspended, and when she lowered her torso to move her stiffening nipples afront his face his mouth opened, jaw slack as she gently brushed her tits across his sweating face.

'What about you, Mr Allan? Do you have anything to say?'

He shook his head as she rose, eyes fixed on her nipples as she fingered his sweat across her protruding points, slightly tweaking at the buds to ease their growth. She gave him a smile which was intended to be reassuring, but his face retained its stunned expression.

Dieter's flesh was starting to show the signs of the thrashing – broad scarlet welts formed a set of overlapping parallel lines from the middle of his thighs to the small of his back, the reddest sector spanning his tightly clenched cheeks. Charlotte raised a hand to stop Seona, and the rubber-clad servant stepped back as Charlotte gently patted his backside.

'Open up, dear, there's a good boy,' she said, smiling now as she anticipated his fear and confusion.

He complied instantly, perhaps grateful that the beating had ceased. His cock was shrunken as if making an effort to retreat entirely into his body, but she located the testes easily, wrapped her fingers about them and pulled down to stretch the skin, make the entire package easier to grip. His thighs were shaking badly, but from nervous energy or the effects of the strap she could not tell. She raised the gathered cock and balls, pulled them up between his arse cheeks and tapped him again to indicate that he should close his legs. Compliance was not so swift, but he did bring the long thick thighs together, thus trapping his genitals between his tightened buttocks. He groaned low and hard and long into the mattress, the strain telling now. If he started to swell at all then the pain would increase. He would have to overcome mentally any stimulation, fight the natural reactions she was about to spark in him.

It was awkward for Seona to direct Petra beneath Dieter. With her hands and ankles sill tied it was a test of her athleticism to shift herself under him, raising her tied legs above and over him to rest her calves on his back as she brought her hands up over his head, trapping his head close against her sex. He was perspiring heavily, his fair hair matted and dark, and his nostrils were gaping, flaring wildly as he hyperventilated, breathing in his partner's scent.

Seona gripped the tight package of trapped balls and cock, gave him an experimental squeeze which made him whimper dully, and Charlotte mounted the bed. He closed his eyes, perhaps anticipating what was about to happen, but Charlotte knew full well that merely blocking out the visuals would provide little relief. He would hear Petra being face-fucked by Charlotte, be unable to avoid the sound, the smell of it.

She drew the black cotton fully up her thighs, baring herself completely. Her lightly haired pubis was showing signs of arousal but it would be Petra's task to service her. Seona was still gripping his genitals, gently twisting them, securing her grip. Charlotte was aware of movement in the corner, in the dimness where Gerry Allan's hands were smoothing, pressing into his crotch. He was finally relaxing. Charlotte straddled Petra's face, facing Dieter, facing Seona, angled so that Gerry would also enjoy a full view of what was going on. It only remained to remove the gag which Petra had been wearing for almost an hour, and the swift rasping sound of the velcro strap being unfixed signalled a long appreciative moan from the blonde which was soon muffled by Charlotte's descending pussy.

Dieter buried his head into Petra's flesh as if trying to escape the sight before him only inches from his face, but his groans confirmed that he was struggling, Seona's hand filling with his dick as he started to swell despite the constriction caused by his tightly joined buttocks. And she started to increase the severity of the twisting, pulling at him, drawing the bundle of engorged flesh away from his body, stretching his beleaguered dick as Petra started to buck against his face in the rhythm dictated by Charlotte's own quickening movements.

Charlotte beckoned to Gerry to get up, and as he did so his cock sprung from beneath his cupped hands, bloated and darkly red. Seona's yanking of

Dieter's balls intensified, his desperate grunts and gargles muffled by the gag and Petra's circling pussy as she ground into him, her legs hauling him nearer.

'Ready to talk yet?' Charlotte demanded, her voice quivering as her exertions vibrated through her, Petra's tongue lapping deeply, probing between her gyrating lips, but the notion that the big man would be able to form any intelligible reply was a nonsense. Seona pulled hard on his balls, raising them directly above the cleft of his arse, then released them to snap elastically, painfully against his behind. He released a long howl against the gag, every visible muscle raised and strained to fight the pain, but he had no sooner parted his legs, his crimson sack falling into a more natural position, than Seona had him and was squeezing again as his dick filled, long and thick beneath him. Gerry had already mounted the bed, was following Seona's instructions to help her slap the man's buttocks, and Gerry did so enthusiastically, his broad hand creating a deeper, harder report than Seona's comparatively light but undoubtedly more painful and effective smacks.

Gerry continued to slap at Dieter's arse as Seona used both hands now, one tormenting Dieter's balls as she brought Gerry to fullness too, pulling at his stubby thickness, lightly slapping his cock-end to further bloat it before slipping on the thick rubber cock-shield, thickly ribbed and gnarled with ugly knotted bumps. The device thickened him, the strap cupping below his balls to tighten about his shaft-base, bolstering his erection.

Charlotte raised herself slightly, giving Petra the chance to gulp in some air. The blonde was clearly in a rhythm of her own now and was bucking hard against Dieter, his pathetic cries now little more than a continuous whimper as Seona poked at his arsehole with gloved finger, prodding him open for what he must now know was coming. Petra's face was glowing, reddened with Charlotte's attention and the natural arousal, the genuine unmistakable flush of lust high on her cheeks as she started to come.

'Maybe loosening your arse will help loosen your tongue,' said Charlotte, the signal for Seona to move aside, her hand still gripping Gerry's hardened cock as she guided it towards Dieter's behind. The big man winced, tried to clench himself against the invasion but Seona was on hand to part him, raise him, and watch closely as Gerry's cock was pressed home, the black rubber shaft gradually disappearing from view as Gerry drove himself inside.

Charlotte raised her face, smiled at the ceiling, and resumed riding Petra's face as her own orgasm started to spark and blossom. Dieter's howls and Gerry's gasps added to her own repressed sounds as she savoured the pulsing arrival at the peak, the crescendo of sensation which made her cup the blonde's face in her hands, precisely grinding the nub of her sex against the hard wet tongue.

The come faded, the scene came back into focus, clear now, unsullied once again. Gerry was fucking Dieter, and the big gagged man was all but spent, his shoulders slack now, all resistance gone, and Seona was smiling too, crouched back on her own booted calves, massaging the fingers she had used to such effect, leaving Gerry to pound frantically, brutally into the man's arse.

Charlotte smiled at her assistant, her loyal beautiful Seona, and knew from her eyes, just knew, that nothing had changed between them. They still had it, they were still the ultimate team, and if Dieter didn't talk after this, he surely had nothing to say.

Seven

Imogen replaced the scarf on the rack and strolled across to view the various hats on show. So nice to get out, enjoy the normality of shopping.

The mall was busy with weekend customers, many idly ambling along the huge concourses, some laden with bags, others merely escaping from the blizzard which had descended without warning. The city centre itself was freezing beneath the heaviest snowfall in years, but the suburban mall was a cocoon, warm and dry.

She chose a seat near the window of a French-style brasserie and ordered some coffee. Only three hours to go. She had not been able to contact Goodstone directly all morning, the annoying answerphone message spewing forth a list of alternative numbers at which he could be reached. But she suspected he was there, listening, wondering, probably afraid to speak to her directly but unable to block out her simple instructions.

So she would be there at the time specified. If he chose to decline her invitation, fair enough, but she had never been refused before, and there was no reason to imagine he would set any precedent. His ignoring the calls could easily be understood on the grounds of personal security, a wise precaution in the event of any embarrassment further down the line.

But he would be there, she had no doubt. It had once appalled her how naïve men could be, how utterly transparent their behaviour. They adorned themselves with the trappings of success and power in some vain effort to distance themselves from the venal, primitive urges which were so crucial to that progress, and yet could not simultaneously develop anything more than an adolescent understanding of what made women tick. If Goodstone was even remotely like the vast majority of men she had seduced over the years then he would be no different. If anything, she mused as the coffee arrived, Goodstone and his ilk, so elevated, so puffed up with self-righteousness, were precisely those in whom appeal to the bestial was most effective. So yes, he would be there, despite his position, despite the security which surrounded him, despite his public protestations regarding the sanctity of his office and the moral responsibility he bore. He had seen what she had to offer and she had seen his eyes receive it with unabashed relish.

But if he didn't turn up? Then she would have to admit defeat. However, she would do so with no regrets. The threat she still posed to Charlotte was real, and she knew that even defeat at this stage would detract little from the damage already inflicted. Charlotte might return to England convinced that she had seen off the challenge, that her role was secure, but she would never again feel safe as Kayla so long as a viable competitor was out there.

The coffee was hot and strong. She sipped at it and watched the passers-by. The call from England had been brief and to the point. Charlotte had not attended the function at the weekend, but a deputy had. It could only be Seona. The misinformation had clearly worked, and although they were getting closer there was no indication whatever that they were anywhere near tracing her. And now time would be weighing heavily on Charlotte's hands, she would be finding it difficult to contain her anxiety and anger. The longer she stayed, the greater her frustration would become.

Imogen licked the trace of chocolate dust from her lower lip, savoured the light grittiness. How sweet it would be to bump into Charlotte in years to come, to pass her and merely smile, both of them knowing who had won. It was worth the planning, the danger, the temporary suspension of her career, just the simple anticipation of that moment, one which would surely come in time. Perhaps they would be elderly by then, but no matter. She knew Charlotte so well, so intimately, knew that the prospect of her having to face that moment, of having to concede that she had finally been beaten was something which she had feared ever since the mantle of Kayla had been passed to her, and its removal would be much, so much more than the relief of a burden – it would be taken as confirmation, endorsed by those who had installed her, that she was finally past it. Imogen's only regret was that she would not be there to witness that moment, to see Charlotte's face as she realised, as it all sank in, as she fell so far and hard that she would curse the day she'd ever been raised so high.

The mobile buzzed into life, and she took it from her bag, waiting until the little screen indicated the name of the caller. Hans again. She stared into the coffee as he spoke, emitting sporadic affirmative hums to indicate that she was listening, and when he had confirmed what she wanted to hear she switched the phone off.

All was in place. This was it. Butterflies fluttered across her belly, and she breathed in deeply to set

157

them to rest again. Not like her to get nervous, but you didn't get many days like this – perhaps a handful in a lifetime, days when you knew everything was going to change, that nothing would ever be the same again. Only a few hours to go, and by late evening at latest she would know for sure whether or not Charlotte's reign as Kayla was over.

Win or lose, Imogen knew that for Goodstone, Charlotte, Seona and everyone else involved, this was going to be an evening that – for a whole variety of reasons – none of them would ever forget.

She summoned the number for the base back home – time to call in for her daily update, find out what Charlotte had been up to, whether she was still confined to her little suite with her dearest Seona and their little continental friends.

The shaved pussy is right there in front of you, wet and reddened lips flanging about your finger as you maintain the posture steady, allowing her to fuck it with rapid short jerks, every so often her lunges forcing her sex completely over the thumb. Your fingers savour the texture of the stocking hem clasping her upper thigh, you curl a finger beneath the hem of the elasticated lacy band and pull the material higher, allowing it gently to snap back onto her skin as she tightens her grip about your cock, her tongue lapping at your cock-head. Yes, she's already guided you into her friend, the one you can't see because of the flesh dominating your view, but you can see the friend in your mind's eye, her gleaming blonde wig, her bared teeth, hear her sounds, bestial and aggressive as she parts her buttocks with the gloved hands, stretching her anus open for the tongue of the friend who is gripping you hard, steadily wanking you to fullness. They haven't let up, they won't stop, and although you came less than an hour ago you know this next climax will be even more intense. Thankfully they'd known you wouldn't last long and had brought the first come from you quickly, making sure you were overloaded with the sight of their faces working at your cock the instant it had been pulled from the blonde's pussy. It had been gratifying, the patient expressions they wore as that first come surged and burst over their faces, tongues lapping at your spurting shaft as they moaned ever louder, theatrically aping your noises as the white stickiness arched high, dropping onto gleaming cheeks, stringing thickly across gaping scarlet lips, perfect teeth parting, pink tongues widely protruding to gather the supplementary gushes.

But now they've brought you to a steady, reliable hardness which they've taken turns to use on one another as they might normally use an artificial tool. Your throbbing balls yearn to be emptied again, but these women know, they sense your building need for release and thwart your desire whenever orgasm is imminent.

Her fingers appear below her pussy, slender and pale and kneading roughly into the open shaved gash, her labia slipping between the joined fingers as she frigs herself, bucking harder against your thumb as it sinks fully into her, the lightly ribbed passage of her wider inside now registering against the sensitive pad of your broad finger. Your cock has already been in there, must have helped to loosen and expand the flesh, but it seems to be so spacious that bringing your other fingers together to push at her seems acceptable, and she responds instantly, drawing her hand away to allow you to bunch your fingers altogether to form an insanely thick target for her.

159

Her hand reappears at her anus, gingerly poking, reaming herself as she groans and pushed harder against your hand. Your arm is starting to ache with the pressure being exerted, but she's getting there, and you watch the shiny smooth wet pussy lips expanding, draining of colour as they stretch about your fingers, first knuckles almost completely accommodated. You draw your hand back slightly, convinced that it cannot be done, that it will damage her, but another hand appears then. It's not hers though – it's her friend's, and she's urging her, assuring her that she's getting there, ordering her to push harder and take more. You raise your other hand to feel at hers as they finger her arse. She grabs that higher hand, bucks further. Her pussy feels tight about your fingers, she's getting so close to the thickest juncture that you can only gape and wonder at how painful it must be. The friend's cries are rising with her own building excitement as she witnesses the fist fuck, and you glance up to see the widened eyes staring from beneath the blonde fringe as she exhorts her friend to go for it, take it all.

Your fingers are in her arse as well now, she's slapping your hand as you get a second finger into the widening slackening backside. The friend's also got a grip on your higher arm, urging you to fuck her with it, get the movement going.

And then, so suddenly that her cries come as a shock even as your hand is enveloped, her pussy has taken all of your hand and you are fully inside the heat of her, twisting, your fingers bunched and compressed by her, the warm flesh contracting about your wrist. The fingers in her arse can feel the back of your own hand through the narrow membranes separating her passages, and it is with these fingers that you fuck her anally, savouring the knowledge

*that her pussy is stuffed with you, but at a remove,
twin sensations throbbing and swelling from both
areas as she resumes sucking you, taking you deeply,
teeth active, nibbling and gently biting as the friend
maintains that maddeningly tight grip on your
pulsing balls.*

*Her cries coincide with the sporadic rush of cool
air about your cock-end as she starts riding your
hand, your forearm screaming for relief now, shoulder starting to cramp as her insistence intensifies.
She's riding your hands, forcing you deeper, willing
you to pound her as her friend's hands tighten about
your wrists to steady you. And then, above you,
directly, the dark waving shape nears, confusing at
first. Thick and drooping, the black cock seems
unreal, artificial, but the scent of it is genuine,
unmistakably manly, and it is only then that you
realise he is there, behind you, nearing the girl in
whose sex your hands are buried. His scrotum, heavy
and thickly haired, is brushing your crown, his darkly
purple bulb swinging ever closer to your face,
hovering above that short gap between you and the
bucking sex of the girl impaled on your hands. He
wants to enter her, that much is clear, but you will
have to accede, vacate the holes occupied. The cock
is directed further down to tentatively poke about the
junctures where your flesh has become conjoined with
that of the woman, almost as if the unnaturally long
dick has some mind of its own and is sniffing,
assessing the situation before acting.*

*And she's taken you in her mouth again, her lips
searing down your hardened dick, biting hard into
the base of you as you feel her throat contract about
your upper shaft, her friend's hand tightening about
your balls yet again as the heavy cock-end is slowly
lowered, clearly now in the man's hard grip, the*

*moistened end of it closing in, nearing your lips. You
don't want to, you've never done it before, never even
thought about such things, but it seems now the most
natural and logical thing to do, to get this fat cock
ready for entrance to the already well-widened holes.
It's surprisingly fat, wide, so you have to gape, your
neck muscles straining as your jaw widens, teeth
unable to avoid the smoothness of its intrusion as it
is carefully sunk into your mouth. You will gag, no
doubt about it, if you even attempt to suck, so you
merely hold the ball of flesh in your mouth, your
tongue-tip steadfast against the moist eye of it,
denying it further access, but you feel the thing swell,
blood pulsing into it as the strong fingers cradle your
head, angling your face the better to make the entry
comfortable.*

*You hear the man's voice and his language is
unknown to you, but the girls understand, they know
what he wants, and so the dark-haired one pulls at
your fingers, urging you to withdraw. The blonde
raises herself, groaning now as she tries to remove
herself from your hand. Your fingers slip easily out
of the tight arse, the dark hole contracting as you
watch her tense and pull harder, your hand fully
wedged inside her pussy. The dark-haired girl
reaches down, grabs the gleaming smeared buttocks
and hauls at her, helping her as you pull back, feel
her flesh tighten about your hand again as she
reaches that fullest point, the broadest expansion she
can bear, and it is with an anguished shriek that she
is free, her flesh slipping away swiftly, your hand
disgorged. She continues to twitch and moan, hands
smoothing her behind and pussy as she slumps
forward, trying to get up. The man's cock is
hardening in your mouth, he's stabbing it into you,
but you can tell he's only using you to get some*

lubrication, there's little expectation that you'll try to take any more, but with your hands free now it seems to make sense to take it, grip it, and attempt a deeper suck. The man releases his cock when you grab it, allows you to stretch your head further back, widening your mouth further. Now you can feel the size of it, and it is enormous, obscenely long, the sheer weight surprising in itself. The man appears content to let you suck hard on the bulbous helmet as the blonde gets off your body, her hand still idly rubbing at you but her concentration clearly affected now as she follows whatever instructions the black man has been giving to the brunette.

You close your eyes again, exhaustion washing over, and the heavy cock is drawn from you, the man moves away. The saltiness on your lips is suddenly nauseating, you must get a drink and, shifting to the side, hand reaching for the floor, you slip from the platform onto the carpet. There is a glass of cool, still bubbling iced water on the table. You must have it. You crawl, torso racked with dull pain, cock still solid, throbbing and swaying, the wettened head nudging your belly as you get to the water and drink, drink it all down, taking a cube into your mouth, sucking the coolness to ease your stretched lips.

When you turn, resting your back against the sofa, it's clear that the blonde is still recovering, lying flat out on the floor, her chest heaving, hand wiping the sweat-soaked hair from her temple as the other pads gently at her sex. She's still groaning, but whether she achieved climax or not you cannot tell.

The brunette has taken up a position close to her friend, but she's standing, hands high against the wall as the man pushes the long cock into her from behind, urging her to rise onto tiptoes as his length is semi-sunken, carefully brought to the point where her warning sounds indicate that she cannot comfortably take any more. He seems content though, the musclebound man, and grips the brunette's hips with broad hands, steadying her as he starts to fuck her pussy. You watch, engrossed, as she turns to face you, her teeth bared, eyes half-shut. She's smiling at you, sticking her tongue out as you drop a hand to your cock and gently rub at the hardness. You want to get up, go across and force her to bend and take you in between those painted lips, caress her glossed hair as you empty yourself again, but the fatigue is intense, you must stay put for now. The thirst returns, you have drained the glass, the cube has splintered and gone, none left, reach for that other glass, dark liquid, maybe it's wine, no matter, drink that down too, quench the dryness, get rid of that blasted saltiness. You can't believe what you just did, what you allowed to happen, and watching the man as he pumps the woman from behind, her face now concealed once again, her arms flexing against the wall as she takes his powerful lunges, it seems incredible that the thick glossy shaft was in your mouth.

The appearance of the guy from the right should be a surprise, but for some reason you knew he was there, watching and waiting. He is tanned, looks to be of Mediterranean origin. In fact, with that small neat moustache, the belly, the broad shoulders covered with a fine layer of dark hair, he could be you, and something about his posture is so similar to yours that you could be forgiven for believing that you'd just had your first sight of a long-lost brother. But he seems ignorant of your presence, steps over the prone body of the still-groaning blonde. He's clearly interested in only one thing, and that's getting his cock into the brunette's mouth as the black man sinks a bit deeper, quickening his strokes.

She takes him awkwardly, her petite body now visibly shuddering with the impact of the fucking she is receiving, but the white man grips his cock with both hands, holding himself as her target, her open mouth slipping over him, cheeks depressing as she sucks hard, her hands finding support at his hips as she tries to maintain a constant contact.

But the black man stops her, slapping her arse to indicate that he is coming out of her. He wants her to rise, and as she does so, her saliva gleaming silver on her chin, eyes shut, he lifts her, the big hands cupping her thighs as he brings her up his body, his solid black rod springing out between her legs. And with her now positioned thus, her stockinged legs in his hands, her sex settling on the almost perpendicular staff, you can see just how big the man is. The heavy black scrotum hangs slack, swaying lightly as the white man grips the base of the black cock and holds it firm. The brunette whimpers, clearly aware that she is going to be lowered onto the thing, and this time it will be her behind that is filled. The white man stoops, fingers probing at her back entrance, but she is protesting, eyes shut, moaning a complaint, and the black man's voice is soothing as he speaks into her hair, the words strange and slow. She raises her arms high, wrapping them about the black man's head as if hopeful that by so gripping him she may be able to restrict the depth of his invasion, but the white man has already positioned the fat velvety cock-head at her anus and is gently pressing her thighs down as he maintains a grip on the upper thickness of the dick. The black man turns with her, moves towards you, and the blonde is up now, can see what is happening to her friend.

The brunette's long high cry signals the entry of the black cock into her behind, and he holds her steady, waiting for her to calm a little before allowing her to be impaled another inch or so, her fingers dropping to assess the size of the thing now about to fill her.

The blonde rises to her knees, grabs the white man's cock and starts frantically rubbing at it, lapping at his scrotum as he parts his legs and allows her to stiffen him further. You know what's about to happen, but the expectation doesn't lessen the shock of seeing the blonde guide the stiff member towards the brunette's pussy. He enters easily, fully embedded in her as the blonde attempts to get her tongue near the filled holes, pleading for access as the men start to establish a rhythm, strong arms surely, carefully bringing the petite woman up and down on their joined dicks. The blonde appears to be close to tears, her frustration surely boiling now as she witnesses at such close quarters the dual entry of her friend. The sound of their flesh filling her is surprisingly loud, the silky wetness of their pumping only overridden by the gathering cries of the females.

It's becoming unbearable. Your cock feels ready to explode at the merest touch, but you don't want to do it yourself. The blonde will do, surely she will take you. You get up and near the fucking quartet, the blonde's head hidden below the conjunction of so much flesh, but she responds when you stoop to bring your cock-head down the crevice of her arse, her body shifting to make access easier. You straddle her, forced now to lean against the strong thighs of the men for support as you locate your helmet at her wet anus, the hole which your fingers had been reaming so deeply before the black man entered and took centre stage. She's tightened now, but still slack enough there, raised and jerking with desire to be filled, so it's a long, slow, easy lunge. You fill her *completely, your balls settling against her distended pussy lips as she releases a low hard growl which vibrates right through her. You start to fuck her hard and fast, ramming into the tender pale flesh with renewed energy. The men seem oblivious to your presence, unconcerned that you are relying on them for support as you lean further to deepen the entry into the blonde's arse, forcing her to raise herself higher, her squeals now perfectly synchronised with those of her dark-haired friend.*

You look up to see the twin sets of bollocks, the cocks now covered completely, and no wonder the brunette is howling, screaming for release as her orgasm sparks the blonde, and you can feel her fingers rabidly frigging her pussy as you quicken still further, gliding in and out of her tight passage so fast that the heat is becoming uncomfortable. No going back now. The brunette's shuddering cry coincides with the release of the white cock from her pussy and you see the white spunk spattering across her pussy, dripping down onto the knotted base of the black cock as the blonde helps to wank the discharge from him, scattering the semen to hit your belly and her own face as the white man grunts the rhythm of his climax. He drops to his knees, stuffing the already wilting cock back into the blonde's mouth as you reach your own peak, the orgasm a series of painful long spurts, your balls tight now as they empty, her sphincter tightening spasmodically, milking the cock into her behind.

The black man lowers the brunette to the ground, his cock bending, still stuck in her arse as she moans, limp and sated now, and he palms her buttocks as he withdraws, settling his heavy penis hard into the gentle crevice of her cheeks. His come erupts from the dark purple eye, jetting thickly across her back.

*The blonde sees what is happening and helps him too,
her thin white fingers rapidly working up and down
the long tapering blackness as his remaining fluid is
expertly pumped onto the sobbing brunette . . .*

Gerry snapped awake, the faces and sounds of the
dream somehow persisting, overlapping with the
realisation that he was still in the penthouse, that he was
in the broad cool bed previously occupied by Dieter and
Petra, and he had just come all over his belly.

His scalp and chest were soaked with sweat, his
body clinging to the thin cotton sheets. That hadn't
happened since he was a teenager.

He listened to his own rapid breathing, wondered
what the day would bring. It had been another late
night, the humiliation of Dieter and Petra had
continued despite their confession: yes, they'd been in
contact with England on a regular basis, taking turns
to call back for updates and further instructions.
Charlotte's suspicions had been confirmed, and now,
who knew what might happen?

He sat up and listened hard – distant traffic,
virtually silenced by the triple glazing, and soft wintry
sunlight illuminating the fully drawn blinds. Impossible even to guess what time it might be, what time
they had eventually retired for the night. Impossible
also to guess what had happened to the young couple
– Charlotte had made it quite clear that she would
welcome their staying on condition that they utterly
submitted to her complete control, that they assisted
in finally nailing Imogen. The pledge had been
forthcoming, he had witnessed it along with Seona,
but there was no telling what value Charlotte would
place on the promises, whether she was just playing a
careful game designed to keep the treacherous duo
close until business had been satisfactorily concluded.

The dull whirr of the extractor fan, the barely audible splashing of water indicated that someone was using the shower next door.

Flashes of the dream returned, fully coloured, obscenely explicit and starkly lit. The faces of the strange characters were unknown to him, but remembering the curve of the brunette's thighs, the strong wide arse of the blonde, it was clear that the experiences of the past few days were becoming impossibly tangled with his deepest, most long-standing fantasies, even those he'd briefly entertained but dismissed so many years ago through a combination of guilt and self-loathing. He wasn't gay, never had been, and the nocturnal fumblings at the boarding school were so distant now that he could barely recall the details, recall whether or not there was any genuine enjoyment involved. But to imagine having a huge black cock stuffed into his mouth? To actually dream of such a thing? Surely now, under the strict instruction of Charlotte and Seona, there was every chance that the final business might well involve similar action. He had gladly fucked Dieter, eager to impress Charlotte with his devotion, but perhaps he would have to make sure she knew that he was not, never had been, homosexual. It would surely have to speak for his devotion that he unquestioningly shagged the backside of a man and did so with apparent relish when in any other circumstances he would have been nauseated and angered by such a request.

The worry with which he had fallen asleep suddenly resurfaced: how the hell could he go back home now? What price this exotic experience, this strange carnival in the autumn of his life? It would never, could never be the same, and although the life he led was surely as pedestrian and predictable as that of any other suburban-based reasonably successful businessman, it had its good points too. The family was happy and healthy and secure. The savings and shares were there, working away to ensure the impending retirement would be comfortable. No worries on that score. But the Sunday morning fifteen-minute embrace which constituted a sex life? He still loved her dearly, that was not in question, and she was devoted to him too. It was impossible to imagine that they would go their separate ways now, not after all they'd been through. But perhaps their compatibility was too complete, too good. She would awake him with her hand, gently pumping him full as he kissed her breasts, sucking at her nipples. She'd always loved that. She would steadily wank him to the appropriate stiffness before slipping atop him, all the time staying close, their bodies touching at all possible points, and she would slowly open her legs, easing her warmth over him gradually as he fingered her behind. For more than twenty-five years they had been doing this, the same sequence of foreplay, and they had been content to adhere to that pattern because it worked. He would wait until her fingers tightening in his hair indicated that her orgasm was starting, he would slip one finger into her behind and hold it steady as her short sharp jerks became a rapid circular motion, she would release her muffled cries into the pillow over his left shoulder and he would pull himself out, spurting into the crevice of her buttocks, smearing himself over her rear hole. Mutual satisfaction guaranteed every time and only occasionally did they ever depart from the tried and tested routine. On his birthday, their anniversary and on the first night of their twice-yearly holidays she would give him a blow job, but even then she would not allow him to lick her. She had always found it unbearably ticklish despite his strenuous efforts to find a way of pleasuring her orally.

The guilt welled within him again like some awful indigestion, untreatable and intense. She would be at home right now, watching her beloved soap operas, occasionally wondering how he was getting on, what he might bring her back from this latest business trip.

He would find something for her, perhaps a piece of jewellery. But he also knew he would be bringing back something altogether more important and potentially lethal to their long marriage. The memory of involvement with these strange, driven women would not be easily dismissed as an interesting lapse in his fidelity. He knew that Charlotte and Seona had already, in some fundamental way, changed his life.

And still, he pondered as he moved to the window and parted the blinds slightly to allow a partial view of the cityscape, they hadn't finished with him.

Goodstone twisted the cap back on the whiskey bottle and screwed it as tightly as he could, as if by sheer will alone he might somehow weld the thin metal into the glass, thus making the liquid unreachable.

He had avoided all calls, but Kyle had been unable to field her and the message had been waiting for him, buried among the routine requests, memos and updates. If she was as determined as she appeared to be then he had no doubt whatever that she would be there at the appointed time and place, but he still hadn't made that definite commitment that could not be explained away.

He had always been so careful, ultra-cautious. On more than one occasion he had been the target of seduction attempts, and even now, years after the approaches from those beautiful women, he could recall the stomach-flipping pleasure, the thrill of contemplating the gamble, taking that one chance. But he'd never succumbed. It was nothing more than self-flattery to imagine that those women had found anything even remotely physically attractive about him. If anything his looks had improved with age, he had grown into the awkwardly shaped body, the years had mellowed and softened his unpleasantly angular face, lent him an air of authority and wisdom. But he was no Adonis, never had been, and so it had always been relatively easy to see through the brazen efforts to get access to him via his weaknesses.

But this woman was different. It wasn't simply that she had demonstrated such gall by even contacting him in the first place – he admired that in any person, but to find it in a woman so young was remarkable. Nor was it that she was undoubtedly beautiful, that stunning white-blonde hair, the flawless visage, perfect presentation, lithe yet pleasantly rounded figure. There was something indefinably attractive about her carriage, her way of looking, maintaining intense eye contact which he found at once mesmerising and disturbing, as though she was capable of subjecting those who caught her stare with a powerful remote hypnotism whose effects persisted long after she had gone. It also helped that she was English and clearly of good stock. He had, ever since his Oxbridge years, harboured a love of that accent, the rather clipped and stern manner which these women used. It was all to do with background, class, and he'd seen enough of the English and their curious ways to know that she frequented the upper echelons of the carefully graded society; she was used to being in the company of powerful people and it showed in the easy manner she demonstrated, even in his presence. It had been a long time since he'd seen anyone behave without inhibition so close to him – he had long been aware that the persona he projected was coldly critical, perpetually challenging, and although the trait had not hindered his career it had certainly helped enhance his image as a cynical and sometimes cruel bully. Kayla's apparent acceptance of him, warts and all, appeared genuine and unforced. She was good. But Kyle was not so impressed, had warned that he would be running checks on her. Kyle's concept of 'running checks' would involve much more than requesting a minion to finger through some old files; the woman and her friends would, even now, be under intense scrutiny, their every move monitored and recorded. She may well have done her homework, made good contacts, and even the fact that she knew the current whereabouts of the yacht was in itself an impressive feat of detective work. But Kyle would take it as a personal challenge, the very idea that some English girl was pestering him, poking at the security apparatus surrounding him. Whether aware of it or not, the young lady had already made a powerful and dangerous enemy. It was so tempting to tell Kyle to back off, to let him deal with Kayla in his own way, but he knew full well that even if Kyle did agree, there was no way he would allow such unmonitored contact with a relative stranger. No way.

Yes, he did get exasperated by the constant security, and yes he had long ago learned to completely ignore those designated to his well-being. They too understood that he was not interested in forming any kind of a relationship with any of them, that he regarded their omnipresence as unnecessary and personally offensive. But even the trips to the beach house required a team of six, and he suspected that many more were assigned without his knowledge.

Even now, a mere three hours before the appointment with Kayla, he hadn't informed Kyle whether or not he would be attending. Kyle would be sitting next door, waiting for updates on the movements of the woman, receiving background reports on her dating years back, and he'd be worrying, worrying, always worrying. Whether he agreed to meet her or not, she was already a marked woman. Time to make his mind up – the drive to the marina was two hours. Of course the 'copter was always an option, but its use always attracted attention.

Of course Kyle was worried – deeply worried – about the contact with this peculiar English woman, and he had made his disapproval plain in the course of a blistering exchange which also involved Tom. Kyle had even requested permission to detain the woman and her strange friends – one of whom was a well-known actor specialising in adult movies – for some informal interviews, but Goodstone had been adamant. He had never made detailed inquiries into what Kyle meant when he requested permission to 'detain for informal interviews', but he did know that it involved the use of agencies which Goodstone had always detested and under no circumstances would he sanction their use in dealing with this woman. She had done nothing wrong, and although her motives could always be held up to question, he was sufficiently intrigued to feel that, for now at least, she deserved some form of protection from the paranoid security apparatus surrounding him.

He stabbed a stubby finger at the console and Kyle replied instantly.

'Blank the diary for this evening. Issue a statement, regretfully et cetera, recurrence of something or other, nothing too serious but I need a couple of days R and R, you might as well come too. Fancy a spot

174

of fishing? Yeah, tell them to get the yacht ready, we might take it out tonight, get some sea air.'

He returned to the drinks cabinet, took out the bottle and, with some effort, displaced the cap. Just one for the road. He swirled it in the glass, savoured the slightly acrid scent of it wafting up towards his face. Another stab at the console.

'And Kyle, get back to that young woman. Tell her I'll be there, I'll see her.'

Dieter looked utterly exhausted. Charlotte and Seona had taken turns to continue the interrogation while the other catnapped, and now that they had swapped notes and double checked the various names and conspiracies he had outlined, all that remained was to determine that he knew precisely what he was not required to do.

There was no longer any need to tether him: the humiliation he had already endured voluntarily proved, if nothing else, that he was a natural submissive, that he would stay with them regardless. But discovering the nature of his relationship with Petra begged the question how far were they prepared to go? They had already participated in an effort to unseat Charlotte and install Imogen as her replacement. That much was clear. But their insistence that their loyalty now lay with Charlotte still rang hollow, and even if it was genuine, she had to consider carefully whether she would now be able to trust a couple who had so swiftly switched sides. If a little corporal punishment was enough to secure their allegiance then there was no telling what they might be persuaded to do under greater pressure or inducement by others.

'You can sleep soon,' said Charlotte, and Dieter looked up at her from the sofa, bleary-eyed and pale as she stood before him.

'Just tell me, one last time, what you're going to do.'

He sat up, frowning, folded his arms and stared hard at some imaginary spot way beyond the floor, as if his instructions had been written far away and he was trying to bring them into focus.

Wearily, pausing frequently to make sure he was getting the sequence of possible actions correct, Dieter advanced through the scenarios Charlotte and Seona had briefed him on. She stopped him only occasionally, asking what he would do in the event of some unforeseen problem, and was delighted to find that he had wit enough to think for himself, was capable of acting on his own initiative should it be required.

Charlotte poured him a large glass of iced water and watched him sip at it. Seona came in to report that Petra had finally fallen into a deep sleep. She had also briefed Gerry, he knew what he had to do in their absence.

'You must sleep too,' Charlotte told Dieter, 'but you won't have long. And remember, when you wake we will be gone. But Mr Allan will be here, and you are to follow his orders. You will do exactly as he tells you. Understood?'

Dieter nodded, eyes already closing in anticipation of some peace, the chance to sleep.

'Very well,' Charlotte said, raising her hand to gently clasp Seona's, 'it's time for us to get ready.'

Eight

Imogen slipped her arm through the cocked elbow offered by Hans and held on tightly as they made their way gingerly down the frost-coated path towards the jetty.

Thousands of tiny lights traced the outline of the bay, the heavier concentrations indicating the clusters of homes about the wealthy and secluded coastal resort. It should, of course, be quiet at this time of year, but several of the larger yachts were ablaze with light, the dull reverberation of bass emanating from on-board parties proving that there were many who preferred to escape the city at every opportunity regardless of the weather. It really was bitterly cold, and although the sensation of icy air nipping her bare thighs beneath the outfit was not unpleasant, she would be glad to get inside.

The three figures manning the gate at the jetty's end would have been virtual statues had they not rocked from foot to foot, arms locked rigidly at their sides, the heavy dark overcoats reaching almost to the ground, their faces shielded from the cold with snugly positioned scarves. They maintained their curious movements, rocking gently like some grotesque mobile in the still winter air, only becoming slightly more animated as Hans and Imogen approached. The tallest of the three advanced, extended a gloved hand. Hans took his ID from his pocket, delved again to locate Imogen's passport, and passed them without comment. The man turned with the documents in hand, angling them into the light cast by the moorings lamps as he checked the tiny portraits, keenly scanning for appropriate matches with the cold faces before him.

'I was told your name is Kayla,' he said, the words distinct and clear despite the muzzling scarf.

Imogen smiled at the tall figure, staring into the shaded area beneath the peak of the baseball cap, difficult to locate his eyes with the glaring lights behind.

'Paul knows me as Kayla,' she said, and the big man cleared his throat, as if the mention of Goodstone's first name was somehow inappropriate, distasteful.

'Follow me,' he instructed, turning as he slipped the papers into his pocket, the burlier of the two others holding the gate open as they entered.

The sheer size of the yachts was impressive. She'd been on many, of course, but she could tell by Hans' constantly faltering steps, his scanning of the vessels as they advanced along the broad concourse, that he was overawed by the size of them. The sea washed between the massive boats, the dull watery clinking creating an almost musical effect, the slight movements of the white bulks disconcerting in their subtlety.

After negotiating what appeared to be almost a maze of narrower passages, each and every one of them crowded with increasingly impressive vessels, the greatcoated man stopped and indicated that they had arrived. Another two figures on board, shaded and still, waited patiently as Hans led Imogen up the steep, lightly sanded ramp, followed closely by the scarved guard.

The smaller of the figures was female, the visible features perhaps Latin-American, sharp dark eyes scanning them closely as she used her hands to mime that they should open their coats.

'It's a little cold for that,' Imogen heard herself say, amazed at her own impertinence given the circumstances, but the mime was merely repeated with more urgency as the scarved man's hand appeared over her shoulder, passing the ID to the other sentinel.

Imogen had no sooner unhitched the lowest button of the warm overcoat than the girl's bare hands were upon her, swiftly tracing the contours of her body, every crevice scanned, the lining of her coat checked. A circling finger indicated that she should turn, arms raised, and the process continued, nimble fingers barely brushing over the small of her back, between her shoulder-blades, down over her stockinged legs, even feeling along the thick fur coat collar. With Hans similarly checked by the girl's male companion, their identities checked once again, they were led inside the vessel, along a corridor, up a short flight of stairs and into a lounge where the massive pull-down digital screen on the wall was silently showing the garishly coloured highlights of the day's world events.

Imogen opened her coat, still unbuttoned, and allowed the warm air to caress her legs and chest. Hans stood rubbing his hands together, his nose a curious shade of crimson.

'Well,' Imogen said as she scanned the framed portraits of Goodstone in a variety of situations, most involving handshakes with extremely well-known people, several clearly taken on the yacht, itself 'we're finally here.'

Hans's tone was cautious, guarded, but she would've been surprised had it been anything but.

'Yes,' he said as the bright screen illuminated his profile, reflected in narrowed eyes beneath the now steam-smeared spectacles, 'we are here, Miss Imogen. And may God help us.'

His words were still hanging in the air, as perplexing as they were melodramatic, when the tall ginger-haired man entered from the door to Imogen's immediate left, an entrance she was unaware of, so perfectly had the portal been designed to form part of the mahogany-lined wall.

Imogen felt herself retreat, although she did little more than draw back a leg to steady herself against the curiously disorientating movement of the vessel. She had always been one to rely on the earliest of first impressions, and the overwhelming effect of the man's eyes was one of extreme trepidation. The eyes were light, perhaps grey but difficult to tell as they caught the glaring electronic light from the screen on the wall opposite. There was a smile there, but it was one of those nurtured over many years, one devoid of warmth, of natural curiosity in meeting another human being. He was interested, certainly, and she saw him scan her from toe-tip to crown, blatantly weighing her up as he rattled out his introduction and invitation to make themselves comfortable.

His name was Kyle, but he declined to explain his position in relation to Goodstone. She took his hand and was surprised how cold it was – perhaps he too had just arrived. The casual top and jeans were classy, but did not sit well on him. Clearly he was a man who lived most of his life inside a suit with tie tight about his neck, reining him forever to his role.

'You'll understand the security, of course,' he said, advancing across to Hans, hand extended, kept stock-steady as the PI struggled to release his arms from the thick overcoat. Even as he did eventually

take Hans's hand, the perfunctory gesture embarrassingly brief, almost insulting, she recognised the sparking of an intense distrust – this man was dangerous,
and he did not do a good job of concealing it. It
emanated from his every move, from the tone of his
voice and the excruciating self-confidence. Even in the
space of what – ten, fifteen seconds? – he could not
have possibly made it any plainer that he did not
want them there and would do everything to ensure
they were removed as soon as possible.

'We have to be very careful,' he said as his smile was
temporarily shifted to allow an appropriately earnest
expression, 'these are trying times for all of us.'

'Of course,' Imogen agreed as she slipped the coat
off, 'we understand. It sometimes seems that everyone
has an agenda.'

Kyle's eyes locked on hers. The shiver made her
shoulders tremble, but she rubbed her hands together,
making light of her visceral reaction to his glare.

'And how about you?' he asked, the reptilian smile
back in place. Imogen knotted her fingers together,
willed the blood to return to dispel the numbing cold.

'Well, let's just say that whatever my agenda may
or may not be, it's for Paul to decide whether or not
it merits his attention.'

Kyle nodded along with her every word as a
nursery-school teacher might encourage the fantastic
ramblings of a toddler, and he even pursed his lips as
if preparing to swallow something particularly unpleasant. When he next spoke, she could tell that he
was not even going to give her the courtesy of
recalling the smile, and his tone was flat, robotic.

'I will have to ask that your friend stay here during
the meeting.'

Imogen glanced at Hans. He would not be happy
to lose sight of her, would be even unhappier if he felt

that she was going to be alone with this creepy character, but she smiled reassuringly at him as he awaited her response.

'I take it my meeting will be private?' she asked politely, cocking her head to accentuate the overtly mannerly riposte to his rudeness.

Kyle nodded grimly, not even bothering to conceal his frown, the blatant contempt. He reminded her of a teacher who had been infatuated with her but had concealed the fixation by being astonishingly cruel to her at every opportunity. Although his motive could not possibly be the same, Imogen would not have been surprised to find this man capable of extreme sadism – he had the dead eyes of an accomplished assassin.

'My understanding is that you are not to be disturbed, so, yes, I can give that assurance.'

'Very well,' Imogen said chirpily, gathering her coat over her folded arms, 'let's go then.'

Charlotte's mind was made up. It was going to be her final appearance as Kayla. The game had gone on too long. Whatever excitement and fun there had been in the early years had long since dissipated, and this whole tedious episode with Imogen had only exacerbated the frustrations she now realised had been steadily increasing for years.

She closed her eyes and exhaled through pursed lips as Seona shifted herself slightly up her back, her strong fingers now kneading the tense tendons about her neck. The shower had been relaxing, but clearly not sufficiently to dispel the accumulated stress, and Seona was clearly aware of the effect, concentrating on easing the musculature, probing about the vertebrae.

And the very thought that Imogen had gone to such unbelievable trouble to cause all of this fuss would be funny if it wasn't tragic. All those years together: so many times they'd depended on her, and she on them; so much laughter, so many tears shared; so many fantastic sex sessions, some serious, some deadly dangerous, but so many just for the sheer joy of it; the early years when they had, surely, been in love – it was all now set at naught, and Charlotte could only close her eyes and hold back the grief, unable truly to believe that, for Imogen, it had been little more than a charade.

Yes, Imogen had been upset when Charlotte had been selected, and understandably so, but now to discover that she must have been harbouring a jealousy so intense that she was prepared to jeopardise their safety as well as the hallowed role of Kayla? It was as enraging as it was bewildering. It would only have taken one phone call, one night out, one look between them to sort it all out, to fall into bed laughing at the absurdity of it, and the faint hope that the whole sorry mess might yet be so resolved was the only remaining light at the end of the proverbial tunnel.

Well, now it would all come to an end – the festering envy, the misunderstandings, the awful, shocking waste of precious time. This final task, with dearest Seona on hand to ensure that it went exactly as she wanted it, if successful could achieve all of it. The years of living as Kayla would now be tested for their worth and the investment of so much time and energy would simply have to see a return. Then and only then could they return to England and tell Dark Eyes that it was all over, that it was time for him to find someone else.

Charlotte groaned. Seona's hands were at the nape of her neck, slowly but firmly pressing deep as if burying in search of the individual knots causing the stiffness, but the fatigue she was inducing was so difficult to fight against that she knew sleep was imminent. And yet, there was so little time now. It wouldn't be long, and the building trepidation would surely bring the tension flooding back no sooner than Seona's fingers had dispelled it.

Charlotte started to shift and Seona dismounted, allowing her to turn over onto her back.

'Will she yield?' Seona asked, and Charlotte pondered the question before answering.

'What choice does she have?'

Charlotte propped herself up on her elbows and watched as Seona rubbed herself down with the small towel. It was so nice to get away from that dammed apartment. Gerry would have things under control for now: Dieter and Petra really didn't have anywhere to run to, and knew full well that they could never hide anyway. But just how well would they manage when Imogen's people arrived? That remained to be seen. It would all unfold as it would and, as had happened so many times before, Charlotte could do little but trust to providence, fate, whatever it might be.

For now, it was enough to savour the new surroundings, the elegant circular bathroom suite, the opulent dressing room supplied. The faint undulating motion had been disconcerting, faintly nauseating at first, but the man's people had been welcoming and helpful, assured them not to worry, that everything was being taken care of. Yes, she was due to arrive, and yes, the object of Imogen's attention knew now who she really was, had been fully appraised of the situation. They were in safe hands.

Seona moved into the dressing room, out of sight. Not long now. Time to get dressed, get mentally prepared for the confrontation. It might be messy, it would certainly be emotional and quite possibly explosive, but whatever happened, Charlotte had only to know for sure that Seona was on her side and everything would be all right. It had been a trying time, all things considered. Now, in a matter of a few hours, it would all be resolved.

She got off the raised massage bench and drew a large towel from the warming rack, wrapped it about her and joined her friend, her lover. Seona was already laying out their outfits, giving the leather and rubber time to breathe, absorb some warmth from the air.

'I wonder what she'll be wearing,' mused Seona.

Charlotte did not answer, but also wondered. Imogen had always been the most extreme of the three when it came to donning unusual garb, but given the circumstances she would surely opt for a more conservative ensemble. She would've anticipated the likely preferences of the older man, tried to cater for him. Knowing Imogen as well as she did, Charlotte guessed that she would select something understated but sensuous; a simple black dress would be appropriate, something silky, perhaps velvety-textured, and of course she would wear stockings, probably seamed too to give that period air; shoes would be high-heeled slingbacks, possibly a pearly necklace. It would all be very simple and she would rely on her natural beauty to sway events, ensure a successful seduction. Her hair? No idea how it looked these days at all, not even sure if she would've retained her natural colour or plumped for a tint of some kind. If she really was pushing her luck then she would be wearing a Kayla-style hairpiece, but her confidence would have to be sky-high even to consider it. Then again, the man might be expecting it, and if his people had done their homework as well as that horrible man Kyle had implied then perhaps he would be expecting the platinum-blonde wig, the pale make-up and large darkly painted eyes. If so, then he would also expect to see the 'real' Kayla in order to judge for himself who really was worthy of the title.

In any event, Charlotte had resolved to wear the most shocking outfit she had, and would be wearing her wig if for no other reason than because she was entitled to. Imogen's treachery would find its most potent symbolism in the misuse of that one very special article, and if she was unwise enough to have worn it then she would very quickly find it removed.

Seona was rummaging in one of the end pockets of the large holdall, and Charlotte was just about to ask her what she was looking for when she withdrew the small brown bottle. Of course. She'd almost forgotten.

They only ever used the lotion for really important jobs, and she couldn't, off-hand, recall the last time. It had certainly been years. Dark Eyes had given Charlotte a tiny sample after a particularly draining Far East trip, but was unable to give her the recipe, just a contact name in Beijing. It was his present to her. It was herbal, of Himalayan origin, and quite unbelievably expensive, so she only ever used it when she knew she was liable to be pushing her mental and physical capacities to the limit. It had been Seona's idea to bring it – Charlotte might well have forgotten all about it otherwise – and now, she was thankful.

'I'll do you first,' Charlotte said, and Seona obligingly positioned herself for its application, placing her hands on the rim of the handbasin and stepping back to raise her backside.

Charlotte screwed off the little metal top, allowed five drops of the viscous liquid to drop into the centre of her palm, then covered the little greenish pool with her other palm and gently compressed her hands.

Seona was looking at Charlotte in the round mirror, waiting, and Charlotte held her stare, smiling sympathetically. She looked tired. They both did. But not to worry – once the lotion had been applied, they had dressed one another and got some make-up on, they would be energised and ready to go. It would all be fine.

The heat generated by the lotion was already pulsing pleasantly in Charlotte's hands as she started to smooth it down the cleft of Seona's bum cheeks, delving deep to cover her tight pussy, careful not to allow her fingers to slip inside. It would take a little while for the liquid to penetrate the flesh, but when it did the sensation would be not unlike a standard muscle-rub, but not quite as hot.

Seona turned around to face Charlotte as she did her front – another careful, slow light massage of the open palm against Seona's pussy, the gentle bud of her clitoris barely detectable for now, and then the residual traces wiped into her nipples.

Charlotte dropped her hands to herself as Seona repeated the process with the bottle – best not to waste any. The merest tingle was already spreading across her pubis as Seona's hands started to work the lotion into her behind. She was still working at her buttocks, smearing the wetness as high as her coccyx, when Charlotte started to kiss her.

Seona had paused at the heavy leather plug stuck in Charlotte's behind and was gently poking it, pressing it to create the maddening vibration they both loved, and Charlotte reciprocated, reaching down to find the leather flange at her friend's back passage, wiggling it in tandem with Seona's movements.

They nuzzled one another's necks, aping one another's motions, now clenching their buttocks with fingers still between, toying at the plug-ends, raising a scented palm to further tease and swell the tingling hardening nipples. It would be good. The pressure, the tension of anticipating what lay ahead could only sharpen and focus their energy, channel the adrenalin which was now starting to build in both of them.

Poor Imogen was working alone, and although Charlotte couldn't help feeling a subdued admiration for her ex-friend, she also knew that the aspiring Kayla would be no match for the two of them, not when they had the advantage now, the upper hand, that priceless element of surprise.

Charlotte closed her eyes and allowed Seona's mouth to work down her neck, to start kissing her chest. She wouldn't go too far, not for now, but this was heavenly, to receive such sweet caresses from the one she loved and had been so afraid of losing.

'Come on, let's get ready,' Charlotte whispered, afraid that she might succumb to Seona right now, end up grabbing the opportunity to release some of the building frustration.

They helped one another: they powdered one another's limbs lightly – the cool unscented talcum made drawing on the rubber stockings so much easier. And the corsets had to be tightly laced, pulled strenuously to pinch the waist, force the diaphragm and breasts as high as their physiques allowed. It was certainly uncomfortable, caused temporary giddiness, but once they had adapted to the constriction, modified their breathing to accept the unnatural pressure, the effect was exhilarating. Seona had brought her favoured thigh boots, the ones Charlotte had bought her ages ago, but Charlotte had opted for her very best black shoes, the ones with tiny gold eyelets for the laces and beautifully spiked heels. Seona helped her to get them on, lace them tightly, and Charlotte returned the favour by zipping up the boots so that they snugly encompassed Seona's strong, rubber-coated thighs. Seona also wore the gloves which extended to beyond the elbow, but Charlotte decided not to wear hers – she wanted to feel as much as possible, be sure not to numb any of her already heightened senses.

They made one another up simultaneously, taking turns to apply the foundation, the eye-shadows, the eyeliners and lipstick. Imogen would recognise them immediately of course, despite the make-up, despite the outfits, but they were not disguising themselves at all. There was no need for concealment here, not when the very reason for their presence had already been established, understood.

Seona applied a final dusting of talcum to the inside of the dress and squatted, swaying and tottering slightly in her boots, to pull the material apart for Charlotte to step into. The ankle-length skirt was slashed completely up the front so that her sex would be intermittently visible as she walked, but in all probability the blueish-black swathe of darkly gleaming fleshlike material would soon be discarded. Seona drew on her skintight leather jacket, completely buttoning it as far as the high collar which folded neatly below her chin. But she was not wearing any skirt today. There would be little time for her to start fiddling with extraneous clothing, and better by far if her thighs were left completely free as their unfettered strength might be required in the event of Imogen having to be restrained.

But there was one final addition to Seona's outfit, one which Charlotte had to help her with: the strap-on matched Seona's clothing wonderfully well, matte-black rubber with tightly fitting black leather harness. The dildo belonged to Charlotte, but Seona always ended up using the thing and so had taken custody of it. With it firmly in place, protruding from her crotch like some fantastic extension of her clitoris, Charlotte could only wonder how Imogen would react when she clapped eyes on it, realised who was wearing it and what was about to be done with it. She wouldn't need three guesses on any count.

And then, finally, the pièce de résistance: for the very last time, Seona drew Kayla's trademark from the battered old box. The wig was well travelled, had served Charlotte well, but the moment was strangely unemotional for her. She stood watching in the mirror as Seona raised the shimmering hairpiece and carefully adjusted it into place. It was as snug and comfortable as an old glove, required only light brushing to restore the familiar shape, the uniform curl about the fringe. Charlotte kept her eyes fixed on her own eyes as the piece was fitted, and although she could detect no visible difference in her stare, her colouring or any other physical aspect of her, the psychological transformation was instant – she was prepared now, as fully as she could be, and her decision to relinquish the role of Kayla now seemed exactly right. There was an undeniable relief that, after what was to follow, whatever it might be and whoever perceived themselves as winners or losers, she would never wear the damned thing again. It had caused enough trouble, broken enough friendships, but she would return it to its rightful owners with a clear conscience. She had fulfilled the role dutifully, responsibly, and never had she jeopardised the tradition which it represented. And now, in her final act as Kayla, she would see the job through to the very end, regardless of the consequences.

Imogen shifted in the broad leather chair, so comfortable that she would have loved to have curled up and snoozed. But there was no question of it: the antici-pation was so sharp, the natural buzz of adrenalin so exhilarating that she couldn't remember ever experi-encing a similar high. He was here, she was here, they were alone, and if she played her cards right she would soon have seduced a man so powerful that the efforts of all previous Kaylas would seem as nothing in comparison.

Goodstone had clearly had a drink, but he was one of those men in whom the signs were difficult to read; years of imbibing had affected his carriage and speech so that the effects were assimilated within a general attitude of relaxed but precise nonchalance. Her father had been precisely the same – a clever, accomplished actor when it came to concealing his addiction.

Not that she could make the same assumption about this man. He would not, could not, have risen to the position he enjoyed if permanently inebriated, but she could also appreciate that the recent reports regarding his failing health were probably exag-gerated. He was overweight, certainly, and the baggy black silk shirt did little to conceal his paunch, but he had the confidence that comes with power, that easy style which she had always found attractive. He was not handsome, but then again, the term was relative.

He replenished her glass, carefully pinching the ice-shards from the small wooden bucket, allowing them to slide down the glass rather than clatter. The room was perfectly circular, was surely in the very bowels of the vessel – they had descended three flights to reach it – and now, with the door closed, she could not be quite sure exactly where it was in relation to the small lounge where she had left Hans. The room's one continuous wall and circular ceiling were lined with what appeared to be huge slabs of polished, slightly curved darkly gleaming marble, and the seemingly infinite refractions and reflections created by the splintering of the little available artificial light caused a disorienting weightlessness, an almost hallucinogenic impression of being at the epicentre of some dark explosion. The low glass table was enormous, held a couple of ashtrays and a scattering of current magazines, a thin sheaf of well-thumbed papers lying atop a closed clear plastic folder. Perhaps he'd been doing some work while he waited for her.

She settled back further in the leather armchair, felt the tension in her shoulders, the nape of her neck. Although she didn't feel particularly nervous she was aware of a steadily increasing tension. He had asked some polite questions about her latest projects, the University Fellowship, the various contacts she had made since her arrival three months ago, but she knew that the civil chatter could not continue indefinitely. He took his seat directly opposite her, the broad thick circle of glass between them partially reflecting his bright shirt in the mosaic of dark swirls cast by the dimly lit marble wall.

He peered into his drink, his expression almost forlorn, but she resisted the temptation to ask him what was on his mind. Although sheer temerity had got her this far she did not want to become overbearingly familiar – the appropriate tone had to be maintained until he decided otherwise. For now, he was in control, and she had to give him his place.

'The performance at the beach house was, well, shall I say, memorable?' he said, but his tone was formal, like the considered conclusion of a paid critic.

'I should take that as a compliment?' she asked, unsmiling.

'Yes. I think you should,' he replied, swirling the golden liquid in the heavy round tumbler. 'I have many questions,' he continued, frowning as he settled himself deeper in the seat, legs crossed, hands cupping the tumbler atop the peak of his belly as he stared at her.

'No one has all the answers, but I'm happy to try,' she offered, anticipating a query as to the background of her alter-ego.

'Why are you doing this?' he asked, his slight smile incredulous, genuinely curious. She felt herself colour, totally wrong-footed, unprepared, and her awkwardness had obviously been noted as he leaned forward, sipping at the drink, clearly keen to hear her answer.

'Why?' she heard herself wonder aloud.

He nodded as he placed the glass on the table, then opened his palms wide as if embracing her from afar.

'Look at you,' he said, 'you are young and beautiful and intelligent. What would compel one such as you to seek a furtive rendezvous with a man twice your age? You must know that you would never have been able to get within several miles of here had your background not been investigated in every detail. I know as much as I need to know regarding your family, your friends, your bank accounts, your contacts in England. I know the hows, wheres, whens, the whos – you name it. I probably know things about you you don't even know yourself. The only reason you're here, the solitary reason I allowed this meeting, is because I would like to know why. Why are you doing this, and why me?'

She sat forward, aping his movement, and also placed her glass carefully on the table. It was hard now to meet his curious gaze, harder still to deny her quickening breathing, the mild panic which was gripping her.

'You say you know so much,' she said, still staring down at the inverted reflection of his face on the glassy surface. 'Perhaps you'll tell me something, answer a question I've been asking for many years.'

He grunted that she should continue.

'Why does Kayla have to exist?'

He laughed, and she looked up to see the twinkle bright in his eyes as the laugh became a cough and he noisily cleared his throat before answering.

'Answering a question with another is not the easiest of skills to acquire my dear,' he said, face reddened with the sudden exertion, 'but I will indulge your boldness this once. Fact is, Kayla is a creature from your part of the world, she is a creation of your culture. Of course, we do have similarly influential women here, but they do not enjoy the same mythical status. For me to answer your question with any authority, I would have to belong to that culture, understand the nature of the thing you have come to know as Kayla. Of course, Kayla is not real, not in the accepted sense of the word. There is no address for her, no taxes are collected from her. She exists only insofar as men like me want her to, perhaps need her to. In any event, I can understand your question, even if my answer may be lacking. I also understand that you have not answered mine.'

Imogen hastily raised the glass. Her hand was shaking now, the flush had become a cool and clammy sweat.

'I'm doing it because, well,' she stammered, 'because I have to.'

'You *have* to?' he said, and she detected the disbelieving tone, the scepticism. She would have to do better.

'All right, I suppose that, well, strictly speaking, I don't have to, but I feel as if I should, that I have no choice.'

His expression had become grim, lips pursed as he sat forward again and reached for the tiny remote control. He jabbed the unit at an area of wall and the screen flickered briefly before pulsing into bright life, the sudden display of garish colour momentarily dazzling in the dim circular room.

'I would like you to watch this, my dear,' he said, 'and I would like you to explain why you feel compelled to follow in the footsteps of these women.'

Imogen could only sit and stare as the compendium of roughly edited clips showed a variety of blonde women indulging in the acts she had come to know so well. It was all there. Some still photos had obviously been culled from the master directory of images kept back in England, but most of the footage appeared to have been surreptitiously captured, the camera angles suggesting that the participants were, in all likelihood, unaware that their enjoyment was being recorded. The lack of any soundtrack made the viewing uncomfortable, embarrassing, and she was aware of him rising from his seat to return to the shelf where the bottle stood, uncapped. He poured another generous measure as she watched a recent clip, and there was Seona, face hovering over a small but spitting cock and the pussy she had just pulled it from was unmistakably Charlotte's. It had to be recent – Seona's make-up was, as ever, light, but those tiny lines about her eyes were new, must've developed sometime over the past five years. The shock of seeing them again, so close, so utterly bared, was suddenly sickening, and she stared down into the glass, quelling the urge to demand that he switch off the offensive proof of Kayla's obscene reality.

She cursed her naivety. Why she had ever contemplated trying to get close to such a man now appeared nonsensically ambitious, but it had made perfect sense and, truth be told, been surprisingly easy. But whatever had sparked his interest, it now seemed clear that he was playing her at her own game, changing the rules she thought she'd learned so well, imposing his own agenda on the meeting she'd imagined would be a relatively straightforward seduction.

He was back in his seat. She glanced up to see that he was watching the imagery with a faintly amused expression. Suddenly he reached forward, grabbed the remote control and stabbed it again at the pulsing coloured pane of light, freezing the image on the large screen. She looked up to be met with an image she vaguely recalled from those days in the House so long ago – an etching, perhaps late Victorian judging by the style, of a woman being sandwiched by two men, her pale skin thrown into sharp contrast by the thick black woollen stockings, both of her passages filled. The work was well executed, although Imogen could detect no artist's name, no date or other information relating to the scene. Most striking of all though, was the fact that woman's face could not be seen, and although the hairpiece was curly and rather long, intricately piled atop her head, it had clearly been rendered by the artist as very light, perhaps blonde.

'The report I was given suggests that this is the original Kayla,' Goodstone said, the interest obvious in his voice, his tone academic rather than excited, 'although it's entirely possible that she was just the earliest recipient we know of, that there were others before her. This woman was, in fact, the wife of a senior clergyman in England. We know that she travelled extensively, sometimes with her husband on official duties, but more often in the company of several very close female friends. She died near the start of the last century, but presumably the title of Kayla had been passed on well before that date.'

Imogen's hands were shaking so badly that she knotted her fingers together and buried them hard into her lap. He noticed the gesture and frowned.

'My dear, you seem unhappy, ill at ease. You may have thought that my agreeing to meet you like this would have a different outcome. Perhaps you imagined that by now I would be, well, how should I say it? That I would have succumbed to your charms?'

It felt like being back at school, being reprimanded for a prank as yet unexecuted but easily anticipated.

'Of course, I am merely human, a simple man like any other. And yes, I would enjoy it, perhaps I would even allow you closer than would be safe for me. But my safety is not the prime concern here. What you have done is seek power for selfish ends, and that is common, it is understandable. But you have to understand that it comes at a heavy price.'

He was threatening her? The shiver raced through her, seemed to bolster the film of sweat on her brow. Of course, he could kill her if he wanted to – there would be no trace, no trail to follow. Perhaps they had already disposed of poor Hans, dropped him overboard to sink into the freezing water between the tethered yachts.

Goodstone got up and adjusted the belt suspending his slacks beneath the paunch.

'I'm no saint, my dear,' he said, but the tone was matter-of-fact rather than menacing. 'I've exercised great power in my time, sometimes wrongly. I live with that. But what I have always tried to avoid is treachery. Friends are very important. They're not to be taken for granted or lightly dismissed. I think you know what I'm talking about.'

Imogen sniffed, trying to hold back the tears. But the wetness brimmed at her eyelids and she no longer made any effort to prevent it from trickling down her cheeks as Goodstone crossed towards the place where the door must be. He raised a hand and pressed, perhaps a buzzer – a signal of some kind.

'Punishment has its place. You deserve punishment, but it isn't for me to dispense it. That's not to say I won't enjoy it, but you'll forgive me if I watch from a safe distance. For men of my age it is safer to enjoy such activity vicariously. I wish you well, young Imogen. Goodbye.'

And then he was gone. The door remained open. She slumped forward into her cupped hands and sobbed miserably, the tears spilling readily as they hadn't for years. She felt so utterly wretched, so riven with humiliation and self-disgust that she could not begin to imagine what was going to happen to her, how she was going to get out of the bloody mess she'd created for herself. What punishment was to be administered? And if not by him, who?

She was just about to reach into her coat pocket in search of a tissue when the movement at the door alerted her, and when she did glance up, fearful, her breath suspended, the snot gathering at the end of her nose and the tears drying on her cheeks, she exhaled in astonishment as Charlotte and Seona walked in and shut the door.

Goodstone settled back in the recliner, hand cupping the glass Kyle had just replenished.

'Her people have arrived at the complex,' he said quietly, and Goodstone looked up at him, frowning.

'That's fine then. Leave them be. Pick them up if they decide not to stay. Otherwise, stay well back.'

Kyle made affirmative noises, hovered, hands clasped behind his back. Perhaps he was waiting to see if he would be permitted to stay and watch what was happening in the circular lounge. Goodstone didn't have to glower at him, say anything, he merely turned his head slightly to indicate that he was looking at Kyle's feet, as if wondering what they were still doing there. The PA quietly left.

He switched on the monitor using the remote, reclined the seat a little further and took a sip of the whiskey.

It hadn't taken them long at all. The impostor, the one he'd so very nearly fallen for, had removed her dress and was being interrogated. It was clear, by the posture of the beautiful petite wig-wearing female, that there was no competition regarding the identity of the true Kayla. Imogen was sitting with knees tight together, eyes downcast, feet drawn close as far beneath the chair as she could manage, her hands knotting together in her lap as the dark-haired, dildo-wearing girl stood with her hands behind her back, watching and waiting for instructions.

He faded up the sound, took the cigar from his breast pocket and started peeling the wrapper off. If only old Tom could be here, he thought, he would love it. Still, he mused, as Kayla's voice, clear and menacing, filled the room via the microphones, his old friend would relish every last detail.

'. . . and you really thought we wouldn't find out? I know you hate me but, my God, Imogen, you know me inside out, we grew up together. It's bad enough that you became obsessed enough to go ahead with this crazy scheme, but you know what really hurts? You know what's so offensive?'

Imogen's face was raised only slightly. Seona stepped forward, the strap-on wobbling and swaying before her, and placed a gloved forefinger gently below Imogen's chin, easing her face up to meet Charlotte's stern gaze.

Imogen's eye make-up was streaked down her cheeks, her chin was quivering.

'I didn't, I mean, I wouldn't have . . .'

'You thought you could humiliate me. But you wouldn't have dared do it unless you had help, and that help had to come from somewhere. You're going to tell me, dearest, make no mistake about it.'

'But I didn't know it would go this far!'

Imogen was pleading, desperate, her eyes bolstered with fresh tears as she raised her palms as if showing how clean her hands were. Charlotte merely shook her head and shifted her weight to the other leg, twisting her toe-point into the carpet as if stubbing out a cigarette.

'No. Of course you didn't. That's why you recruited two actresses to pose as your slaves, that's why you dragged some tired porn star out of retirement, that's why you hired a private investigator to do the donkey work of infiltrating high society for you? That's why you had arranged for us to be spied upon from the moment we arrived here?'

Imogen's eyes seemed to widen at this last statement, and Charlotte pounced on it.

'Yes, we know. We know you've sent your merry little band to our apartment. They'll be expecting to find us there, they'll be hoping to interest us in buying information on your whereabouts. Another chapter in your game, keep them guessing, keep them distracted, and most importantly of all, keep them as far away from here as possible while you crown yourself Kayla by taking an impressive scalp. Would that be a fair summary of what you had in mind for this evening?'

Imogen seemed unable to answer, stunned, mouth agape, the tears still dribbling down her face, dripping from her chin as she stared up at her ex lover and best friend.

'How?' Imogen mouthed rather than said, her hands falling limply into her lap, fingers nervously tracing the edges of her stocking hems.

'How? Oh dear, dear Imogen, wouldn't you just love to know. Suffice it to say, your grand plan is now in tatters. And before we go any further, let me make one thing perfectly clear.'

Charlotte took a step nearer Seona and reached out to smooth her fingertips across the end of the thick wobbling black cock sticking out from the rubber-clad assistant's groin. She gently stroked it, miming the act of masturbation as she stared at Imogen, spelling out her order.

'You will ask me no further questions. You will provide me with answers as and when I demand them, and otherwise you will say nothing. Is that understood?'

Imogen was staring blankly at Charlotte's fingers as they moved up and down the black rubber shaft, her expression utterly blank, as if she had somehow mentally removed herself to another time and place.

'Is that understood!' Charlotte yelled, and Imogen sat bolt upright, her strict training in the role of submissive now returning after so long acting as dominatrix.

'Yes, mistress,' she smartly replied.

'That's better. Now get on your knees and bend over. Seona is going to give you a little fuck to soften you up.'

Imogen did as she was told without hesitation, slipping from the broad soft chair, turning to fold her arms on the expanse of leather as she raised her behind to Seona's attention. Charlotte allowed herself an audible laugh.

'Very nice, dear,' she said, placing one of her heeled feet on Imogen's right buttock, prodding the fullness of her flesh with her toe-point before lifting the garter belt clear of the indentation it had formed in the succulent skin, then allowing to snap back into place.

'You've been looking after yourself, I see. Perhaps just a couple of pounds here and there, but overall I'd say you've done rather well. Do you still have such a penchant for buggery these days?'

Imogen did not answer.

'You may answer, slave,' Charlotte said, the smile evident in her voice.

'Yes, mistress,' Imogen replied, the emotion welling again in her throat as Seona brusquely kicked at her heels, parting them further.

Seona got to her knees, placed the heavy rubber black shaft upon Imogen's behind and allowed it to sit there, darkly contrasting with the pale bum-flesh. Charlotte paced behind the chair, staring down at Imogen's buried face, the arms folded beneath her, tense and trembling.

'Whose idea was it?' Charlotte asked, and Seona started gently to push the dildo up Imogen's cleft. The tool rose, poking upwards at the height of the movement before gently retracing the motion in reverse, the dry rubber juddering slightly as it passed over her skin.

The slap from Seona came as an obvious shock, causing Imogen to jerk forward as the latexed hand stung the fullest curve of her right buttock.

'Answer,' said Seona quietly, and Imogen raised her face slightly, sniffing deeply before responding.

'It was my suggestion,' she said, and there was just an iota of pride in her tone. Perhaps she was considering defiance now that the initial shock had worn off.

'I beg your pardon?' Charlotte snapped, and even as her words emerged Seona was parting Imogen's cheeks roughly, aiming the thick dildo-end at the juncture between her pussy and anus, prodding hard.

'It was my suggestion, mistress,' Imogen said, but now the tone of bitterness and anger was clearly evident. No doubt now, she was going to make a fight of it.

'Get that thing inside her and fuck her,' Charlotte snapped, and Seona complied with some difficulty, pushing hard but unable to penetrate Imogen's dryness despite broadening the woman's pussy lips with extended fingers.

Seona leaned forward, carefully positioned her face over the juncture of tool and flesh, and released a long thick dribble of saliva which connected with the smooth cleft of Imogen's cheeks before coursing down to envelop the bulbous black lump. She retracted the stiff shaft without losing the contact already established, watched as the saliva wrapped itself about the rubber, then pushed again. Imogen stuck her head down, and the cry was barely muffled deep in her chest as Seona pushed again, slowly, deliberately driving the strap-on home, one hand steadying the shaft as the other held the flanging base hard against her own pussy.

'Years of lies and deceit,' Charlotte hissed, 'and all you ever had to do was call me, get in touch, clear the air. We could still have stayed friends, we could have been just the way we were. But no, you had to go it alone, you had to try and go one better, didn't you?'

Seona was in now. The entry had been slow and quite obviously painful for the resisting Imogen, but now, as she withdrew the tool, Imogen's pussy flesh distending along with it, puffing out as if unwilling to release it, Seona allowed more spittle to drop into the cleft, further lubricating the dimly gleaming blackness.

'And why shouldn't I?' Imogen cried in between sobs.

'Fuck her,' said Charlotte quietly, and Seona gripped the hips where the suspender belt was sunken, darkly outlining the fullness of the woman's peachy globes, the tool stuck and steady. Then she lunged hard and deep, burying the thing completely inside her, eliciting a throaty gasp which became a high staccato shriek.

Charlotte stood as near the chair as she could get and reached down to grip Imogen's hair tightly. The dark brown shiny locks formed a wild ponytail over her forearm as she pulled the panting woman's face up, her grimace now visible.

'Open your eyes,' Charlotte said, and Imogen did so, her lips bared, tongue nipped between her white teeth. Her head shifted, bobbed in Charlotte's grip as Seona established a rhythm, sliding the dildo in and out of her, the withdrawals slow, the entries hard and ever-deeper, each making Imogen screw her eyes shut momentarily as the tool, now wet and moving easily, reached greater depths with every stroke.

'I'm not playing any more,' Charlotte said, her eyes only inches from Imogen's, 'and I didn't come halfway around the world to listen to your insolence. If you think the fact that we were once friends will have any bearing whatsoever on the severity of your punishment, then you must be even more deluded than I thought.'

Imogen's eyes suddenly bared, pupils dilating dramatically as she closed her mouth, sucked in her cheeks, then spat at Charlotte furiously. The spittle sprayed messily across Charlotte's upper chest and neck.

The slap across her face was swift and hard and anticipated, Imogen closing her eyes, twisting her face as far as she was able under Charlotte's tight grip.

'Get that thing off,' Charlotte said, releasing Imogen's hair to allow the woman to slump back into folded arms.

Seona stood, unhitched the strap of the dildo and allowed the harness to slide over her rubber-clad thighs, carefully drawing it over the thigh-boots. Charlotte was going to do it herself now, take out some of her building anger on the helpless Imogen.

The rage was clear in Charlotte's voice as she spoke, but Imogen turned her face, staring defiantly, eyes now twinkling with that familiar energy and mischief. She was surely enjoying it in some strange way, savouring the confrontation despite the fact that she was clearly not in a strong position.

'Put it on me,' Charlotte commanded as Seona stepped out of the harness and lifted it, the wettened shaft now scented, more pliable. Imogen raised herself, her expression struggling to contain the discomfort Seona had caused, and she took the tool with trembling hands, leaning down towards Charlotte's feet.

Charlotte raised her right foot, placed her shoe on Imogen's shoulder and pressed, pushing her down further until her face was on the carpet. Imogen's hands came to encompass the leatherbound feet, smoothing about the warmth, the slender tapering heels, the delicate lacework along the face of them.

'Kiss them,' Charlotte commanded, and Imogen did so, licking at the black leather, hands caressing the rubberbound ankles as she wet the shoes, nibbling and pressing her tongue against the toes. Charlotte lifted the first foot slightly, allowing Imogen to slip the harness under the heel. The motion was repeated, Imogen careful to keep her face low and busy. Charlotte parted the long skirt more fully, gazing down as the enslaved Imogen worshipped her feet, now carefully drawing the leather harness up over her calves, the obscene dick swaying and dipping as it was moved slowly upwards.

Imogen gaped, allowing the wobbling end of the shaft to enter her mouth. She steadied it between her teeth, gripping it tight as she drew the harness higher, over the breadth of Charlotte's hips as she parted the gashed rubber dress more fully, like some awful cape about to engulf the hapless victim.

Seona moved behind Charlotte and unhitched the skirt, drew it away from the mistress with a flourish, discarding it over the back of the armchair.

The thing was almost in place when Seona gripped the back of it, pulled it high up the small of Charlotte's back and secured it tightly just beneath the lower fringe of the jet-black corset. Imogen released it from her mouth, her gaze still on Charlotte's as the dildo was further tightened, pulled into place to press hard against Charlotte's own pussy.

Charlotte rubbed at the tool, her hand snaking back into Imogen's hair, and she parted her legs a little for greater stability before gripping the thing tightly, poking it at Imogen's lips. Imogen resisted at first, lips tightening, eyes shut, but Charlotte merely repeated the action, harder this time, and Imogen opened her mouth with what sounded distinctly like a snarl, eyes still closed. There was something resolute, aggressive about her attitude as Charlotte plunged the rubber into her mouth, pushing, demanding that she take it as fully and as quickly as possible.

Seona got to her knees behind Imogen and gave her a couple of preliminary, almost tentative slaps, as if merely testing the texture of the buttocks. The punishment proper seemed set to begin.

'You remember this,' stated Charlotte, not a question – whatever memory she was hoping to spark, Imogen could not acknowledge it, her lips stretched, throat swelling as the dildo was stuffed into her face, filling her, eyes rimming with tears borne of sheer effort and discomfort as she strained to accommodate the thing, her hair still firmly in Charlotte's grasp.

Seona slapped the inner thighs of Imogen, urging her to part further. As she did so Seona's hands were kneading at her pussy and arse, no caution now, fingers pressing, probing, pulling at the tender flesh as she sought to further moisten and widen the already broached lips. Then Seona's palms were curving about Imogen's right thigh, her pale fingers gripping the back-lace stocking tops as if securing a greater grip through the material as she brought the leg off the ground, contorting Imogen's torso as she struggled, the rubber cock still stuck inside her throat as she curved her spine further to accommodate Seona's latest move. And the raising of the leg to Seona's shoulder drew the other leg away from the ground, Seona's strong arms lifting her, hauling her higher up her body, her pussy now gaping openly, red and wet and wide as Seona palmed Imogen's legs over her shoulders, about her neck, her mouth now only inches away from the woman's open sex and twitching backside.

Charlotte dropped to her knees as Seona completed the manoeuvre, allowing Imogen to plant her palms into the deep carpet for support as her behind was raised to envelop Seona's face, and whatever Seona was doing now, it was sending Imogen wild. Her thighs jerked, spasming together about Seona's moaning mouth as she struggled to maintain the oral clamp on Charlotte's dildo.

Charlotte gripped the hair again and started to pull and push, dictating the pace at which she expected the tool to be throated, and Imogen complied, whining as the shaft pumped in and out of her face, her buttocks bucking, hips gyrating as Seona ate her pussy, nose barely visible at the peak of Imogen's arse-cleft, the strong gloved hands supporting her by the hips as her legs flailed, one shoe already kicked off, the other hanging loosely, ready to fall.

'Yes, you remember, you remember where you learned how to do this, who encouraged you and helped you and made you stay when you'd had enough, when you wanted to go running home. You remember when you lost your cherry? You remember when one of these things went into your arse for the first time and we watched one another as it happened? You remember all that for sure,' Charlotte said rapidly, her own memories clearly now shaping the severity of her actions, the desperate, almost rabid face-fucking she was forcing Imogen to endure.

'But you've forgotten all of that now? Is that it?' Charlotte demanded, her voice rising in pitch and speed as she brought two hands to Imogen's head, gripping the hair tightly as she rode into the reddened lips. Imogen protested pathetically, her whines weakening as Seona buried her face ever deeper between the raised sex lips.

'Well, maybe this will help you remember it all, dear Imogen, and when you do remember I hope you will see fit to give the both of us the kind of apology we deserve. By the time we've finished with you you'll curse the day you ever clapped eyes on that blasted dildo, because it was you, dear, it was you who started all of this with your little mail-order surprise. I'm sure you'll remember that, if nothing else.'

Charlotte pulled the black rubber shaft from Imogen's mouth and she slumped forward into the carpet, sex still wrapped about Seona's face. Charlotte reached down to where Seona was barely visible, still busy at Imogen's sex, and she wasted no time in plunging two fingers into Imogen's arse as the dildo wobbled, dripping with the woman's saliva, ready to go in there as soon as Seona lowered her.

Imogen groaned into the carpet, her noises weakened and sporadic, seemingly unrelated to Seona's oral actions or the brusque anal finger-fuck Charlotte was now administering.

Charlotte kept her fingers inside the tight dark hole, pumping steadily as she lowered a hand to locate Imogen's right breast, and the immediate high cry from the prone girl indicated that the nipple had been located and was being pinched, tweaked, pulled. Seona lowered the hips and gently brought Imogen's body back down to within fucking distance of the dildo, and Charlotte leaned her face towards Seona, tongue protruding, to lick at the glowing cheeks where the viscous evidence of her pussy-licking was glistening, shining beautifully as Seona puffed, taking huge breaths of fresh air.

Seona shifted away to make space for Charlotte, and Imogen barely moved, her face rubbing into the carpet as if seeking an exit deep down in the floor, willing an escape route to be revealed below her. But Seona was already upon her, gripping her shoulders, hauling her upright and propping her as she sought her breasts, savagely manipulating them in her black latexed fingers. Charlotte prepared to bugger her with the dildo, circling the wet black head against the red-rimmed hole, spreading the juice from the open pussy below, tenderising and reaming in advance of what would surely be a painful invasion.

Charlotte worked quickly, positioning herself square and solid on the carpet, parting her legs, twisting her shoe-tips into the deep pile to secure an unmoveable stance as she gripped Imogen's stocking tops and hauled then up, tighter and higher about the strong thick thighs, savouring the breadth of her raised posterior, smeared and open and ready for the tool. She palmed the cheeks further apart and leaned back to survey the puffed and crimson-tinged pussy, the dark depression of her slackening behind as she tapped the heavy rubber cock against one cheek, then the other before placing it into the crevice, using her hands to close the voluptuous buttocks about it, the lower half of it almost completely concealed by the pale flesh as the saliva-coated upper thickness protruded, wedged between the taunted muscles.

'Get your tongue into Seona's pussy and think yourself lucky, dear. Be grateful you're getting this chance,' Charlotte said as she allowed Imogen's buttocks to spring back open and firmly placed the broad black bulb at the dark and already closing anus.

Seona perched herself on the edge of the armchair, opened her legs fully and used her shining black digits to pull her labia wide, raising her heels to the chair's edge to support herself as she raised her arse, also bringing it within tonguing-distance of Imogen as Charlotte urged her forward, staying close all the while, the dildo poised to invade.

Imogen raised her hands, spanned the juncture of rubber stocking and flesh, breathlessly puffing directly onto Seona's open pussy as she prepared to taste her. Charlotte placed a hand firmly on the small of Imogen's back, the suspender belt under her palm, her other hand trembling with the effort of gripping the dildo, steadying it as she started to press it into the gently jerking behind. Seona waited until Charlotte gave the signal, then grabbed Imogen by the hair and hauled her flushed face directly into her. Her back arched with the impact, crying aloud as Imogen's tongue plunged into her, her nose grazing her clitoris. Charlotte raised herself slightly, one hand now clutching Imogen's shoulder for added grip, and she sank the dildo fully, completely into Imogen's behind in one deliberate, brutal stroke which made the woman howl into Seona's pussy.

'Remember now?!' Charlotte cried, face raised, eyes shut as her fingers about the withdrawing shaft measured the length she had plunged into her ex-friend. Imogen's noises were distant, wretched as the arse-fucking commenced in earnest, but there was to be no respite for her. Seona pulled the face away from her for just a second or two, enough for Imogen to seize an intake of breath, but then she was buried again, her mouth and nose enveloped, ground into the openness.

Charlotte stopped the fucking motion and carefully rose, moving herself forward, the dildo still stuck fully inside Imogen's arse, and she straddled the woman, both hands now on her shoulders as she stepped, crouching, to deepen the invasion, bring the tool as fully into her as possible. Imogen writhed, raising her behind in a vain effort to relieve the increasing tension on her anus. But Charlotte merely moved with her, defying her even to attempt to ease the tension, and when Imogen did stop, unable to contort herself any further, Charlotte resumed the hard, unforgiving fuck, the tool not becoming visible between strokes now, merely repeatedly, incessantly pounding against the filled flesh-ring as if trying to lift her off the ground completely. Seona was beginning to lose control, her hands using Imogen's head like a gigantic sex toy, her own fingers now working along with Imogen's tongue to flick and expand her already protuberant clitoris, the darkly red bud standing out starkly from the light covering of clipped auburn hair.

'Please,' Imogen begged, pressing against Seona's thighs to force herself back from the onslaught, but Charlotte pushed her face back into Seona's pussy, holding her there as the sobs racked her torso, only the occasional splutter audible as Seona started to buck and ride the face in close pursuit of her climax.

And when Seona's come did arrive it was swiftly, noiselessly, but the frantic hauling at Imogen's head reached a manic, almost unhinged intensity as she thrust herself against the smothered face.

The sound of Imogen gagging on whatever fluid Seona had released signalled an appropriate juncture at which to allow her some mild relief, and Seona retreated further up the chair, clasping and rubbing at herself as the orgasm subsided, her eyes closed, mouth open, utterly spent and racked with spasmodic aftershocks.

Imogen folded, shoulders dropping away from Charlotte's hands as she drooped onto the carpet between Seona's boots, her hands on the leatherclad feet. She panted and gasped, only a slight gurgle indicating that she had indeed received Seona's spurting come.

Charlotte, now motionless, the tool still buried, reached down to palm Imogen's hair briefly, and the gesture appeared gentle, almost affectionate, as if she had forgotten that the woman was meant to be receiving punishment. But then, so swiftly that Imogen released one final pained and desperate cry, Charlotte stood up, the dildo straining impossibly inside Imogen before bending and springing from the gaping hole with an alarmingly loud sound.

Imogen curled herself into a ball, hands covering her sex as she whimpered and writhed. Charlotte stepped back, chest heaving, the perspiration already working its way through the make-up, the dildo still bobbing up and down.

'Right, dear,' Charlotte said, grabbing a quick breath between each word, 'now we can try again.'

Nine

Gerry yanked another moisturising wipe from the little plastic box on the table and covered his brow with the cooling tissue.

Dieter was sitting in what had become his customary chair by the ornamental hearth, staring down at the tiny chess set, apparently engrossed, but Gerry couldn't help wondering if he was thinking about what Gerry had done to him rather than the predicament his rook appeared to be in.

The big man hadn't mentioned the incident at all, had perhaps already wiped the whole episode from his memory banks. But the notion that he might suddenly recall Gerry fucking him and decide to take instant retribution was one that Gerry could not totally discount nor shift from the forefront of his mind.

Another glance at the clock – already fifteen minutes past the time that Charlotte had warned him to expect the arrival of Imogen's people. What details Dieter and Petra had gleaned from their secretive exchanges with home base were scant and unrevealing. One of them would probably be a man called Orlo who used to be a porn star. The other two were actresses recruited by Imogen via a West-Coast agency, and they had already made something of a name for themselves as Kayla's supposed 'slaves'. Of course, they were coming in the hope of tempting Charlotte to part with some serious cash in exchange for the whereabouts of Imogen, but they would not, could not, know that both Charlotte and Imogen were long gone, having successfully established contact with Hans and arranging the sting which, even now, might well be complete.

But what if it was all a treble bluff? Gerry had known his fair share of dodgy dealings, had even tentatively dipped a toe or two into the murkiness of that growth industry known as 'insider dealing', but this was entirely different. At stake here was so much more than cash, and Charlotte's impressively prolonged and intense debasement of both Dieter and Petra had proved how seriously she regarded any betrayal of her trust.

If Dieter's eventual confession was to be believed – and he was so mentally and physically shattered when he delivered it that there seemed no reason seriously to doubt it – it was either Dark Eyes or the Librarian who had instigated Imogen's trip, planted the idea in her head years ago. They had arranged the intermediaries who helped her secure the Fellowship, fund the entire venture and maintain the elaborate concentrically structured secrecy apparatus which distanced them from any obvious involvement.

If Charlotte's dumb, almost robotic reaction to the confession had been open to any analysis whatever, it was surely safe to say that she was both stunned and disgusted by the news. She had made the trip to prevent treachery, but the trip itself was an act of betrayal designed to accelerate, not prevent, her downfall as Kayla. Seona had also been deeply upset by the confession, and stayed up a little longer than Charlotte that evening, begging Dieter to deny his own confession, adamant that he had to be lying.

However, their extended, intense cross-examination of Dieter and Petra seemed to confirm what he had said beyond any reasonable doubt, and his eager participation in the intense push to save the entire trip from disaster had been wholehearted and demanding. If he was still on the other side then he was doing a splendid job of pretending that his loyalties now lay with Charlotte.

Petra entered, dressed and ready. Her silk kimono was a beautiful garment, but gave no hint as to the powerfully athletic body it concealed. She seemed strangely relaxed given the circumstances, but then, Gerry mused as he watched her move across to the windows, she, as well as Dieter, had willingly committed themselves to involvement in this business. If what he had heard was true then they would be using this as a learning experience, part of the study necessary to become established in the field. He measured his own involvement against theirs: for him it had been a fantastic, unbelievable adventure, one which he would never forget. And it still wasn't over.

'How are you?' came Petra's voice, strong and keen, and Gerry looked up to see her staring right at him. He nodded, opened his palms, raised his eyebrows and smiled. She crossed her arms.

'Don't be afraid of this,' she said, 'it is nothing. We are only playthings, these people coming are also playthings of others. It is not important.'

Dieter hummed agreement of what his statuesque partner was saying. 'I'm sure I saw that man's movie, but it was a long time ago.'

'Orlo,' Petra said wistfully, and Dieter laughed.

'I think you know what movie I am talking about,' he said, leaning forward to raise the little lid of the chess set as it emitted a shrill beep to indicate the game was suspended.

Gerry got up.

'Would either of you like a drink?' he asked, but Petra tutted loudly, advancing quickly down the three broad steps and ushering him back to his seat.

'You are to stay, I will get your drink. Remember what Charlotte said: you are in charge, so you must act in charge. You do not fetch drinks for others, they do it for you.'

She was serious. Gerry met Dieter's smile uneasily, unsure whether smiling and being friendly was also *verboten*.

'It is an art of sorts, this dominance and submission,' Dieter said slowly, as if it was a sentence he had created all by himself and was particularly proud of. 'That is why it is easy to see that Charlotte is Kayla. If she was not worthy of the title then she would not have resisted so fiercely, she would have avoided such a confrontation. It is time consuming, it is costly. It is also dangerous. But she knows that she is in charge, that she cannot allow any challenge, however slight, however serious. To bow to any challenge is to admit defeat, to become the submissive. And she cannot do that.'

Gerry was still struggling to compose a sophisticated response to Dieter's observation when the phone buzzed into life and Petra answered it quickly.

'Yes, thank you, yes, we have been expecting them. Please do. Thank you.'

She replaced the receiver, passed Dieter and handed Gerry his long vodka.

'They are on their way up,' she said.

Gerry slurped at the drink, managed to swallow an awkward ice-lump and continued swallowing until the glass was empty.

Remember you're in charge, he said to himself. Remember – you are in charge.

* * *

Goodstone was drunk, but very merrily so, and he could only close his eyes and savour the sweetness of the tumbling memories as he lay back on his recliner. Tom would not believe it, not until he saw the tape. But there would be fun to be had there too, some concessions would be wrung from his oldest friend before he would be allowed to clap eyes on a single second of it.

He was savouring the various scenarios open to him when Kyle's mild cough alerted him and he pressed the button to straighten the back of the chair, swivelling it as he did so. He had brought her to say goodbye.

It might well have been a completely different woman. She had changed back into the staid dark businesswear. She now resembled any one of a thousand smartly dressed young women he passed on a daily basis. But she was no less beautiful for that.

He indicated that she should sit, but she gracefully declined.

'We really have to be going. As you know, I have people back at our apartment. They're expecting us as soon as possible.'

'I quite understand,' he replied, nodding gravely.

'I just wanted to apologise,' she said, hands clasped afront her, 'for the inconvenience, the intrusion this whole episode surely represents for you. Imogen is already somewhat chastened, but she has caused great upset to a lot of people, not least of all you, and on her behalf I want to convey sincere regret for her actions.'

'For what it's worth, you may tell her that I am happy to accept her apology and I hope she has wisdom enough to learn from her peers. You are a remarkable young lady, to have come this far and taken the chances you have.'

'Some things merit a little extra effort I suppose,' she replied meekly. How extraordinary – the same woman he had just witnessed treating her ex-friend with such bestial ferocity was now as inoffensive as an office temp. It struck him that the mild-mannered, exquisitely polite persona now before him was no disguise, just as her rubberclad dildo-wielding alter-ego was every bit as real and convincing. And what of the real Charlotte? What was she really like?

'With your permission,' he said quietly, avoiding her eyes now, staring into his glass, 'I would like you to lunch with me the next time I'm in England. Would that be possible?'

She smiled so sweetly that he felt his heart skip over a memory of butterflies flitting across his stomach, the forgotten ache of first love.

'I would like that very much,' she said, bowing ever so slightly.

He cleared his throat, gulped the remainder of the drink and barked out Kyle's name. The creepy redhead appeared instantly.

'Have Miss Charlotte and her friends taken back into the city as quickly as possible.'

'Yes, sir. There are reports of black ice on the main freeway but it shouldn't take –'

'I said as quickly as possible, Kyle. What's the point in having a chopper if you don't use the damn thing?'

Kyle muttered another yes-sir as he left.

Goodstone rose, reached out for Charlotte's hand and gently pressed his lips to it.

'Farewell, Miss Charlotte, Miss Kayla.'

'Thank you,' she said.

And then she was gone.

Gerry was sure his voice was still trembling, but the trio seemed content enough to believe that he was in charge, that his assurances regarding Charlotte and Seona's imminent return were genuine.

Petra had been acting as the perfect hostess, dispensing drinks quickly, and he'd noted that she paid particularly close attention to the long-limbed brunette who clearly did not object to the interest.

Orlo had been quiet, content to sip the bourbon and scan the apartment, and Gerry was taken aback at the directness of his question, the first thing he had said since entering.

'So, what's your normal line of work, Gerry?'

Gerry's heart raced and he wanted to say something non-committal about stocks and futures. But Petra's words rushed into his mind – *You are in charge*. He sipped at the vodka and leaned forward as if discussing something rarely spoken of.

'I, well, I help Kayla to sort out problems.'

Orlo stared hard and sharp, searching Gerry's eyes for weakness, aversion, the telltale signs of lying. But Gerry held the stare, even managed a broad smile.

'So, you work for Imogen?' said Orlo, the confusion evident. Gerry sat back, took another sip. He was on safer territory now – the truth.

If Dieter and Petra had orchestrated this whole affair then now was the moment of revelation, and he would be well and truly shafted. He had to believe, he had to trust that they had pledged themselves to Charlotte in good faith, that they would remain faithful during this first real test.

'Imogen isn't Kayla,' Gerry said flatly.

Orlo frowned, drained his glass. The gorgeous Oriental girl appeared to pick up on the news faster than her brunette friend, and the worried glances between the trio confirmed that they too had been deceived by Imogen.

'Kayla is my mistress,' said Petra, and Dieter was

nodding, pushing his specs up and staring at his little chess set as if he'd just realised how to save his rook.

Orlo sat forward and passed his glass to the passing Petra without taking his eyes off Gerry.

'I don't want to talk out of turn, my friend, but if I'm not much mistaken then there's something funny going on here,' he said thickly, his tone so grave, so solemn that Gerry could not help laughing aloud. Perhaps it was just the tension, maybe the vodka, but the whole situation suddenly seemed so utterly absurd, so surreal that he could not restrain himself, and it was with genuine relief that he saw Orlo beginning to smile, albeit bemusedly. Dieter released his own high laugh to join the giggles of the girls as the tension evaporated amidst confusion and no little shock.

Not more than two or three more drinks had been consumed when Petra made the first move, placing herself so provocatively close to the brunette that the dark-haired woman had no option but to look up at the blonde, and when she held the stare, licking her lips, it was clear that she would not refuse the invitation to go to the bedroom.

It was going according to plan – exactly, precisely as Charlotte had assured them it would if they stayed calm and remembered who was in charge.

Gerry realised then that he was not in charge, never had been: Charlotte had merely allocated him some small measure of her power and given him permission to use it in her absence.

The Oriental girl, after watching her brunette friend leave hand in hand with Petra, turned to assess Dieter. He was still smiling, enjoying Gerry's performance, and seemed quite taken aback when she stood and offered him her hand. He finished his drink and made a polite request to be excused before exiting along with the petite long-haired girl.

Gerry went to the drinks cabinet, fetched the bottle of Tennessee whiskey, a fresh tumbler, and returned to his seat.

'Right then,' he said, the relief evident in his voice, 'what say we have a proper drink?'

Orlo rubbed his moustache, smacked his lips and nodded.

Imogen had cried during most of the flight back into the city, alternately attempting to hug Charlotte and get to her knees to beg forgiveness.

It was becoming more difficult to maintain the aloof severity demanded by the role. She had not been punished, not nearly enough at any rate, and yet Charlotte knew she would not be able to spurn the pleas for much longer.

The silence in the elevator had been awful, only punctuated by Imogen's occasional sniffs as she miserably wiped at her puffed eyes. Her hair was hanging in unkempt clumps, she would be in desperate need of a long hot bath and a deep massage. Even the thought made Charlotte tingle – the idea that they might now make up, be friends again. It was so utterly alluring, deliciously exciting that it almost seemed worth the incredible hassle of the past month. And yet, Seona might have other ideas about it all.

The apartment was strangely quiet as Charlotte opened the door. Perhaps it had all gone wrong, they'd been unable to keep Imogen's people on the premises. Or perhaps they had gone to one of the complex's bars. But when she heard the ribald laugh she realised someone was indeed in the main lounge, and it was neither Dieter nor Gerry.

Imogen followed meekly in Charlotte's footsteps, Seona taking up the rear as they entered the main room. Gerry looked up, glass in hand, clearly pissed, and across from him sat a moustached man with his trousers at his ankles, his hand tightly gripping the base of one of the biggest cocks Charlotte had ever seen in her whole life.

'Hi,' said Gerry, clearly drunk, 'I'd like to introduce you to Orlo.'

Cruel as it seemed, the presence of the others made it essential that Charlotte and Seona continue to punish Imogen. She was permitted to bathe quickly and select a change of clothing from among Seona's things, allowed some food and drink, but her plea to be granted some brief period of sleep was turned down flat.

Charlotte knew they were having a good time in the room, and Orlo and Gerry had only just left to join them, but she couldn't go in there without first explaining to Imogen what was going to happen. She had her sit in the centre of the four-seater, Seona just along from her, watching her closely, monitoring her reactions to Charlotte's every word as she stood before her, arms crossed.

'Tonight is the end. I am Kayla and you know it, we all know it, but no more. When we go back home we end this thing once and for all. It brings nothing but hurt and distrust, it breeds envy and poisons relationships which otherwise would last a lifetime. It's not that I don't want it, Imogen, you have to understand that. I despise it, and you should too. If I hadn't had it you wouldn't have wanted it. It was always the same. You didn't ever show any interest in having a bicycle or a pony or an E-type or whatever until and unless I had one. Can't you see that? This whole Kayla business has been just the same, just another thing I have that you want. Well, if that's what's so bloody important to you, take it, have it. I don't care any more. But not until tonight is over. Then, you can stake your claim if you wish, but if you do, I promise you now, any chance there may be of us ever again being friends will be gone for ever.'

Charlotte turned away, gripped with an over-whelming urge to cry, to break down and tell Imogen that she still loved her dearly and wanted things to be just as they were that sunny afternoon, when they first made love for no other reason than they could and wanted to. But they had seeded a jealousy on that day, a warped relationship that had rooted itself ever more firmly with the passing years. She could see that now, but had no idea whether or not Imogen even knew what she was talking about. She drew in a deep breath, quelled the welling tears and cleared her throat. She had to be strong now, right at the final hurdle, she could not show the weakness yet, allow the dam to burst. She turned smartly to face Imogen and Seona.

'Your punishment in nearly complete. Take her in,' she said coldly, quietly, and Seona rose, waiting for Imogen to join her.

When she did get up, still fresh-eyed despite what she had already been through, Imogen took two steps towards Charlotte before dropping to her knees and clasping her hands as if in prayer.

'Forgive me,' she said, and for the first time that night, perhaps the first time ever, Charlotte thought she heard the voice of the real Imogen.

'Not yet,' Charlotte heard herself say, cold and distant, harsher than she'd thought she could ever be.

As Imogen got to her feet and followed Seona from the room, Charlotte remained impassive, staring at the slowly closing door as the tear rolled down her cheek. It would be over soon.

* * *

She had only taken several minutes to use the toilet, remove the anal plug which she'd been wearing now for so long, but by the time she got to the bedroom it was clear that Seona had wasted no time in making sure Imogen's punishment was pushed to the top of everyone's agenda. Not that any of them would've required much encouragement – there was not one among them who had not been lied to, and now, given the opportunity, they were exacting their revenge.

Charlotte moved slowly to the base of the huge bed and watched, arms crossed, as Gerry and Dieter toyed with her, raising her high above Orlo's solid foot-long cock, still being sucked strenuously by Petra. Petra was in turn being reamed by the Oriental girl, and the brunette was standing, eagerly fucking the Oriental with Seona's strap-on. It wasn't clear exactly who was directing proceedings, but Charlotte was content to assess the situation for a minute or so, keen to see just how completely Imogen had surrendered herself to the complete debasement now being inflicted on her.

Indeed, her expression was strangely ecstatic, as though she had somehow resigned herself to being a mere object and was content with that insignificant status. Sympathy welled in Charlotte. The insignificance was, in itself, a precious thing, of inestimable value when unattainable, just as the role of Kayla was impossibly glamorous and desirable to those least likely ever to attain it.

In that respect they were, ultimately, the same: Seona had accepted her status long ago, as Charlotte's unquestioning servant. She was happy with that, and always had been. The devotion she had shown over the years could not be feigned, was borne of genuine love, and Charlotte envied her the simple purity of that self-knowledge. But for poor Imogen, dear deluded jealous Imogen, the years had been dominated by a festering, corrosive jealousy – based on what?

Charlotte unbuttoned the skirt and allowed it to fall to the carpet. She removed the blouse and bra, slipped the shoes off. Time to be bare, utterly bare. There was nothing more to be concealed, disguised. There was no longer any need for fetishes and charms and the trappings of lust. She wanted to be on that cock, to show the others how it should be done, and her arse was slack and ready and the cock looked big, too big – but it had been a long time.

She mounted the bed, lowered her face while gently running her hands over the high tight balls. Petra was still sucking hard and deep, taking as much of Orlo as she could, but the sheer thickness of him made it impossible to accommodate fully. Imogen had probably had him, she had always been the deep-throat expert among them, but for now she was powerless, her breasts being sucked by Dieter and Gerry, Orlo's fingers probing at her behind as she was suspended above the giant cock.

'Turn her,' commanded Charlotte, and the men did so, easily, quickly, so that she was facing away from Charlotte, her behind close now.

Charlotte said no more, but merely reached up to grip Imogen's hips, and she pulled down, the men realising what she wanted to do and complying immediately, lowering Imogen's pussy onto the monstrous dick. She did not cry out, did not gesticulate in any way, but simply allowed herself to be filled with cock as she settled onto him. Charlotte continued to stroke his balls, measure the width of him as Imogen's flesh was stretched about him.

'Dieter,' Charlotte said, and he mounted the bed eagerly, already aware of what would be required.

Charlotte leaned forward. She did not need to part Imogen's cheeks at all, so distended was her sex with the thickness of the penis now stuck fully inside her, and rasped her tongue over the anus once, twice, thrice, each lick interspersed with a gentle finger-poke. She gripped Dieter's long hard cock and briefly wanked it before squeezing hard on the bulb to make it a little thinner. Then she slipped it into Imogen's arse and directed Gerry to get to the bed-head, fill her mouth.

Petra was on her back, the brunette lapping at her pussy as Charlotte directed them to get up and attend to Imogen's breasts. The little Oriental keenly took the right into her mouth, tongue already lashing at the swollen nipple as the brunette slid across the bed and manipulated access to the left tit, squealing with delight at the scene before her. Petra, without even waiting to be instructed, had laid herself flat on her back and was lapping at the heavy sets of testicles as they worked in and out of Imogen, craning her neck back in an effort to tongue the dual entry as she roughly frigged herself.

Imogen was stuffed in every hole, the men only gradually working their way towards some kind of synchronicity as Charlotte got off the bed and beckoned Seona, the tears already welling again.

'This has to end,' she said, holding Seona close, kissing her neck, willing her to make love to her there and then as the noises of Imogen being fucked and teased and tormented seemed to crash about her, crowding, clamouring, chaotic. 'I can't do this any more,' she whispered, the tears now rolling freely. Seona held her close and cuddled her, a reassuring hand smoothing over her hair, the whisper returned saying *it's all right, it's all right*.

'Take her away, look after her, I'll join you soon,' Charlotte said into Seona's ear, and then, for the very final time, she spoke as Kayla.

'Enough,' she said, and everyone stopped. Imogen was all but invisible, buried under the bodies, her limbs limp, all resistance gone. Petra sat up and pulled Orlo's shaft from Imogen's pussy as Dieter also disengaged and moved away. Gerry had already pulled his cock from her mouth and the girls had retreated to the sides of the bed, almost cowering, waiting for further instructions.

Imogen was exhausted, streaked with saliva and pre-come, her eyes shut, hair impossibly messy and a film of greasy sweat coating her face.

'Take her out,' Charlotte said, and Dieter lifted her from Orlo's body easily, as if the fucking had drawn so much energy that she was virtually weightless.

The big man carried her, following Seona. Now she would be fine.

'Right,' Charlotte said sternly, 'this is my final order as Kayla. You have only to follow this last order, and our business is concluded.'

They stared, expectant, fearful, unsure what to expect. Even as she thought the thought she realised that the final order had to be what she had always secretly feared by becoming Kayla in the very first place – the complete loss of control, the absolute surrender to the wishes, desires and lusts of others, and it had to happen right now. It might not set her free, it might not answer many of the questions she still had – questions about herself, about her friendships and loves – but for now a ghost would be slain, an exorcism of sorts could be performed.

She got on the bed, crawling towards Orlo's heavy shaft, now lying semi-erect across his hip.

'I want you all to do to me what you just did to her, and don't stop until you've had enough, each and every one of you. My last order is that there are no further orders. Fuck me.'

She grabbed the giant cock and started gobbling it, no pretence at style or method. She merely stuffed it into her face and sucked it as deeply and roughly as she was able. Hands were on her behind right away, fingers poking into her pussy, her arse, fingers pulling at her nipples, moving her, raising her. Her face was pulled away even as Orlo was reaching fullness, the cock back in his hand. Then they had her in the air, hovering, fingers still pulling at her opening arse, steadying her for the brutal entry she was about to endure. The brunette was standing, legs apart, fucking herself with the strap-on she'd removed for the purpose, her expression desperate, unbelieving as Charlotte was lowered onto the cock, her anus expanding easily about the girth, sliding down over the gnarled vein-work. Her very insides were nudged by the tool as she was raised again, lowered, Gerry and Petra co-operating to ensure that the rhythm of the fuck was constant, measured. The Oriental was at her breasts, the strong tongue lashing wildly at her nipples in between strong nibbles, tweaks and painful sucks.

Then she was being laid down, head resting, the sweet scent of bourbon in her nostrils as the big cock worked in and out of her behind, many fingers flicking at her clitoris, entering her pussy, other more desperate digits trying to get in alongside Orlo's cock as he started to increase the pace of his shafting, his scrotum slapping hard against her with every stroke. Perhaps Dieter had returned, she couldn't be sure. Time was morphing, melting, but a cock was stuffed into her mouth, another nudging for attention on her other cheek, and she briefly opened her eyes to see the brunette high above her, teeth bared like some wild creature, eyes wide as she tried to get the dildo into Charlotte's throat. She turned to find a real cock on the other side, dear Gerry finally getting his chance, his bulb dripping with pre-come as his eyes willed her to take it, and she did, deeply, sucking the saltiness from his as her pussy started to fill. Then there, just a glance, but Dieter right enough, feeding his slender hardness into her to join the shafting of the bigger cock, and soon they got the rhythm going, Gerry's cock was getting too hard to keep sucking at this angle, so she rose, reaching out, grasping, and her hand was taken, used to fuck a pussy. It was the brunette again, using Charlotte's bunched fingers instead of the dildo. It clearly wasn't thick enough and Charlotte's hand was taken in, easily swamped; the woman's cries rang around the room as she gripped Charlotte's forearm tightly, using it to delve deep inside her silky inside. Even Charlotte's other hand had the Oriental's nipple, the tight velvety skin urged into her palm as they all groaned and whined and pumped and sucked and flicked and rubbed, and the two cocks were working well now, getting deeper, their solidity stretching her, forcing her higher up Orlo's body.

The sudden burst of spunk into her mouth was unexpected, and she heard Gerry grunt and felt his fingers under her chin to steady her as he emptied himself into her, his cock-head only being withdrawn to spurt some of his offering across her face. She took him back in, sucked hard again, deeper now, and the gush along her throat was warm, easily taken. He is withdrew, moved away, but there was no respite as she felt her own hands nearing her, the hand still inside the brunette's pussy, and she wanted licked into the bargain, even with the hand still in place. She'd managed to get up there, she'd straddled both Charlotte and Orlo, and Charlotte strained to get her tongue to the aromatic point where her wrist was completely enclosed by hot flesh, the inch-long clit-oris hard and vertical. Charlotte pulled her hand from the pussy, felt the liquid running down her arm, but did not realise that the woman was pissing on her until the dribble became a powerful and pungent gush of urine, splashing into her mouth as she tried to get the clitoris into her mouth. With the nub trapped between her lips and eyes desperately screwed shut against the piss, Charlotte sucked hard on the bulging clitoris, so hard that the woman cried out. She was so close and Charlotte allowed her teeth to vibrate at the peak of the bud, sparking a scream from the woman and her instant retreat. Her continuing cries sugges-ted that she was finishing herself off on the floor, perhaps with the dildo she'd seemed so keen on. It was Dieter next, and his lunges had become frantic, totally out of synch with Orlo's steady pumping. She hadn't strength enough to raise her head to see what he was doing as he pulled out, but felt the spunk scatter in a wide arc across her belly and breasts. The Oriental and Petra were on her instantly, lapping at the discharge, continuing the torment of Charlotte's nipples as they smoothed the creamy sperm into her hard buds, so sensitive now that even the merest touch seemed to send shockwaves of pain through her. It couldn't be long now, it wouldn't be long until she can could through to see Seona and Imogen, and maybe then she would get her come, but Orlo had to finish too, and she concentrated, tightening about him as he entered, slackening as he withdrew, making the entry progressively harder for him when he might well have thought he'd slackened her so well that it wasn't going to get any better. But he responded to her muscles, seemed to get bigger, and then it was Petra at her pussy, lapping wildly, like a dog at a bowl, her hand pushing in, further tightening Orlo's presence, and he clearly knew what was going on, his breathing erratic now, staggered, and Petra delved deeper, her lips starting to close about Charlotte's bud as her slender hand was fully inserted, now twisting, expanding, testing the limits as Orlo signalled that he was ready. Petra pulled the heavy thick cock from Charlotte's behind and Charlotte looked down to see the monstrous thing sticking up between her legs, her clit so close to it. Petra was smiling, lipstick a mess, staring at the cock-head expectantly as she firmly wanked it. The solid white line of thick spunk erupted, Petra shrieked, the snake spiralled and twisted, only partly clinging to Petra's lips before splashing down onto Charlotte's pubis, and the Oriental was there again, clearly an avid spunk-eater, and her lips were as coated as her tongue and teeth, her eyes shut as she fingered more of the milky gel from Charlotte's belly button, stuffing it into her mouth.

Something about Petra's mouth on her clitoris and the sight of the huge cock being wanked and waved as it emptied spurred Charlotte's own come, and they all fell upon her as the first spasm racked her, her cries high and loud as the semi-erect cock was stuffed back into her behind and more fingers filled her pussy, Petra's lips back over her clitoris. Then the brunette was trying to face-fuck her again, the Oriental trying to get herself nearer Orlo's cock, eager to have some of it for herself. Charlotte closed her eyes, wondering at the sparkling array of colours exploding in her mind as the orgasm, irresistible and breath-stopping, reached its peak, the exhaustion swamping her instantly, the cock still inside her, fingers still working as she let the giddiness wash and wave over her.

* * *

231

Seona had bathed and massaged Imogen by the time Charlotte, semen-soaked, reeking of urine and the faint odour of dung, staggered back into the room.

Seona stood, alarmed, arms outstretched, and Charlotte all but collapsed as she was led to the bathroom.

As she recovered from the group fucking, Seona having fixed them both something to drink, she soaked in the tub and allowed the relief to suffuse her every pore. It had finally ended, even if the only people who knew it had been in the apartment that evening. Those others – those who felt they had first claim on Kayla, her identity and behaviour – they would just have to wait.

They would pack their bags and head back home tomorrow. There would, of course, be many loose ends to tie up, and she was quite certain she knew what the priority would be. But that could all wait. It would be a sweet pleasure to return that damned wig, to know that she would never have to wear it again. And the return of that thing would be the chance, perhaps the only chance, to find out why Imogen had been so cruelly used, why the rift in their friendship had been so cynically exploited. If there was an answer she knew she would never rest until she found it. They would evade her, of course, and even if they did not she would be lied to again. Well, she resolved, no more.

For now, she had done what she wanted to do, was expected to do, but in the process had ended up doing something else altogether. An inestimable bonus was within reach. And now, perhaps, there would be some form of understanding, the many questions she had always carried but been unable to answer might not be so daunting, so frightening.

If she could only look at herself, at home, in her own mirror, and know that she was good, that she had done no harm – that would be enough. Mild guilt surfaced at the thought of Steve, but she knew it was only her deep sense of duty which sparked the mild discomfort; it was not love of him, dashing and witty and wealthy as he was. She simply did not love him and never had. He would be one of the first loose ends to be firmly tied up when she got back.

But, exhausted as she was, there was one last piece of business she could conclude before sleep, and it happened to be the most important piece of business for many years.

She drew her weary body from the bath-tub and sat awhile, slowly towelling herself dry, pondering the best way to do it. But the longer she towelled and the longer she pondered the more she realised there was only one way to do it, only one time to do it, and the time was now.

Seona was propped up, staring at their ex-friend when Charlotte went back into their bedroom, but she had kept herself to the other side of the bed from where Imogen was sound asleep. Still that distance, even in bed.

Charlotte pulled the robe about her, tightened the belt and stood watching Imogen's face. Seona said nothing.

Charlotte, pained and stiff, got to her knees and planted a gentle kiss on Imogen's forehead – the eyes opened, tired but aware.

'I'm sorry,' Charlotte said.

'Me too,' Imogen replied.

'And me,' Seona said and, for the first time in years, they all smiled together.

Epilogue

The Librarian shivered and drew the collar of her blouse snugger. With the heating system now shut down the House had become chilly despite the sunshine outside.

The desk drawers had all been emptied of anything personal, the documentation had already been despatched by secure post to the new base. Not much left to do now.

Dark Eyes had been in the new base for the past week, getting things ready for her arrival. He would meet her at the airport, perhaps they would have something to eat before meeting their new staff. She could draw up the agenda for the first full meeting of the Board during the flight. It wouldn't take long – the usual formalities would be observed, then they would move to *Any Other Competent Business*, and there was only one item for discussion: the search for and proper selection of suitable candidates for the vacant position of Kayla.

She smoothed her hand over the bare desk surface, but there was little dust to sweep away. The whole place had already been thoroughly cleaned by the agents' people, the property would be on the market in a few hours' time. It did need some renovation – there were certain structural problems to be dealt with by any prospective buyer – but it would yield a healthy return for the Foundation and help ensure its future. But the old place had served them well, had witnessed many strange and wonderful sights, curious couplings and extraordinary beauties of both sexes. It would reverberate with those memories and ghosts for as long as it remained standing, and she could only wonder at what traces, what resonances might be detectable, sensed by future occupants. In all likelihood it would be developed as a hotel complex, in which case it would see more action. But although it might be more frequent, she was sure it would seldom be as interesting.

She stood, smoothed her skirt, easing the cool cotton material to dispel the ridges where it tightened about her hips. Her heels sounded hollow and loud on the floorboards as she crossed to draw the drapes for the final time.

With the room now dim, the silence becoming rather creepy as it always did, even in brightest daylight, she assessed herself from afar in the long mirror behind her desk. It was the best distance, certainly the most flattering – not close enough for the light wrinkles about her eyes and neck to be unavoidably obvious, but close enough that she could honestly appraise her figure. She had done well despite the passage of the years: she still had the waist, and although her large breasts were becoming more difficult to control she made the most of them, still favouring the light silk blouses which had always shown her assets to best effect while maintaining some modicum of businesslike uniformity. Her hair, ever fairer, had worked loose from the hair-clasp, so she removed the band and held it between her teeth as she shook the shoulder-length locks out, head bowed before her, then threw it back, adroitly gathering it in her fist, her other hand twisting and forming the column into a simple neat bun which the broad clasp would comfortably control. Her make-up was fine, lip-gloss still pretty much intact, but she would have a leisurely touch-up at the airport after check-in. Plenty of time.

She'd always loved travelling, the anonymity offered by departure lounges had been a lifelong passion. Seldom, if ever, had she been annoyed by late flights. Watching all those people: their comings and goings; the interactions between the single and the coupled; wondering about their jobs, their lovers, their passions; it had always been fascinating and she never tired of it. Perhaps she should have long ago followed a career which offered more contact with people, didn't involve being cocooned, stranded in secret locations where every movement was monitored and the element of chance, of natural interaction, was nullified. But it was too late now. She would go to the new HQ, get accustomed to her new desk, the new view, experience the novelty of a new apartment, a new routine, a different drive to the office and some new colleagues. But it would revert, as it always had, to the routine. She knew it, and feared it.

But it would be good to be back in Paris, even if the move was billed as temporary due to 'exceptional circumstances'. She could look up what contacts still stayed there, resume her eternal tour of the Louvre, struggle to decline the culinary treats so easily available. It would be, for a while at least, a welcome change from the silent English greenery.

For one thing, it would be so much easier to take a lover. When she had last stayed, for those three years after the collapse of her first marriage, she had been wild and keen to experiment, had quickly located the bars and coffee shops, most offering views of Notre Dame, where the literary men and women, the artists and musicians from all over the planet flocked to drink and talk and fall in love. And yes, she had gone with many men and women, usually much older, and she had learned a lot from them. Now, she would return as one of those older women, and there would be many young ones more than happy to use her as part of their experiment in experience, just as she had used those who now were surely dead. It was a role she accepted, could easily imagine herself enjoying, and enjoy it she would.

No guarantee that the following HQ would be anywhere near as exciting as Paris, but after what had happened it was extremely unlikely that it would ever be relocated in England. If the Paris move lasted anything more than five years then she would be so close to retirement that it really would make no difference anyway. She would then be free. Free to do with her life whatever she wished. The only problem was, she had long ago stopped wishing for anything.

She smoothed her palms down over her breasts, breathed in deeply and cupped her hands about her waist, pressing the slight belly beneath the skirt. Nothing wrong with a little bit extra thereabouts, certainly hadn't ever done Marilyn any harm. She chided herself at the comparison. It had once been welcome and often heard, but that was then, and she had long since passed the age when Monroe's beauty was at its peak. Still, it had once been the compliment she most often succumbed to, the comparison she secretly pined to hear, and it had been made many times.

The distant crunch of gravel signalled the slow arrival of a car. She moved back to the window bay, parted the drapes enough to allow a view of the vehicle as it moved past the gap between the trimmed bushes fringing the front lawn – a low blue sports car. She checked her watch. The Property Agent had arrived a little early, but no harm done, he must've missed the early heavy traffic on the carriageway, had made the journey from the city in good time. Once she had passed him the master keys and the security codes for the various alarm systems then she could head for the airport.

She slipped on her jacket and buttoned it, adjusting the pinched waist. He'd sounded rather nice on the phone, perhaps about her age. She smiled at herself again, at the reflection in the slender mirror. Last time then.

She was making her way down towards the main staircase when she heard the heels echoing downstairs in the hallway. It wasn't the man then – he must've sent a deputy, clearly a female. No, wait. Two sets of heels, already moving quickly. Two females? No – three!

The thought, more a deep fear than anything rational, had barely manifested itself when she turned the corner, peered cautiously over the handrail to see the figures already heading up the stairs. Three women, all dark-haired, darkly dressed, their bodies instantly familiar.

The Librarian moved back, fingers gripping the slender dark-wooden rail, the panic already knotting in her stomach. She would have to get the heels off, move quickly. Hundreds of places to hide – it would be possible to stay concealed until they got bored searching and left.

But it was too late. She was frozen, unable to let go of the handrail, and when the women turned at the landing, the smallest already looking up, she realised that indeed it was Charlotte, Imogen and Seona close behind.

239

Resistance was pointless. She stood back from the rail, tried to compose herself as the women ascended, mounted the landing.

'You know why we're here?' Charlotte said calmly, and the Librarian nodded.

It would be painful, it would be humiliating, and she knew that any objections she may have would be ignored, but they should at least know she hadn't acted on her own initiative. They would get her side of the story, one way or another – of that there was no doubt.

'He's gone,' said the Librarian, anticipating Charlotte's next question.

'I know, dear,' Charlotte said, 'we'll get to him in due course. I'm sure you'll be happy to show us exactly where he is as and when the chance arises.'

The Librarian lowered her gaze, waiting. Charlotte unbuttoned her jacket. The suit was normal, but the thick belt about her waist was not. Charlotte's red-painted fingernails moved slowly over the huge buckle, gingerly located the broad steel hoop and, with a steady movement, she drew the band even tighter about her waist, pinching it while releasing the buckle and allowing it to slide down, her grip about the thick end of it.

The Librarian stared hard into Charlotte's eyes, realising that this time it would be serious. There would be no role-playing, no quarter given, no allowances for age or status or anything else. The game was over.

Within minutes the skirt had been hauled off, Imogen was licking at her pussy, fingers already probing at her arse. There was no tenderness, no affection there. Seona had ripped the blouse open with one terrifying wrench, and now, as Charlotte lashed her bared raised buttocks with the broad stinging belt and Seona twisted and squeezed her aching nipples, the Librarian raised her face and let her cries ring about the empty, memory-soaked House, tears streaming down her cheeks as, inside, she felt she might now die of sheer joy.

NEXUS NEW BOOKS

To be published in October

VAMP
Wendy Swanscombe

A beautiful dark-haired lesbian lawyer from central Europe travels across the sea to the legend-haunted realm of Transmarynia, where she is to help a mysterious blonde stranger prepare for residence in Bucharest. What she discovers is beyond her most erotic nightmares and may mean the end of the world as she and her sisters know it. Bram Stoker's tale of obsession and desire is turned on its head and comes up dripping with something quite other than blood. Read it and stiffen with much more than fright.

£6.99   ISBN 0 352 33848 2

GIRL GOVERNESS
Yolanda Celbridge

Sloaney blonde ice maiden Tamara Rhydden, nineteeen, thrills to her own exhibitionism and teasing. Working for a London escort agency, her aptitudes fit the job description, but Tamara doesn't 'go with' clients; she finds that some men – and women too – prefer to be spanked for their insolence. A rich slave gets her appointed as governess of Swinburne's, a bizarre academy for grown-up schoolgirls in the earthy West Country, where maids come to study 'etiquette. The etiquette, she uneasily discovers, is that of discipline. The maids practise a role-playing, spanking cult of Arthurian chivalry . . . Tamara tries to put her past behind her, but the cheeky minxes compel her to exercise her caning arm, despite the governess's new-found tastes for being governed. How will Tamara make sure her *real* needs are taken care of?

£6.99   ISBN 0 352 33849 0

THE MISTRESS OF STERNWOOD GRANGE
Arabella Knight

Amanda Silk suspects that she is being cheated out of her late aunt's legacy. Determined to discover the true value of Sternwood Grange, she enters its private world disguised as a maid. Menial tasks are soon replaced by more delicious duties – drawing Amanda deep into the dark delights of dominance and discipline.

£6.99   ISBN 0 352 33850 4

To be published in November

JULIA C
Laura Bowen

When Julia Dixon marries her boyfriend Andrew she knows nothing of his association with 'The Syndicate', a secretive organisation devoted to the exploration of sex. Unwittingly becoming an apprentice to this clandestine corporation – where all new recruits are given a name beginning with C – Julia, now known as Caroline, is made to re-examine her clear-cut feminist principles as she confronts her innermost desires through a series of strange erotic challenges.

£6.99   ISBN 0 352 33852 0

WHEN SHE WAS BAD
Penny Birch

Penny's friend Natasha Linnett is a minx, and when she's bad she's very, very good. When a dominant, wealthy American wine buyer takes an interest in Natasha, she realises she can pretend to secure for him some bottles of real Napoleon-era brandy. She doesn't realise, however, just how many are the bizarre and lewd sex acts in which she must collude to maintain deception. Will Natasha manage to line her pockets as she wishes, or will she be caught out ignominiously like the bad girl she really is?

£6.99   ISBN 0 352 33859 8

THE SUBMISSION OF STELLA
Yolanda Celbridge

Stella Shawn, dominant Headmistress of Kernece College, crabes to rediscover the joys of submission. Her friend Morag suggests an instructive leave of absence, and enrols her at High Towers, a finishing school in Devon, whose regime is the total submission of women to women. The strict rules and stern discipline at High Towers ensures that even Stella can learn once more how to submit to the lash.

£6.99   ISBN 0 352 33854 7

If you would like more information about Nexus titles, please visit our website at www.nexus-books.co.uk, or send a stamped addressed envelope to:

Nexus, Thames Wharf Studios,
Rainville Road, London W6 9HA

NEXUS BACKLIST

This information is correct at time of printing. For up-to-date information, please visit our website at www.nexus-books.co.uk

All books are priced at £5.99 unless another price is given.

Nexus Classics

A new imprint dedicated to putting the finest works of erotic fiction back in print.

------- ✄ ---------------------------

Please send me the books I have ticked above.

Name   ....

Address   ....

            ....

            ....

            .... Post code...................

Send to: Cash Sales, Nexus Books, Thames Wharf Studios, Rainville Road, London W6 9HA

US customers: for prices and details of how to order books for delivery by mail, call 1-800-343-4499.

Please enclose a cheque or postal order, made payable to **Nexus Books Ltd**, to the value of the books you have ordered plus postage and packing costs as follows:

UK and BFPO – £1.00 for the first book, 50p for each subsequent book.

Overseas (including Republic of Ireland) – £2.00 for the first book, £1.00 for each subsequent book.

If you would prefer to pay by VISA, ACCESS/MASTERCARD, AMEX, DINERS CLUB or SWITCH, please write your card number and expiry date here:

....

Please allow up to 28 days for delivery.

Signature ....

Our privacy policy

We will not disclose information you supply us to any other parties. We will not disclose any information which identifies you personally to any person without your express consent.

From time to time we may send out information about Nexus books and special offers. Please tick here if you do *not* wish to receive Nexus information.   ☐

------- ✄ ---------------------------